Esther stared after Craig, feeling frightened and disappointed all at once.

Something had happened in the past few moments. She had seen it in the sudden fire of his gaze, in the way he had loomed over her as if she were prey and he the hunter, as if she were all that existed in the universe.

The moment had passed quickly, but she knew she hadn't imagined it. The air was almost too thick to breathe, and her body was responding to something powerful. Deep down inside, she knew she wanted his possession, and damn the consequences.

Just once, whispered some pleading voice in her mind, just this once. Let me know. Let him teach me. Take me. She was willing to give herself completely, if only she could have one taste of the forbidden fruit....

Dear Reader,

I'm not going to waste any time before I give you the good news: This month begins with a book I know you've all been waiting for. *Nighthawk* is the latest in Rachel Lee's ultrapopular CONARD COUNTY miniseries. Craig Nighthawk has never quite overcome the stigma of the false accusations that have dogged his steps, and now he might not live to get the chance. Because in setting himself up as reclusive Esther Jackson's protector—and lover—he's putting himself right in harm's way.

Amnesia is the theme of Linda Randall Wisdom's *In Memory's Shadow*. Sometimes you *can* go home again—if you're willing to face the danger. Luckily for Keely Harper, Sam Barkley comes as part of the package. Two more favorite authors are back—Doreen Roberts with the suspenseful *Every Waking Moment*, and Kay David with *And Daddy Makes Three*, a book to touch your heart. And welcome a couple of new names, too. Though each has written elsewhere, Maggie Simpson and Wendy Haley make their Intimate Moments debuts with *McCain's Memories* (oh, those cowboys!) and *Gabriel Is No Angel* (expect to laugh), respectively.

So that's it for this time around, but be sure to come back next month for more of the best romance reading around, right here in Silhouette Intimate Moments.

Yours,

Leslie Wainger

Leslie Wainger
Senior Editor and Editorial Coordinator

Please address questions and book requests to:
Silhouette Reader Service
U.S.: 3010 Walden Ave., P.O. Box 1325, Buffalo, NY 14269
Canadian: P.O. Box 609, Fort Erie, Ont. L2A 5X3

RACHEL LEE

NIGHTHAWK

Silhouette
INTIMATE MOMENTS

Published by Silhouette Books

America's Publisher of Contemporary Romance

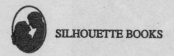 SILHOUETTE BOOKS

ISBN 0-373-07781-5

NIGHTHAWK

RACHEL LEE

wrote her first play in the third grade for a school assembly, and by the age of twelve she was hooked on writing. She's lived all over the United States, on both the East and West coasts, and now resides in Florida.

Having held jobs as a security officer, real estate agent and optician, she uses these, as well as her natural flair for creativity, to write stories that are undeniably romantic. "After all, life is the biggest romantic adventure of all—and if you're open and aware, the most marvelous things are just waiting to be discovered."

To Rita Mackin Fox and Vicki Badik,
my dear sisters of the heart.
And to Bev Morgan,
Who oughtta live 180 miles closer!

God blessed me with your friendship.

ACKNOWLEDGMENTS

My deepest thanks to the dear friends who generously
helped me with research: Sally Gregory, Vicki Badik
and Susan Moore.

Special thanks to the people who generously shared their
technical and professional expertise: occupational
therapist Susan Jackson and physical therapists
Elaine (Gigi) Kafka and Ron Brooks.

Any errors are mine, of course.

Prologue

Craig Nighthawk didn't look like a man who was in the process of giving up half of his life. He looked dark and powerful, even a little wild with his long, flowing black hair and his hard-as-obsidian eyes. Coppery skin was drawn snugly over a face that was unmistakably Indian, a landscape of rocky ridges and deep hollows. Something about him brought to mind a shaman of yore, a being of night and magic.

He sat casually now, as if nothing in the world were wrong or unusual in what he was doing. He wore a comfortable chambray shirt, a pair of jeans that were almost white from wear and washing, and ropers, the boot favored by truckers, America's modern cowboys. He had his powerful legs casually crossed, right ankle resting on left knee, and his hands, strong and lean, were relaxed as they lay in his lap.

He looked comfortable. In charge. No one would ever imagine that he was giving up a lifelong dream and love affair. No one would ever imagine that he was on the edge of desperation.

"I'm sorry, Mr. Nighthawk, but I really can't give you more

than that," the dealer said. "I have to prep it, I have to keep it on my lot, and I have to sell it for a profit."

Nighthawk never took his eyes from the man. "I know what that cab's worth, Mr. Gifford. I know to the penny what someone will pay for it. It's in perfect condition and you know it. The only prep you'll have to do is rinse the dust off it from time to time."

Gifford spread his hands. "There's nowhere else you can sell it."

"I can always drive it to Des Moines. Or Denver." He pointed to the piece of paper on which he had scrawled a figure. "That's my bottom line."

Twenty minutes later, Nighthawk stepped out of the dealership with a check in his pocket for the exact amount of his share of the sale price. The rest would go to the company that had financed his original purchase.

He stood in the sun for several minutes, feeling the hot, dry breeze of the Great Plains summer brush against his cheeks, watching the small dust devils dance across the pavement. Then he walked over to the big black Kenworth cab that had been his home for more than two hundred thousand miles. Losing her hurt every bit as bad as he'd known it would.

He cleaned the last of his personal stuff out of the roomy cab and the sleeper behind, checking to make sure he overlooked nothing. Then he unhitched his pickup truck from the tow bar, climbed into it, and drove away, never looking back.

Behind him, the wind blew dust devils across the hot pavement, and with it blew away the ashes of his dreams.

Chapter 1

Esther Jackson sat on her front porch and watched with be-mused irritation as a sheep devoured her flower garden. As far as the eye could see there was nothing but grass, a few huge old cottonwood trees, the distant mountains...and the fence that should have kept that sheep on the other side, off her property.

The August wind blew steadily. Hot and dry, it seemed to be turning her skin to parchment. She ought to go in and put some cream on her face, but she couldn't make herself get out of the rocking chair. The sheep, trespasser though it was, was too amusing. Too irritating. Too...out of place. It seemed to have a passion for marigolds and geraniums. Esther wondered in a detached sort of fashion whether it was going to get an upset stomach.

She supposed she ought to do something—shoo it back be-yond the fence perhaps, except that she couldn't see where it had managed to break through. Except that she'd never dealt with any animal other than dogs and cats in her life and she wasn't quite sure what to do. Did sheep bite?

The image of herself stumbling around on her gimpy leg

trying to shoo a recalcitrant sheep out of her garden made her chuckle into her iced tea. The further thought of the sheep snarling back at her almost made her laugh out loud.

Of course, she shouldn't find this amusing at all. Planting those flowers had been expensive. But worse, it had been difficult labor for a woman who had to wear a brace on her leg. Not impossible, just difficult, and she really ought to be angry.

Except that she found herself enchanted. The sheep was just being a sheep, after all, and doing a sheep thing. Just then, looking up, she saw what was presumably the rest of the flock coming over a rise. Still firmly on their own side of the fence, they were slowly heading this way, bleating a little as if calling to their sister or brother. She had no way of knowing whether the animal in her garden was male or female, and she didn't propose to get close enough to find out.

The stray sheep lifted its head briefly, as if taking note of the calls of the flock, then resumed its placid dining.

Too, too much, Esther thought. She rather liked the little fellow's temperament. Easygoing.

More and more sheep were coming over the rise. There must be several hundred of them at least, she calculated. Funny, she'd lived here almost three years and had never realized her nearest neighbor was a sheep farmer. Or was it sheep rancher? She was hopelessly lost when it came to such things, having been a city girl until she relocated to Conard County, Wyoming.

But while she might not understand much about what people did hereabouts to earn their living, she loved her new home. She liked the wide-open spaces, and the purple range of mountains to her west, and that silly sheep that was dining on her geraniums. It was a sight she never would have seen in Seattle.

A whine and a jingle of chain from behind her drew her attention. Her shorthaired Saint Bernard, Guinevere, was at the door, begging to be let out.

"Absolutely not," Esther told her. "You'll just chase that poor sheep and ruin its digestion."

Guinevere looked offended.

"All right, maybe you wouldn't chase it, but what if it chases you?"

Although, upon reflection, she didn't think that was too likely. Sheep weren't rumored to be very aggressive, at least not that she'd heard. But what did she know? Maybe Wyoming sheep were fierce.

The tinkle of a bell reached her on the ceaseless wind. She looked up again to see that the flock of sheep had come closer. Herding them was an animal that looked like a gigantic string mop with feet. Another sheep? But no, it didn't have the neat curly coat of the sheep, but rather long thick strings of off-white fur that honestly did look like a cotton string mop.

And it barked. When it *woofed* the sheep obeyed, heading away from the…dog, she guessed. It had to be a dog. It was nearly as big as the sheep it was guarding, probably as big as Guinevere. She wondered what breed it was.

Guinevere whined again, and chuffed quietly. She wasn't ordinarily a difficult or noisy dog, but the presence of a sheep in her front yard was exciting her. Or perhaps it was the scent of that strange dog which was approaching.

"I hope you have better taste than that, Guinevere," Esther said to her dog. "That animal looks positively scruffy."

Guinevere barked loudly. The sheep looked up from a marigold blossom as if trying to determine what the bark meant. The sheepdog—or whatever it was—just totally ignored it. Moments later, the woolly invader returned to grazing. Guinevere whined impatiently.

"Sorry, girl, but I'm not going to let you argue with scruffy strangers or strange animals. I have no idea how violent a sheep might get. Maybe it's a qualified kickboxer. You never know with strangers. Those hooves might well be lethal weapons."

Guinevere didn't seem particularly impressed with her mistress's reasoning, but Esther had already forgotten her dog. In fact, she'd already forgotten the sheep on her front lawn and her rapidly diminishing garden.

Because behind the flock of sheep came a man on horseback. With the bright sun behind him, she couldn't tell much except that he looked big and powerful on the back of an equally big and powerful horse. It was an image straight out of a western, the tall rider silhouetted against the brilliant sky.

And just that suddenly, the tranquillity of the day was shattered. Not that anything happened, but she couldn't remain relaxed and amused when a strange man was approaching. When *any* man was approaching.

Instead, the sour taste of fear filled her mouth, and she was suddenly painfully aware that there was not another soul for miles in any direction. Just this strange cowboy and his flock of sheep.

God, it was terrible to feel so vulnerable. And so ridiculous. That cowboy had no interest in her whatever. He would come to collect his sheep and then go.

But never had she been so aware of her isolation.

Guinevere whined again. Esther considered letting her out—Guin was very protective of her—but decided against it.

The cowboy spied the sheep in her yard and spurred his horse, riding to the head of the flock and coming to a halt on the far side of the fence. The fence was fifty yards from where she sat, so she shouldn't have felt threatened. She did anyway. Her hands tightened around the arms of her wooden rocker and every muscle in her body seemed to tense.

"Howdy," he called, and touched a finger to the brim of his hat. "Mind if I come get my stray?"

"No. No, certainly I don't mind." Even if her mouth was dry and her heart was hammering. She tried to scold herself for overreacting, but for some reason the bracing words didn't help. She was a woman alone, and she'd been taught at a very early age what a man could do to her.

He dismounted, tethered his horse to one of the fence posts, and climbed carefully through the barbed wire. The dog that looked like a mop was still patiently herding the sheep down the hillside. Other than to make sure the dog knew which direction to move the sheep, there didn't seem to be any need for the rider.

He crossed the hard ground toward her, moving with a surprisingly easy stride. Esther caught herself staring, her artist's eye picking out details almost hungrily. He wore a navy blue western shirt and denim vest, and blue jeans that were more faded in the knees and seat than elsewhere. Jeans that had seen as much hard work as his boots.

But she couldn't avoid looking at his face. She tried, of course, noting other details such as the fact that his shirt snapped rather than buttoned, and that his hair, black as coal, was long, falling below his shoulders. But finally she met his gaze, finding eyes as black as midnight.

She caught her breath and for one insane moment the world seemed to stop in its course as she tumbled headlong into dark pools. But almost as soon as the impression hit her, it was gone, drifting away on the dry, hot breeze.

"Hell," said the cowboy as he reached the edge of her small lawn and garden. "Cromwell, what the heck do you think you're doing eating the lady's flowers?"

The sheep, recognizing the voice, deigned to look at him a moment before tugging another geranium blossom off the nearest plant.

"You should have shooed her away," the man told Esther.

"Well, that's a matter of opinion," she replied, hoping she didn't sound as nervous as she felt. "I have no idea how a sheep would react if I were to try to prevent it from dining."

The cowboy cocked his head a little, looking at her as if she were some kind of surprising puzzle that had just been dropped into his lap. "Cromwell wouldn't hurt a fly."

"You name your sheep?"

"Some of 'em. There's too damn many to name 'em all."

"So I should have thought." The flock must number several hundred. The thought of naming them all made her head whirl. "Why Cromwell? That's really not a girl's name, is it?"

"No, but Cromwell isn't your ordinary ewe."

"Apparently not." Relaxing a little as the cowboy didn't come any closer than the sheep, Esther began to enjoy herself again. "I've been worrying that she might become ill from eating my garden. Do you have any idea if geraniums and marigolds will make her sick?"

He shrugged, spreading his leather gloved hands.

"Flowers aren't exactly on her regular diet—except for wildflowers maybe. I guess we'll just have to see."

"I suppose." He must be American Indian, she thought, judging by the inky blackness of his hair and the coppery tone to his skin. She found herself wishing she could paint him. It would be such a challenge to capture his skin tone in watercolor.

She must have been staring too intently because he shifted uncomfortably and looked away for just an instant.

"I'm Craig Nighthawk, by the way. I own the spread next to yours." He indicated the land behind him with a jerk of his thumb over his shoulder.

"I'm pleased to meet you. I'm Esther Jackson."

"Well, Miss Jackson, I'm real sorry about your flower beds. I'll get Cromwell out of here and replace all the plants she ate."

"Oh, that won't be necessary, Mr. Nighthawk. It's getting late in the summer and I'm sure a frost would have killed them before much longer anyway."

Esther hesitated, feeling rude for sitting in her rocker and not budging even a little to shake his hand or offer him a drink. But there was her limp, her terrible limp, and as long as she stayed seated, her long denim skirt covered the brace on her leg completely. When she stood, long though her skirt was, the brace would become visible, and for some reason she didn't want him to see it. Of course, she didn't want most people to see it, but she'd long since become accustomed to the fact that there was really no way to avoid it.

But she just kept sitting there, rocking, giving him what must certainly appear to be a vapid smile, not even offering him a glass of cold water.

"I'll replace the flowers, ma'am."

"That really won't be necessary, Mr. Nighthawk."

He looked at her for a long moment, as if he were pondering her behavior, then he turned and swatted the sheep on the rump. "Come on, Cromwell. Enough is enough."

The sheep looked at him, then returned to nibble another geranium. Guinevere woofed softly from the door.

"Nice dog," Nighthawk remarked. "Saint Bernard?"

"Yes." Which reminded her. "Your dog...*is* it a dog?"

A slow smile creased his face, softening an expression that had been as unyielding as stone. "He's a dog, all right. A komondor."

"He looks like a string mop."

His smile widened another notch. "I call him Mop."

At that Esther chuckled. "How apropos. Now what about Cromwell?"

"I call her Cromwell after Oliver Cromwell because she's always bothering the neighbors."

Esther laughed outright, and her opinion of this man underwent a great shift. He might well be a cowboy who talked plain and herded sheep, but he was clearly well-read. And she rather liked his sense of humor. At that moment she decided to get up, brace or no brace, and offer him a drink.

"Would you like a glass of water, Mr. Nighthawk? Or some iced tea?"

He looked surprised again, and Esther found herself wondering if this man was unused to common civility from his neighbors—and if so, why.

"That's kind of you," he said, giving her a crooked smile. "A glass of cold water would be great."

For an instant she feared her body was going to refuse to obey her, but after the briefest hesitation, her muscles resumed functioning. She rose, feeling the exact instant his eyes spied the brace visible beneath her skirt. There was a buzzing sound in her ears, and she felt her cheeks heat painfully as she turned and limped toward the door.

There was absolutely no reason to feel humiliated, and so she had been telling herself for years. So therapists had told her on countless occasions. She hadn't done anything wrong. She wasn't wearing the mark of Cain, just a brace.

But somewhere deep in her soul she felt defective and undeserving, and each time someone saw her limp and her brace, she felt exposed, embarrassed. The whole world could see she wasn't normal. That she was imperfect.

Nonetheless, feeling Craig Nighthawk's eyes on her like a

burning brand, she made it to the door. Guinevere, seeing that Esther was coming inside, backed away to make room for her.

Once inside the comparative coolness of the shadowy house, Esther released a long breath and relaxed. It was silly to feel this way, she scolded herself. She'd been limping for the better part of twenty years, and she really ought to have gotten used to it by now.

But she hadn't. She loathed the looks of pity that came her way, and she hated the inevitable questions. Out here in the middle of nowhere she'd finally found a comfortable hideaway. The only people she dealt with regularly—the sheriff's department, for whom she worked as a freelance artist, and the few stores she frequented—had all grown used to her disability. But instead of making her more comfortable with her condition, it only seemed to have heightened her sensitivity. Apparently what few calluses she'd been able to build had vanished.

But it was always worse when she came under the scrutiny of one of life's rare perfect physical specimens. The man standing in her garden appeared to be as close to physically perfect as most mortals ever get.

In her yellow-and-white kitchen, she filled a large tumbler with water from the bottle she kept in the refrigerator, then limped her way back to the front door. Guinevere whined again, but when Esther told her to stay she sighed and obediently sat down.

Craig Nighthawk was on the porch now, standing back respectfully so she didn't feel crowded, but saving her unnecessary steps. She felt her cheeks burn with shame, and was grateful to be able to sink back into her rocker. He tipped his head back, downing the water in one long draft, then looked straight at her.

"Does it hurt?"

The bluntness of his question startled her. Her hand flew to her throat and she blinked rapidly.

"Your leg," he repeated quietly. "Does it hurt?"

"No. No."

"That's good. Pain isn't a whole lot of fun. Thanks for the

water." Giving her a nod, he set the glass down on the porch railing, then walked down the steps. "Come on, Cromwell. Let's get you back where you belong before you ruin any more of Miss Jackson's garden." He paused to look back at Esther, touching a finger to the brim of his hat. Then he grabbed the sheep by the wool at the back of her neck, and tugged her toward the fence. Cromwell obviously decided she wasn't going to win this one, and trotted along beside him docilely enough.

Esther was amazed that he managed to get the sheep through the fence. He made it look almost easy. Well, perhaps Cromwell had figured out how to do it, too, which would explain what the animal was doing in her garden.

As for its owner, Mr. Nighthawk... Well, the man was in a class by himself. People had stared at her over the years, sometimes rudely, but no one had ever been quite so blunt about her leg. She didn't know whether to be amused or offended. Amused, she decided finally. Just amused. It was a far more comfortable emotion, and generally stood her in good stead.

Rocking gently, she closed her eyes and tilted her head back a little, letting the breeze caress her face. It was so nice out here, she thought. So isolated. No one from her past could find her here unless she wanted them to. *He* couldn't find her.

The fear that never left her seemed far away right now.

Strange woman, Craig Nighthawk thought as he shepherded his flock toward the next pasture. Very strange. Pretty enough in a quiet way, with the finest pair of hazel eyes he could recall ever seeing. And that auburn hair of hers, tumbling down past her hips—he had wanted to gather it up by the handfuls and see if it was as soft as it looked.

Well, she'd probably acted a little funny because she'd heard about him. Sooner or later everyone who passed through Conard County heard that Craig Nighthawk had been charged with kidnapping and raping a five-year-old girl. Didn't matter that he'd been released when they found the real culprit. Didn't matter that Dud Willis had actually done it, that he'd confessed and been sentenced to life in prison. Nope, didn't matter a snowball in hell. For all folks claimed to believe in "innocent until proven guilty," once the finger was pointed, a person stayed guilty for the rest of his days. The old "where there's smoke there's fire" view of life.

Not that it mattered to him. He'd always been a loner, and always would be. It was easy enough to ignore the looks, stares and whispers when you spent most of your time herding sheep.

Craig glanced back over his shoulder and saw that Esther Jackson's house was disappearing behind the lip of another rise. She was still sitting on the front porch in her rocker, watching the afternoon wane. What a strange and lonely woman.

But he had things he needed to be more concerned about, like getting his sheep ranch on a solid financial footing. He wasn't a rancher by nature, and all that he knew about raising sheep had come from books, magazines and USDA pamphlets. Thank God for his sister Paula and her husband Enoch Small Elk. They, at least, had some hands-on experience—although, after the last two years, he was getting a damn sight better at it himself.

No, he was a trucker by nature and experience, a wanderer who had always lived his life on the road. Now he preferred to spend most of his time on the range, communing with the sheep, the sun, the wind and the earth. He supposed ranching was basically the same thing, just more limited in scope. Instead of seeing a bunch of different mountains in the course of a day, he saw the same mountains from a different perspective. He could live with it.

But what a greenhorn he'd been at the outset. Hell, he hadn't even realized that all those acres of grazing land he'd been counting on were in such bad shape. He was still working at reconditioning it with the help of his flock. They chewed down the overgrowth so that he could fertilize and seed with better vegetation. Right now he was moving this group over to an unreclaimed area from the section they'd just prepared for seeding.

Little by little he was getting his land into the kind of shape that should eventually allow him to enlarge his flock and yield an excellent return in terms of wool. For now, though, his little flock were mostly lawnmowers who were helping him break even.

He and Enoch had been out here last week, laying the electrified wire around the section where the sheep would be grazing for the next month. He didn't use the fence to keep the sheep in—he already had barbed wire that was supposed to do that—but to keep predators out. An electrified wire running outside the fence about eight inches above the ground would keep out coyotes and wolves. There were wolves up on Thunder Mountain, he'd heard, and while he hadn't heard of any livestock kills, it was always a possibility. What really worried him, though, were the coyotes. They played hell with a sheep rancher's bottom line. The electrified fence had so far done a good job of keeping them out.

And then there was Mop. His komondor was the world's best sheepdog, he figured. Not only did the dog keep the flock in line, but the breed was famed for its ferocity on guard duty, reputedly capable of winning a fight with a bear.

Not to mention Mop was just a good friend.

Cromwell, on the other hand...well, that damn sheep just didn't act like a sheep. Now he was going to have to figure out how he could afford to replace Esther Jackson's decimated garden. That had been strange, the way she just sat there and watched Cromwell devour her plants. He couldn't imagine anyone being too afraid of a sheep to try to shoo it away. Of course, she did have that bad leg. Maybe she wasn't too steady on her feet.

Well, it didn't matter. Point was, he had to repair her garden. And that was probably going to cost a few dollars that he could ill afford to spare. Damn that Cromwell, why couldn't she ever be content to stay with the rest of the flock? Why was she always wandering off to be by herself and do her own thing?

Sort of like himself, Craig thought. The flock went one way, and Cromwell and Nighthawk went another. Loners by nature.

Damn it, a sheep wasn't supposed to be a loner. But then neither was a man.

And both of them seemed to be doing just fine in spite of it.

Several days later, Esther Jackson awoke feeling that a magical day lay ahead of her. It was a feeling she associated with special times, special events, and particularly her youngest years. Her earliest memory of feeling this way had been on the first day of summer vacation when she was seven years old. She had climbed stealthily out of bed, taking care not to wake her mother, or most especially her father, and had slipped her feet into brand-new sneakers.

Sitting on the edge of her bed this morning, she vividly remembered how exciting and beautiful the day had seemed. It had been early, no one else was up and about yet, and the day was little more than a pink glow in the east. Everything was fresh and new, just waiting for her to discover it.

That feeling had been scarce enough in childhood, and it was even rarer now. Looking out through the uncurtained window of her bedroom—no need for curtains on the second story when no one was around for miles—she watched the pink light wash the eastern sky, staining the high wisps of clouds the exact, unreproducible orangish pink of a flamingo's feathers.

Just the sight of that incredible color, the gift of nature's prism, filled her with a sense of awe and magic, and a need to hurry to her studio to see if she could possibly capture even a small part of that beauty.

She dressed swiftly, almost haphazardly. After all, one of the great things about living in the middle of nowhere was that there was almost no one but an occasional hawk to see what she was wearing. At times she had even gone out to her studio in her flannel nightgown—although she'd been reluctant to do that ever since she had started helping the sheriff out as a sketch artist because deputies had begun dropping by to make sure she was okay and didn't need anything.

Not that there was much call for her work as a police artist. More than two years ago she had volunteered to sketch a kidnapper from the description of his five-year-old victim. The man who had eventually confessed had proved her ability to translate a verbal description into a charcoal sketch. Since then, the sheriff had called on her expertise another half-dozen times.

The police work was a sharp contrast to her usual milieu of watercolor landscapes and still lifes. An interesting contrast, she thought, because it gave her the opportunity to do something so completely different. It was even refreshing. And it was rather surprising that she could excel in an area so diametrically different.

Since she wasn't expecting to see a soul, except possibly a sheriff's deputy later in the day, she pulled on a pair of jeans and strapped her brace on over the denim. The brace was an ugly contraption of metal and leather, but the only alternatives to it were crutches or a wheelchair and neither one would suit her. Crutches would occupy her hands so that she couldn't paint, and a wheelchair was simply too immobile for her needs. Besides, she didn't care to paint sitting down. She was a pacer, walking back and forth as she viewed both her work and her subject from different angles, stepping back to see more clearly how translucent smears of color were coming together.

This morning she was as eager as she had ever been to get down to her studio. There had been a time when finding opportunities to paint had been like discovering nuggets of gold. Since she had become successful enough to support herself at it, however, the opportunity to paint was available every morning, and no longer excited her as it once had. There were even days, much as it embarrassed her to admit, when she didn't want to paint at all.

So much for her lifelong dream of never having to do anything except paint. What was that old saying? Be careful what you wish for, because you might actually get it?

She laughed at herself and made her way cautiously down the stairs. Today was going to be an absolutely perfect day. She could feel the magic on the air.

Pink light poured into the kitchen through the open café

curtains. How different from Portland, where she'd always drawn her curtains at night. Here she never feared that anything except a coyote would peer into her window. The highway was a good mile down a rutted driveway, and nobody came this way by accident.

She had time, she decided, for a cup of coffee on the porch before the day brightened enough to give her the best light. All her life she'd been a morning person, cherishing the quieter colors of dawn over the more florid hues of sunset, loving the crystalline clarity of the dew-scrubbed air and the stillness of a world not yet fully awake.

In the time between the first lightening of the eastern sky and full day, the world underwent a gradual transformation of colors that thrilled her. Nature was the world's premier watercolorist, shifting hues in gentle gradations that she was ever struggling to imitate. Always an acolyte, she sat at the feet of Nature in the morning, and watched the hand of a true master at work.

Her work reflected her appreciation of dawn, and one critic had remarked that when viewing an Esther Jackson painting, it was possible to tell to the minute how old the day was.

That wasn't true, of course, and no one recognized that better than Esther herself. She was always striving, and never quite achieving her goal.

But that was what kept life interesting, she mused. With nothing to strive for, life would be pointless.

The porch on her house was both exquisite and extravagant, and it was one of the two things that had convinced her to buy this place. She loved the way it wrapped around the entire house, providing a vista in every direction. It was always possible to find a spot that was sheltered from the ceaseless wind, or dry in the heaviest rain.

This morning she stepped out the back door, facing east, and watched the subtle shifts of pink in the wispy clouds as the day steadily brightened. The coffee was hot and the morning was chilly, and the contrast caused a sensual humming in her nerves. It was hard to imagine that life could be any better.

At some point she noticed an unusual sound. It was faint,

but so regular it couldn't be natural. Sort of metallic, sort of scrapey... She cocked her head a few times, trying to place it as a new, uncomfortable tension began to sing along her nerves. No one, she reminded herself, could find her here. No one outside of Conard County knew she was here except her agent, and Jo would never betray her.

But the foreign sound continued, unnerving her. The beauty of the morning was irretrievably shattered, leaving only ugly fear in its wake. Clutching her mug in both hands, she debated whether to check it out or just go inside and call the police. At last she decided to walk around the house to see what she could find.

She tried to move silently—a nearly impossible task in her brace which creaked and made her movements awkward. She consoled herself that whoever was out front wasn't trying to be quiet and probably couldn't hear the small sounds she made.

When she reached the front corner, she halted and listened to sounds which could only be made by someone digging with a shovel. Who the hell would be digging in her front yard? And why? A raft of unpleasant possibilities occurred to her, most of them involving bodies and graves.

Her heart was pounding and her mouth was desert dry. For the first time since moving here, she wished she owned a gun. For the first time she questioned whether isolation was safe.

Drawing a deep breath, she gathered her courage and peered around the corner...and found Craig Nighthawk digging up her ruined flower beds with a spade. Staring in disbelief, she stepped out into plain view.

He paused, reaching up to wipe the sweat from his brow, and saw her. "Mornin'," he said.

Several seconds ticked by before she could even find her voice to reply. "My God, you scared me!"

He looked surprised, as if such a notion had never occurred to him.

"I had no idea anyone was out here," she told him angrily. "Then I heard someone digging and had all kinds of horrible thoughts!"

He nodded, leaning on his spade. "Sorry. I guess I should've rung the bell when I got here."

The easy way he apologized stymied her anger, leaving her wound as tight as a top with no way to expend the energy. Inwardly she struggled for equilibrium.

"I didn't realize you were so edgy."

"Edgy?" For some reason she felt as if he had just insulted her. "Why wouldn't I be edgy? I live all alone in the middle of nowhere, and nobody is supposed to be digging in my garden at dawn! Of course I'm edgy!"

He tipped his head back a little, studying her with an intensity that somehow left her feeling emotionally naked. She wanted to turn and flee, or at least kick something, but good behavior forbade it. She scowled at him. "What are you doing in my garden?"

"Digging up the plants Cromwell ruined."

"It must run in the family."

"What do you mean?"

"First Cromwell devours my flowers, and now *you're* digging them up with a spade. My karma must really stink."

He wanted to laugh. She could see it in the sudden lightening of his obsidian eyes, and in the twitch of the corner of his mouth. The sight helped ease her irritation. But apparently laughter didn't come easily to him, because he never unleashed it. "I told you I'd repair the damage. Sorry I couldn't get out here right away."

Four days had passed since her garden had become a gourmet feast, and she thought she had told him to forget about it altogether. "I must be overlooking something," she said. "Since you weren't expected, there's no need to apologize for tardiness."

"I'm apologizing for not fixing your flower beds sooner."

Esther shook her head, wondering if this man was a little slow. "I believe I told you not to worry about it. The frost will kill everything shortly anyway."

"Maybe not for a couple more months, and it seems wrong that you should have to look at dead plants for that long just because my sheep strayed."

"Really, I think I can handle the trauma. This is just a minor catastrophe, after all, and I *did* rather enjoy watching Cromwell dine. So please, don't feel obliged to do anything at all about it."

"I can at least dig up the dead plants so you don't have to."

In her present mood it would have been so easy to take amiss his insistence. She almost did, in fact, until she remembered this was the man who had bluntly asked if her leg hurt. If he could be that blunt, then he wouldn't likely pussyfoot around telling her that he'd dug up the remains because she couldn't possibly do it with her gimpy leg.

She opened her mouth to tell him about the man with the small tilling machine who, for a reasonable fee, would take care of the garden, but instead was astonished to hear herself say, "Would you like some coffee?" Well, she told herself, it would be churlish not to offer him *something* when he was working so hard on her garden. Never mind that she hadn't wanted him to do it. He was plainly doing what he felt to be the right thing.

"Sure. Thanks." The smile that touched his lips looked as if it weren't used to being there. "Just black will do."

As she limped back into the house, she heard his spade slide into the dirt again.

Damn, she wished he hadn't come back. Now she would feel beholden to him for cleaning up that mess. She hated to feel beholden.

Worse, he had made her realize that her fears hadn't been left behind. For all she had hidden herself in the middle of nowhere, her fears had managed to follow her and still waited, ready to pounce in an instant. Wasn't there any way to escape?

Mugs in hand, she limped back down the hall and onto the front porch.

"Thanks." He gave her a nod as he accepted the steaming mug of coffee, then sat on the top step and leaned back against the porch railing. "It's a beautiful morning."

Esther agreed. She settled into her rocker and watched the western mountains slowly transform from a dark purple to a gray blue as the light shifted steadily from pink to the whiteness of day. Little by little, her tension and irritation seeped away.

"I already bought the flowers for the flower beds," Nighthawk told her presently. This morning he had his long inky hair tied back with a piece of twine and had doffed his gloves to drink his coffee. He had strong, lean hands. Esther wondered why they kept drawing her attention.

"Really," she started to say, "you don't need to—"

"I know I don't," he interrupted. "You made that clear. But I've already paid for them, so I'll plant them. I couldn't get any of those flowers you had before, though. Too late in the season. They gave me something else, but I don't remember what they're called." Actually, he just hadn't paid attention. He'd only been at the shop because he needed flowers to replace the ones Cromwell had eaten, and if they didn't have the original varieties, then he was willing to plant whatever was available.

"Whatever they are, I'm sure they'll be lovely." She gave up the fight. This man was bound and determined to plant replacement flowers, and short of summoning the sheriff to evict him, she wasn't going to be able to stop him. Nor could she find it in her to continue to be annoyed by his insistence. He felt he had to do the right thing, and that was a quality to be admired.

He rose from the step and went to the bed of his pickup, returning a moment later with a flat full of darling little purple flowers. "I should have asked the guy to write down the name. Do you know what they are?"

Esther shook her head. "I haven't a clue. My knowledge of flowers is limited to a half-dozen really common plants. These are very pretty, though. If you'll leave one unplanted for me, I think I'll paint it."

"You paint?" He looked at her with real interest as he set the flat down on the lower step and reclaimed his seat.

"Watercolors."

"Is that your job?"

She nodded.

"Now that's impressive. I've never met a real artist before."

Esther braced herself for the usual questions about how many paintings she'd sold and how much she made in a year, but they never came. Craig Nighthawk took another sip of coffee and looked out over the gently rolling prairie toward the mountains. "It's nice to make your living the way you want."

"Yes, it is. Do you?"

He gave an almost undetectable shrug. "I used to. But what I'm doing now isn't so bad. It's a heck of a lot better than some jobs I've worked. At least I'm out in the open."

"I've been here almost three years," she told him, "but I'm still startled by how wide-open everything is. At first I thought it looked so barren but now..." She spread her hand expressively. "This summer I found myself standing on the porch and watching the way the wind ripples across the grass. It looks exactly like waves on a sea."

"Sure does. You've got some good grassland here. Looks like it hasn't been neglected as long as my place has." He jerked his head toward the scrubby land on the other side of the fence. "Somebody overgrazed it, then let it go wild. It'll be years before I get it back in shape."

Esther blinked. "Really? I never thought about that."

"Neither did I. I thought when I bought the place that I was getting a lot of good land." He glanced her way and gave her a rueful smile. "Course, what did I know about grazing sheep? I drove a truck."

"Big occupational change."

"Still should've read up before I jumped into it."

"So what do you do about it?"

"Little by little we're getting the pasturage in shape. Then we'll be able to increase the flock. Might even bring in some cattle."

"Cattle? But they can't graze with sheep, can they?"

"That's a commonly held belief, but the fact is you can graze 'em side by side. They mostly eat different plants, and between 'em they'll help keep the pasture healthier." He shrugged. "Then again, maybe I won't get in any deeper than sheep. Ransom Laird has a spread up north of here where he raises sheep, and he seems to be doing well enough."

"I met him once," Esther remarked. "When I was doing something for the sheriff. He seems like a nice man."

"Yeah." Tipping his head back, Nighthawk downed the last of the coffee, closing the subject immediately. He set the mug on the porch with a thump. "I'd better get back to work," he said. Rising, he returned to the garden and started digging.

Esther stared after him, wondering what she had said wrong.

Chapter 2

Esther really needed to get to work. She had a gallery show-ing in London coming up in a couple of months, and she still had several of the promised paintings to complete, not to men-tion one she hadn't even started yet. Instead she was standing in her kitchen cooking a huge breakfast for a man she didn't know who plainly just wanted to be left alone.

She couldn't quite explain why she thought that. He'd been sociable enough, but had given her the distinct feeling that it wasn't easy for him. Of course, it wasn't easy for her either, so perhaps she'd been guilty of projecting her feelings onto him.

And what the hell did it matter? Obviously she was losing her mind, cooking breakfast for a man she didn't know when she made it a rule to avoid men as much as humanly possible. Something must have shaken a few of her screws loose.

Even so, she kept right on cooking, frying slices of the small ham she'd meant to use for her dinners, making home fries because she was out of bread for toast, and finally scrambling some eggs.

And something inside her quivered with unease. Was she

doing this for Mr. Nighthawk because he'd been kind enough to restore her garden—or was she doing this because it was what a woman was supposed to do for a man? The mere thought nauseated her.

But she finished cooking breakfast anyway. When she went out front to get him, he was just finishing. Her garden plots were a riot of pink and purple blossoms and Nighthawk was putting the spade in the back of his truck.

"Come in for breakfast," she called to him. "I have home fries, ham and eggs."

He turned slowly, his inscrutable face betraying just a smidgen of surprise. "I don't think I ought to come in."

It was as if his words snapped her into a bird's-eye position, looking down on the two of them, seeing herself as a woman alone in the middle of nowhere with a man she didn't know. Of course he didn't want to come into the house. "I'll bring it out onto the porch then."

He hesitated, then nodded. "Thanks. I appreciate it."

Of course he was hesitant. He had no idea what kind of person she was. The realization eased her own apprehension. If he was concerned about such things, then she probably had nothing to fear from him.

She had a round table and chairs at one corner of the porch, and it was there she served them both breakfast. The breeze blew gently, carrying the fresh scents of the morning earth to them, enhancing the already delicious aroma of ham, potatoes and eggs.

Craig ate with obvious appreciation. "You eat like this every morning?" he asked her.

She felt a laugh quiver on her lips and in the pit of her stomach. "Of course not."

He looked straight at her then, his dark eyes holding her. "Thank you. You didn't need to go to this trouble for me."

"It was the least I could do."

The breeze gusted, snatching a tendril of her auburn hair and dragging it across her face. She tucked it back behind her ear and tried to ignore the way this man's attention made her feel. Little butterflies had settled in her stomach and she felt exhilarated somehow. But then he returned his attention to his plate, and she felt strangely deflated.

The silence felt awkward, so she searched for some safe topic of conversation. "How is Cromwell doing?"

He looked up again and smiled, an expression that took her breath away. When he was straight-faced, he looked stern and proud, but now he looked...welcoming and warm in a way that made her feel she could trust him. A little warning sounded in some corner of her mind, reminding her that looks could be deceiving. After all, hadn't her father been as handsome as the devil himself?

"Cromwell is Cromwell." He shook his head slightly and shrugged. "I'm beginning to think I should have named her Marco Polo, or Magellan. She managed to cross the fence again and when I found her yesterday she was maybe a quarter mile from the rest of the flock."

"How does she get through that barbed wire?"

"When I figure it out, I'll let you know. The really amazing thing is that she crossed the electrified fence, too. Sometimes I think she teleports."

A bubble of laughter rose from Esther's stomach and tumbled over her lips, bringing another smile to the harsh landscape of Craig Nighthawk's face. They both apparently had the same thought because at the same instant he whistled and she hummed the opening bars of "The Twilight Zone" theme. And together they burst into laughter.

"Great minds think alike," Craig remarked. "I don't know about that sheep, but I'm honestly beginning to think she jumps the fence."

"It could be. They can jump, can't they?"

"I haven't a clue. It's not something that ever crossed my mind before, but it's clear as day that that ewe couldn't have come *through* the fence, because if she had she would have gotten a serious sting from the electrified fence and wouldn't have gone any farther."

"Why do you electrify the fence? Isn't that dangerous?"

"Only for predators, and Cromwell, if I've done it right. So far it seems to be working and it's easy to move with the flock. These home fries are really great, by the way."

"Glad you like them." She went inside to get the coffeepot and returned to fill his mug, then set the pot on a hot pad beside them.

"What made you move out here?" he asked. It was a casual question, the make conversation kind, and there was no reason she should feel threatened by it. She felt threatened anyway.

Looking away from him, she stared out over the softly rolling land toward the mountains. "I...needed to get away. From everything."

"Well, you can't get much farther than this," he said easily enough. "At times I've gone weeks without seeing another living soul."

She returned her gaze to him then, feeling cautious but curious. "Do you want to get away, too?"

He hesitated, helping himself to another mouthful of potatoes before he answered. "Getting away can mean a lot of things. I wanted to get away from the reservation."

She hardly knew how to respond to that. Being of immigrant stock herself, she bore the guilt of a nation when it came to the treatment of the Native American peoples. At the same time she had very little real notion of the wrongs that had been done to people like Craig Nighthawk, so she felt herself floundering for something that might be an appropriate response. "I come from Seattle," she said finally. "I really don't know a whole lot about reservations...." Even in her own part of the country.

He shrugged. "Most people don't. And some are better than others. The one I was raised on is dirt poor and it kind of encourages kids to dream of escape."

"Is that why you settled on truck driving? To escape?"

"Partly. Partly it had to do with a guy I met when I was about twelve. There was a truck stop on the edge of the res and I hung around over there looking for odd jobs. I could pick up a dollar here and there to do things like empty the trash, wash a windshield—whatever. Anyway, there was this trucker named Chigger who used to lay over there for a day or so every couple of weeks. For some reason he took a shine to me. Taught me how to play poker and introduced me to science fiction. He kept a whole bunch of his favorite books in the cab, said they were his best friends. I'll never forget when he gave me a copy of *The Foundation Trilogy*. I still have it."

Esther was touched. "He sounds like a wonderful man."

"He was." Craig smiled faintly. "He also filled my head with tales of being on the road. Action, adventure, new sights, new people. He made it sound like going on a voyage of discovery. As if truckers are the world's great explorers."

"Do you still feel that way?"

"Oh, maybe not as much as when I was a kid. But I still love it. There's something about climbing up in the cab to set out on a fresh trip that just—" He broke off and shrugged. "I felt free."

Esther pushed her plate to one side, having eaten all she could. She preferred breakfast to be a light meal. "You must feel very confined now, then."

"I reckon."

A sound from the screen door drew her attention. Guinevere stood there, looking expectant. "So you finally decided to get up, sleepyhead?" Esther smiled and explained to Craig, "Guin always sleeps late in the morning. Usually I'm out in my studio and working for hours before she finally decides to get up."

Guin woofed and Esther rose, going to let the dog out for her morning run. But Guinevere had an itinerary of her own and instead came over to make Nighthawk's acquaintance. He greeted the dog with his palm up and Guinevere quickly decided that he was okay. She accepted a scratch behind her ears, then dashed off the porch and out into the fields.

"She loves it here," Esther said. "So much freedom. In Seattle I had only a really tiny fenced yard for her to play in."

Craig rose, stretched mightily, then gathered up his dishes. "I need to be getting back to work. So do you, probably. I'll just carry these things in for you."

Esther stayed where she was on the porch, not wanting to make him uneasy by going into the house with him. He made two trips, even though she told him just to leave things, thanked her for a great breakfast, and drove away.

The morning was suddenly quiet again, except for the harsh cry of a hawk, the whisper of the breeze and the steadily fading growl of the truck engine.

Standing at the porch rail, Esther watched the dust cloud raised by Craig's truck as it traveled down the rutted drive to the road. Finally it vanished and the day was still and empty again.

In his absence, Esther realized what a powerful presence Craig Nighthawk was. Not even Guinevere's eventual return filled the gap.

Strange, she thought, then headed out to her studio to paint before the morning light was gone.

In a burst of extravagance, she had replaced part of the north side of the barn's gambrel roof with skylights, so that light poured into the barn. As long as it wasn't raining, she always had the best light by which to paint. If the day turned gloomy, there were other tasks to fill her time, such as sketching new ideas.

Today she worked on a planned landscape of the Rocky Mountains as they appeared to her from her property. It was one of her most ambitious projects to date, intended to fill a sixty-by-forty-inch sheet of three-hundred pound stock. Contrary to her usual method of painting and then flattening the paper, which rippled from the watercolors, she had decided to stretch this piece on a frame because it was too large to flatten on her usual equipment.

After soaking the paper for several hours, she had stapled it tightly to the frame. Today it was as taut as a drumhead, and dry so she could begin sketching on it.

The sense of magical expectation that had consumed her this morning began to return, filling her with anticipation of the project ahead.

Hours later she was still working steadily when the letter

carrier drove up. Esther had a mailbox out on the road like everyone else hereabouts, but Verna Wilcox had taken one look at Esther's brace and had started delivering the mail right to the studio or house. Verna claimed it was no trouble, especially since Esther didn't receive a whole lot of mail, mainly a flurry of bills toward the end of the month, and an occasional letter the rest of the time.

"Knock knock," Verna called cheerily from the door of the studio.

"Hi, Verna!" Smiling, Esther turned from her work. "What have you got for me?"

"A letter from your agent." Verna carried the white envelope to her and paused to look at the sketch which now covered two-thirds of the paper. "Oh, my, my, my, that's going to be pretty." At forty-five, Verna was a younger version of her mother, Velma Jansen, the dispatcher at the sheriff's office. Both women were thin to the point of emaciation, with lined, leathery skin, and a tendency to smoke too much and speak their minds with complete freedom. "'Bout time you got around to painting a big picture."

"They're certainly increasing in popularity."

"Of course. People need things to hang on the wall over the sofa."

There was no way on earth Esther could take offense at Verna's opinion. Art for the sake of art wasn't important to letter carriers. Verna was practical to the last bone in her body and anything without a utilitarian purpose was a waste.

Esther tucked the letter from her agent into her pocket. "I'm finished for the day. The light's starting to go. Do you have time to come in for a cup of tea?"

Verna glanced at her watch. "Sure thing. You're the last stop on my route and I don't need to get the truck back until four-thirty."

Together they walked back to the house and into the kitchen where Verna settled at the table while Esther put the pot on to boil.

"What happened to your garden out front?" Verna asked her. "I thought you had geraniums and marigolds out there."

"I did, but a sheep ate them."

"A sheep?" Verna barked a laugh. "Let me guess. One of Nighthawk's sheep?"

"A ewe he calls Cromwell."

"Did he pay for your garden?"

"Actually, he came over just this morning and replanted it with all those new flowers."

"He did?" Verna looked surprised. "He hasn't exactly been the sociable sort hereabouts."

"He seemed nice enough to me. In fact he insisted on replacing the flowers even though I told him it wasn't necessary."

Verna nodded slowly, taking in the information. "Well, he hasn't had much call to be sociable around here, I guess. He used to be a truck driver, you know."

"He mentioned that." Esther poured boiling water into the teacups and carried them to the table. She put out three different boxes of herbal tea as well as Earl Grey and Darjeeling.

Verna selected Earl Grey and dipped the bag in and out of the water. "Well, he's not a trucker any more, and if you want my opinion it's because of all that time he spent in jail. Probably lost his job."

"Jail?" Esther sat slowly as her heart skipped uncomfortably. "He's an ex-con?"

"No! No, no, no," Verna said swiftly. "Hell, you was here at the time. Don't you remember? He's the one they arrested first for raping the little Dunbar girl. Before Dud Willis confessed."

"*He* was the one they arrested?" Esther felt stunned.

"You don't remember?"

Esther shook her head. "I didn't really pay a whole lot of attention. Well, I don't get the newspaper, and I don't listen to the radio or anything..."

"But didn't you draw the picture of the kidnapper?"

"Well, yes, but they didn't ever need to use it because the man confessed the same day that I talked to the little girl and did the drawing. The girl's mother was upset because the drawing didn't look at all like the man who was in jail, but I never did pay attention to who he was. By the time I got to the sheriff with the drawing, the real rapist had confessed.''

And she found herself wondering why she felt as if she needed to apologize for not keeping up to the minute on local events. In point of fact, she *hated* the news and avoided it as much as possible. What was the point of listening to an endless litany of pain and suffering when there wasn't a damn thing she could do to prevent any of it?

"Well, it was Craig Nighthawk they arrested," Verna told her. "Kept him for weeks in that jail. He turned down bail, you know."

"Why'd he do that?"

"Because he figured people was so mad he was safer in jail."

Esther nodded her understanding. People had been extremely enraged over Lisa Dunbar's kidnapping and rape. Isolated though Esther was, she had picked up on it whenever she went to town for groceries. "He was probably right about that."

"Course he was."

"But why did they arrest him in the first place?"

"The little girl's clothes were found on his property. If Dud Willis hadn't confessed, Nighthawk'd be in prison for life. Ain't no way a jury around here was gonna let him off."

"I guess not." She could well imagine that the clothes would have been taken as absolute proof, especially when tempers were running high. "It must have been awful for him."

"Reckon so. They's still plenty of folks around here who think he had a hand in it."

"Why? Because the clothes were on his property?"

"That's part of it. They also figure the little girl knew what she was talking about when she said the man who hurt her had long black hair."

Esther felt a chill snake along her spine, and she looked out the window as if seeking a reminder that the rest of the world still existed. She had no trouble believing a man could hurt a small child, but she didn't want to believe Craig Nighthawk could.

"Well," Verna continued, pausing to drain her cup and set it aside, "ol' Willis confessed and never once pointed the finger anywhere else. And there wasn't any other evidence that Nighthawk had any part in it. The sheriff believes he's innocent and that's good enough for me."

But Esther wasn't sure it was good enough for her.

Craig Nighthawk sat down to dinner that evening with his sister Paula, her husband, Enoch, and their two young children. The little girl, Mary, was five but seemed much older because of the quiet way she watched the world from her huge dark eyes. Little Billy was three, and greeted almost all of life with an irresistible belly laugh.

Paula passed a huge bowl of macaroni and cheese to him, then filled the children's mugs with milk. The kids loved this meal, but Craig suffered through it only because it was a cost-saving measure. They simply couldn't afford to serve meat as a main dish every day and Paula balanced the kids' diets with eggs and milk. Still, Craig liked meat. Back in his trucking days, he'd eaten meat two or three times a day. And lately, with fish so expensive, he was beginning to dream of broiled swordfish and fried catfish.

Hell, he was even beginning to think about sacrificing Cromwell, stringy and tough though that old ewe probably was. It'd surely be a hell of a lot easier on his temper to eat her rather than deal with her.

"Did you take care of the woman's garden?" Enoch asked him while they ate.

"Yup."

"That damn ewe is a pain in the butt."

"No kidding."

"Was she happy with the new flowers?"

Craig suddenly realized that he hadn't even asked Esther. "I don't know."

Paula shook her head, giving him a smile of sisterly indulgence. "That was the important thing to find out."

Craig shrugged. "Wasn't much I could do about it one way

or another. They were the only flowers I could get and I'd already bought and paid for 'em. What was I gonna do?''

"I just don't want to get sued," Enoch said.

Enoch had a streak of paranoia, but that wasn't unusual among res Indians. After you'd been kicked two or three dozen times by white folks, you got to expect it. That was one of the main reasons Craig had wanted to get his sister and her children away from there. People in Conard County were still prejudiced, but not to the degree he'd seen where he came from. Hell, there were a couple of Indian sheriff's deputies, one of them a woman.

Which meant that those two bright and shining faces across the table from him had a chance to grow up without feeling hated and terrorized by the world at large. Unfortunately, the price of that was separation from their roots. He still hadn't figured out how they were going to deal with that.

He would never forget his surprise as he'd traveled around the country at discovering that the whole world *didn't* hate Indians. He didn't want these kids discovering that fact with the same surprise; he wanted them to grow up believing it.

"I think we ought to slaughter that damn ewe," Enoch said. "We couldn't afford those flowers. That's food off the table, and some mutton could replace it."

"I figure it'd be like eating rubber bands."

Paula flashed a smile but shook her head. "We don't want to slaughter her, Enoch. She's a good breeder. We'll manage." She spread her arms suddenly, as if to embrace the whole world. "Why are we complaining? Three years ago we didn't have an indoor bathroom or central heat. Three years ago we weren't eating any better and we had a whole lot less hope."

Enoch looked down at his plate, then gave her a smile. "You're right. I'm just impatient."

"Aren't we all," Craig remarked. He passed his nearly untouched plate to Paula and rose. "Let the kids have seconds. I'm not hungry."

Nor should he be, he thought as he stepped outdoors and watched the sun sag toward the mountains. He'd had that bountiful breakfast at Esther Jackson's place this morning and he felt guilty when he thought of those two little kids inside. *He'd* had enough to eat today; now they should go to bed with their tummies as full as possible.

Not that they were starving. God knows, he and Paula and Enoch had all had times in their lives when they'd had nothing to eat. Those kids weren't dining on five-star cuisine, but they had enough food. He just felt guilty because he wasn't giving them any more.

Stupid.

Wishing for a cigarette, he rocked back on his heels and looked up into the blue sky. He'd given up smoking back when he sold his truck because it was a waste of money. What killed him was that all this time later he could still crave a cigarette as strongly as the day he'd quit.

Oh, well, no point thinking about it, he told himself. They'd pulled this ranch through more than two years, and he didn't for a minute doubt that they would pull it through to better times. The pasture was shaping up, and he figured between the lambs his ewes would drop come April, and the profit he expected from wool next year, they ought to be doing better soon.

From where he stood on the porch watching the day dwindle, he could see other signs that this place was just getting by. He'd painted the house five years ago when he bought the place, but Wyoming winters were harsh and it was looking as if it needed another coat.

He and Enoch had done some work inside the barn, making it more useful to their needs, but the outside looked weathered and even a little dilapidated. They were going to have to do something about that before much longer or buy the paint several times over in repairs. The roof was sound, though. They'd seen to that last fall.

Around back of the house, Paula was raising an extensive vegetable garden, canning whatever they didn't immediately need for the coming winter. Her henhouse was making more eggs than they needed, and she'd begun to sell them here and there for less than the supermarket wanted. With those proceeds she bought clothes for the children.

They were doing as well as could be expected, and considering that he owned the spread free and clear, they were doing better than most people.

So what the hell was he feeling gloomy for? Because he wasn't driving a truck any longer?

Nah. He wasn't drowning in self-pity. He'd done what was necessary to take care of the people he cared about, and that wasn't something to pine over.

But for some reason today he just felt…glum. Lonely, actually, which was ridiculous considering his house was full of people, and that he generally preferred to be alone anyway. But being alone and being lonely were two different things, he guessed, and right now he was feeling lonely.

Turning to go back into the house to work on the books, he paused and looked around him.

In the evening light, the place still looked as beautiful as it had the first time he laid eyes on it. Maybe even better because back then it had been run down and left to go to pot. Now there was a lawn and a garden and signs of life everywhere, like that swing hanging from the limb of the big old cottonwood beside the house. It was a home.

For an instant, just one uneasy instant, he wondered what Esther Jackson would think of it.

Then he brushed the thought aside like an annoying fly and went inside to deal with the other part of ranching.

It wasn't until she was about to go to bed that Esther remembered the letter from her agent. She'd shoved it into her pocket when Verna gave it to her, and later had dropped it onto her desk, meaning to get back to it after dinner.

It probably wasn't all that important—Jo generally called when something significant was up—but now that she'd remembered it she knew she wouldn't be able to forget about it until morning. As long as she was busy, she could ignore her curiosity, but not when she was trying to go to sleep.

Sighing, she pulled her flannel nightgown over her head and limped barefoot down the stairs. Without her brace on she had to be exceptionally careful because her knee and ankle were

so unstable, but she leaned heavily on the railing and negotiated the steps successfully.

When she'd considered buying this house, she had hesitated
because of the stairs, but everything else was so perfect that
she had assured herself that one or two trips a day up and
down these stairs was something she could manage. And so
far she had.

With care she crossed to the small room she used as a study.
The letter was waiting for her on the blotter, glowing whitely
in the near-dark. She hesitated to reach for it, however, suddenly feeling strangely reluctant.

Instead she went to the window and looked out at the night.
No city dweller, as she had been most of her life, could possibly imagine how dark the night was out here. Stars sprinkled
the sky in breathtaking profusion, and with only their gentle
light the world appeared to vanish in the black of night.

She could see the hulking shape of the tree at the corner of
the house, and the dark shadow of the barn silhouetted against
the star-spangled sky. She could dimly see the edge of the
porch but little was visible beyond it. From a distance she
heard the lonely hoot of an owl, carried on the soft sigh of
the breeze.

She might have stayed there for hours, admiring the perfec-
tion of the night, except that the envelope on her desk was
like a silent pressure, beckoning to her and tugging at her. Jo
wasn't one to waste paper or telephone calls. If she'd written,
it was important enough to take the time.

Still feeling reluctant, she limped to the desk, taking care
to balance properly on her bad leg. It was a relief to lean
against the desk and know for a few minutes that she wasn't
apt to fall if she didn't pay strict attention.

With a flick of her wrist, she turned on the desk lamp, then
opened the letter. The note was brief and very much to the
point.

Dear Esther,
I'm leaving for Europe in a couple of minutes and don't
have time to call, but I want you to hear this as soon as

possible, and I don't want you to hear it from anyone but me.

You know I have a strict policy of not releasing client addresses or phone numbers, but in this case I'm afraid it has happened. One of my new employees couldn't see any harm in giving your father the information....

Esther crumpled the paper in her hands, unable to read another word. Her father knew where she was. *He knew!*

Her mouth was dry, her palms damp, and her heart was hammering rapidly. The night which had seemed so beautiful only moments before was suddenly filled with threat. Her father might even now be somewhere in Conard County, Wyoming.

How long had he known?

Quickly, with trembling hands, she spread out the crumpled letter and searched frantically for the information. Jo didn't say when the address had been given out, but her letter was dated the tenth, three days ago. That meant Richard Jackson had known his daughter's whereabouts for at least that long and probably longer.

Panic washed over her in hot and cold waves. She had to close the windows and lock them. *Now!* He might be out there watching, waiting, planning.... Oh, God, he had always hurt her at night. Always. Stinking of alcohol and his own vomit, he had filled the night with terror and pain.

She locked the study windows swiftly, sobbing for breath as her heart continued to beat like a jackhammer. Limping painfully now, she hurried toward the living room to close those windows.

Her knee buckled suddenly, sending her sprawling face-down in the hallway at the foot of the stairs. Oh, God, oh, God... Broken prayers wandered through her frightened mind as she gasped for air and waited for the shattering pain to subside. She felt so helpless...she *was* so helpless...

She had no idea how long she lay there. The night whispered about her, touching her with soft hands. Somewhere an owl hooted sadly. Crickets chirped undisturbed. There was nothing in the darkness except her own terrors.

Nothing.

A bubble of laughter rose from her stomach. There was an edge of hysteria to it, and she caught it, refusing to let it escape. Forcing herself to draw slow, deep breaths, she reached for sanity, and found it in an image of her own panic. She had been acting like a damn fool, driven by images out of the past that had little bearing on the reality of now. For God's sake, she was a grown woman, no longer a helpless, frightened child. If Richard Jackson showed his face on her doorstep, she would blow his head off.

All she needed to do was get a gun. Just that. She would be safe then.

Her knee hurt when she stood up again, but she ignored it. Pain was nothing new or frightening to her. It was merely an obstacle to be surmounted. She did, however, take care not to put her weight down wrong again.

She locked the windows and locked the doors, then climbed painfully up to her room. Richard knew better, she told herself. After all these years in prison, he *had* to know better. He wouldn't dare show up out here.

But she couldn't sleep anyway, and lay awake into the wee hours trying to think of something, *anything,* except Richard Jackson and how he probably wanted to kill her.

Chapter 3

"Good afternoon, Miz Jackson." Deputy Sheriff Micah Parish climbed out of his Blazer and walked between her flowerbeds to the porch. He was a big man, bigger even than Craig Nighthawk, with the same inky black hair and dark eyes. His face, too, spoke strongly of his Native American ancestry. "Just thought I'd drop by and see how you're doing."

Over the last three years, Esther had become fond of Micah Parish. He was the deputy who most often dropped by to check on her, claiming it was on his way home. Esther knew better. "I'm doing just fine, Deputy. Would you like something to drink?"

He favored her with a smile. "I could do with some of that iced tea."

"I'll be right back with it."

Guinevere wanted out. She stood impatiently at the door, chuffing eagerly. The dog was fond of Deputy Parish, who always had a minute or two to play fetch.

When she returned a few minutes later with tea for the deputy, man and dog were sitting companionably together on the steps, Guinevere soaking up a good scratch behind her ears.

"Thanks," Parish said as he accepted the tea. "If Guin ever has pups, let me know. My kids would love one."

She knew Micah had three children. He'd mentioned them at one time or another, and she found herself wondering about them. "How old are they?"

"Sally's seven. Jacob and Jeremy are three."

"Twins? Your wife's hands must be full."

"She seems to love it." A smile settled deep in his dark eyes, and Esther felt a twinge of envy for the contentment she saw reflected in his face. "Faith swears her entire purpose in life is to look after me and the kids. I reckon that'll change some when the kids get older, but for now we're all loving it."

"I imagine." For her own part, Esther couldn't imagine spending her life looking after other people. She'd been forced to spend entirely too much of her childhood doing exactly that.

"So, is everything all right with you?" he asked her.

"Well, yes."

But he must have heard her hesitation. His fingers paused on the dog's neck and he turned so he could look directly at her. "That sounded qualified."

"Well…" She hesitated, thinking of the letter that had kept her up most of the last two nights. "I guess it is."

"Anything I can do?"

"I don't know." Much as she wanted some reassurance, she didn't know how much she wanted to explain. Micah Parish seemed like a nice man, but…did she want to bare so much of her soul to him?

He scratched Guinevere's ears again, then ran his palm down the dog's back. "I don't stop by here because I'm uninterested."

"No, I realize that."

He nodded, looking out over the prairie toward the mountains. "Sometimes it's not good to be alone."

She hesitated, not certain if he was speaking obliquely to her or about himself. She waited to see what he might add.

"I spent a good part of my life alone, psychologically and emotionally. That's the worst kind of aloneness, feeling like you have nobody to turn to or depend on. If you need someone, there's more than one person you can turn to. Me. Nate Tate. Janet and Abel Pierce. You're not alone, Miz Jackson.''

"Thank you."

"Nothing to thank me for. I'm just stating a fact. So whatever's troubling you, when you get ready to talk about it, give one of us a call.''

"Actually…" She needed someone to tell her she had nothing to fear. She needed to hear that almost as much as she needed to breathe. Not that she would believe it, but she needed to hear it anyway. "My father…got out of prison a while back. Last year sometime. I don't want him to find me."

"Can he?"

"Someone in my agent's office gave him my address recently. I just found out about it."

He looked at her. "Are you hiding from him?"

"Trying to."

"Why?"

"He was…he was in prison for killing my mother."

He nodded. "I see. But maybe he learned a little something."

"Maybe." But she didn't believe it. She remembered his temper all too well. "Is there any way I could get a restraining order so he has to stay away from me?"

"Well, you'd really have to talk to a lawyer about it, but I don't think so. Not unless he does something."

"Oh." Not that she could imagine how a restraining order would stop Richard Jackson. It never had in the past. Feeling cold despite the warmth of the day, she suppressed a shiver. For the last fifteen years she had lived with the cold comfort of knowing that man was in prison. Now she had to live in a world where there was no comfort at all. Apparently he hadn't forgotten her, as she had desperately hoped. But he wouldn't. He had a big grudge to bear.

"Thanks," she said dismally.

"On the other hand," Micah said slowly, "if you think there's a possibility there might be trouble, we can sure keep an eye out. What's his name?"

"Richard Jackson."

"What was he convicted of? And where?"

Her lips suddenly felt stiff, and she realized how very much she didn't want to speak these words. "Second degree murder. We were in Portland at the time."

"Oregon or Maine?" He pulled a pad out of his pocket and began writing rapidly.

"Oregon." Where it never stopped raining. Her memory of her childhood was one unending blur of pain, fear and wet, dismal days.

"What does he look like?"

Esther shook her head, feeling her heart give an anxious skip. "I can't remember. I honestly can't remember." And that terrified her. Would she remember him if she saw him face-to-face? And if not, how could she possibly protect herself?

Micah stayed a while longer, talking about events of general interest in the county. Esther listened with only half an ear, involved as she was in her own worries. Vaguely she was aware that he pressed her gently for more information but the simple fact was, telling anyone what had been done to her and her mother meant remembering, and she was willing to go to almost any lengths not to do that. She'd spent too many years burying the past to want to exhume it now.

When Micah Parish at last rose to leave, she was truly sorry to see him go. Night was drawing closer, and with night came terror.

Without Guinevere, she would go nuts. That was the first coherent thought in Esther's mind the following morning. The dog kept her sane. Not only did Guin provide companionship, she also provided a sense of safety. If any stranger came up to the house, Guinevere would alert her. The fact that the Saint Bernard would probably love an intruder to death was irrelevant. At least Esther would have a chance to protect herself because of the warning.

Guinevere's presence beside her bed was the only thing that

had made it possible for her to get to sleep last night. Today she was going to go to town and buy a gun. Period.

Before the coffee finished brewing, the phone rang. Sheriff Nate Tate's warm voice poured into her ear. "How's my favorite artist this morning?"

"Let me guess. You've been talking to Micah Parish."

He chuckled. "The man put a little bug in my ear first thing. What can I say? So, how are you doing?"

"I'm sleep deprived and probably hallucinatory as a result," she admitted dryly. "I'm convinced my dog is my only lifeline to sanity."

"Not a little stressed, are you?"

"Just a teeny-weeny bit. I'll be in town later today to get a gun. Maybe then I can sleep."

"Can I talk you out of this? Not coming to town, of course. By all means come to town and I'll buy you a cup of that stuff they call coffee in the front office. But can I talk you out of the gun?"

Esther closed her eyes, suddenly and shockingly wishing Nate Tate had been her father. Or that she could have had a father even a little bit like the sheriff. "Nate, I need to sleep. And even though Guinevere will bark her head off if some stranger shows up, she's a friendly dog. She's not protection."

"You might be surprised what she'll be if she feels you're threatened. But be that as it may, how about the fact that a gun kept for protection is more likely to be used by the criminal against the owner than the other way around?"

Esther felt her stomach sink. "Did you have to tell me that?"

"Yes," Nate said gently. "I did. Because it's true. If you want to buy a gun, you have to be sure you *will* use it to kill, you have to learn how to use it, and then you have to lock it up somewhere so the criminal can't find it before you can get to it. As for Guinevere giving you the time to do so...well, if she's so friendly, she might succumb to a juicy treat."

"Gee, thanks! You're making me feel great."

He chuckled. "I thought I'd perk up your day." He paused a moment, then added, "I'm not opposed to you having a gun,

but you're going to need to learn to use it. You're going to
have to be very careful not to panic and shoot some innocent
person, and you'd damn well better be able to prove self-
defense if you *do* shoot someone, or you're going to spend
the rest of your days in jail. That's the reality of gun owner-
ship.''

"Forget the gun." Her stomach had sunk again, that roller-
coaster feeling of taking a sudden drop. "You're right, it's not
a good idea. I'm not sure I could shoot anyone. Even him.''

"It's not an easy thing to do," Nate agreed. "And do you
really think he wants to hurt you? After all this time?"

Esther closed her eyes, her hand tightening around the receiver until her fingers ached. "I don't know. I honestly don't
know." But he had plenty of reason to want to.

"We'll keep an eye out, Esther. If he shows up in this
county, he won't be here long before we find out about it. I'll
have a word with him, okay?"

"Okay. Thanks.''

A few moments later she hung up, feeling as if she'd just
hit a dead end.

Guinevere had come downstairs and was sitting at her feet,
as if she understood her mistress's distress.

"I'm just being a big baby, aren't I?" Esther asked the dog.
Guin thumped her tail in agreement. "Just because he wanted
my address doesn't mean he'll show up here. He might just
write a letter, right?"

Guin woofed.

"I thought you'd agree. Well, let me get my coffee, and
then we'll make a list for the grocery store.''

When she sat at the table with her coffee and English muffin, she noticed a small smear of blood on the floor where
Guin had been sitting. The dog was in heat. Wonderful. She
looked down at the Saint Bernard, who looked up at her with
sad doggy eyes.

"I guess you're not coming to town with me today, girl,"
Esther said. "We'd wind up being chased by every testoster-
one-laden mutt in town. And you'd spend the whole time try-

ing to get away from me so you could have a roll in the hay, wouldn't you?''

Guinevere yawned.

"That's what I thought. You have this unfortunate tendency to turn into a...well, you know. You don't behave like a lady.''

The dog whined softly.

"Sorry, but I don't approve. I'll find a gentleman for you one of these days, I promise.'' And would have done long ago if they had still been living in Seattle. Registered short-haired Saint Bernards weren't common around here, unfortunately. Maybe she should just give up all hope of breeding Guinevere.

And then it struck her that she might very well have to move soon. If Richard Jackson showed up here, she was going to have to sell this property and move somewhere he couldn't find her. God, would it never end?

Before she went to the supermarket, she stopped in the sheriff's office which was on a corner across from the Courthouse Square. Old men were in their usual seats on the park benches, and a couple of them had brought folding chairs and a table so that they could play chess in the shade of a big tree. The afternoon breeze was dry and pleasant.

Inside the sheriff's office things were moving at a slow, quiet pace.

"Not much going on today,'' Velma Jansen told her from the dispatcher's desk. "Verna says you're working on a big painting of a mountain.''

"I hope it turns out. I've never done anything so big before.''

Velma paused in the act of lighting another one of her endless cigarettes. "Of course it will! Don't even think about anything else. If you do, you'll choke. Go on back. Nate's up to his ears in paper and he'll be glad for any distraction you can give him.''

When she entered the sheriff's office, he rose, greeting her with a big smile. At fifty he was still a handsome man and his smile was one of the warmest she'd ever seen.

"Rescue!" he said with pleasure, pointing at the stacks of paper on his desk. "You couldn't have timed it any better. Coffee?"

"Thanks, but I'll pass. I've already had my quota today."

Gage Dalton, the department's special investigator, stuck his head in the door for a minute, and greeted Esther. They had worked together a couple of times when she had made drawings for the department. "Here's the rap sheet you wanted, Nate. It just came in."

"Thanks."

Gage closed the door behind him as he left, and Nate's brow furrowed as he read the papers he'd been given. Esther looked past him out the window at the square. It was such a beautiful day that it was impossible to believe any threat could lurk out there. If Richard intended to come after her, why hadn't he shown up already? Maybe he'd just been curious about what had happened to her. She clung to the possibility like a straw in the wind.

"Well," Nate said finally, looking up, "Richard Jackson was one hell of a sumbitch."

Esther's heart lurched at the mention of her father.

Nate waved the papers he'd just read. "His rap sheet. I figured since you were nervous I'd find out what you were nervous about. Now I know, judging by this stack of restraining orders to keep him away from you and your mother. They didn't work."

Her mouth felt as dry as sand. "No."

"Eighteen arrests for battery against your mother. Charges dropped every time."

"She was afraid he would kill her."

Nate nodded, looking as if he'd tasted something very unpleasant. "I know the routine. One very big charge of battery against a child. You." His gaze drifted to her lame leg. "Did he do that to you?"

She managed a nod before she looked away, ashamed.

"He did finally kill your mother, I see."

"Yes."

"And now he's out. Since...last May."

She nodded, compressing her lips and trying to leash a whole bunch of suddenly overwhelming emotions. She wanted to cry, to scream, to smash something. If life were at all fair, Richard Jackson would have died in prison. But life wasn't fair. Not even remotely. Hadn't she learned that almost from birth?

Nate continued. "Assorted other crimes, all apparently linked to alcohol. Did your mother drink, too?"

Esther wanted to crawl under a rock and stay forever in a dark place where no one would see her shame.

"Never mind," Nate said. "She probably did. Regardless, it doesn't excuse your father's conduct. I can see why you're afraid of this guy."

She looked at him again, feeling as bleak as a day in the dead of winter. "Deputy Parish said I probably can't get a restraining order."

"That would be my guess, too. It wouldn't do any good anyway. The man never listened to them before. Of course, he's a hell of a lot older now, and maybe a little wiser. It'd shock the bleeding hearts to know this, but sometimes prison *does* have a corrective effect. And sometimes, just getting older is enough to do the trick."

She gave him a strained smile. "I guess I'll just have to hope."

He pursed his lips. "Well, we'll sure keep an eye out. I'll increase the patrols in your area, but until we have something more that's all I can do. If he shows up here, let me know. If he contacts you in any way, let me know. Then we'll talk about what more we can do."

He wasn't being unreasonable, and she knew it. In fact, he was being far more helpful than most lawmen would be, she figured. After all, fifteen years had passed, and in all that time there was absolutely no indication that Richard Jackson intended any further harm to his daughter. He hadn't even made a threat toward her. So maybe he had learned his lesson.

"Thanks, Nate. I really appreciate it."

He spread his hands. "We'll do more the instant there's any indication we need to. Now how's the rest of your life?"

For some reason she found herself telling him about Cromwell and Craig Nighthawk. Maybe she wanted to get some idea of what Nate thought of Nighthawk. Maybe she needed reassurance on that score, too. Trusting men didn't come easily to her, but she trusted Nate Tate. How could any woman not trust a man with a beautiful, loving wife and six obviously happy daughters...not to mention grandchildren.

"He replaced the flowers, huh," Nate said when she finished her tale. He was still smiling over her description of the sheep. "Nighthawk's okay. I don't think you need to worry about him. In fact, I think he might be a good neighbor to have. All his dealings that I know of have been honest and straight."

"What about...his arrest?"

Nate shook his head. "That was a *big* mistake. Some folks won't let go of it, but don't you pay them any mind. They'd believe anything that makes another human being look bad. Hell, I'll bet they read the supermarket tabloids and think they're gospel!"

When she stepped out onto the street a little while later, the sun momentarily blinded her. She paused, and for an instant the world seemed to freeze. Was that Richard Jackson standing on the corner over there?

She blinked hard and looked again, but whoever it was had moved on. It couldn't have been him. How could it be? She didn't even remember what he looked like.

But unease followed her through the supermarket, and all the way home.

When she pulled up to her house, she was astonished to see Craig Nighthawk's dog sitting on her front porch. Then she remembered that Guinevere was in heat. Great. How foolish of her to think that out here in the middle of nowhere this wasn't going to be a problem.

She climbed out of her Jimmy and surveyed the situation. If she tried to get into the house right now, chances were that Mop would slip right past her and get inside. Or maybe Guin would be totally disobedient and slip outside. Either way she was probably going to wind up with some pups she didn't want—assuming Mop didn't hurt her dog.

Limping more than usual because of fatigue, she walked slowly up to the porch. The komondor turned to look at her, his brown eyes hardly visible beneath his thick cords of fur. His snout was dark brown and shorthaired, but the rest of him did indeed resemble a slightly dirty string mop. And he was every bit as big as Guinevere.

"Hello, Mop."

His shaggy head cocked as he recognized his name. Well, that was promising. She didn't have it in her heart to be angry with him. He was only being a dog, after all, and right now Guinevere was irresistible to him, a femme fatale in white-and-brown fur.

"I'm sorry, guy, but the lady is unavailable."

Mop moved something which appeared to be a tail.

"No, I'm afraid you can't persuade me by wagging. I'm hard-hearted, you see. Utterly implacable. Immovable."

Mop appeared unimpressed.

"The Wicked Witch of the West has nothing on me. Trust me. I shall be very angry if Guinevere has a litter. She has registered champion bloodlines, you see."

Mop offered a pleading groan.

"Well, I understand perfectly that you may be a prime example of your breed," Esther told him kindly. "In fact you may come from champion bloodlines as well. But they are *different* lines, you see. Mop, I hate to tell you this, but you *aren't* a Saint Bernard. And while I wouldn't ordinarily have a problem with you, I just don't want to be saddled with four or more puppies that no one else wants! You'll have to find somewhere else to sow your wild oats, I'm afraid."

Mop whimpered softly and wagged his entire body.

"No, I can't be persuaded. Good heavens, Mop, you wouldn't even be around to raise and support them! I know you men! You just run off and leave all the responsibility to the woman. You'd be out there herding sheep as if you hadn't a care in the world and poor Guinevere would be saddled with all these hungry pups. I won't change my mind."

Mop settled down with his head on his paws watching both the door of the house and Esther at the same time.

Cautiously, Esther squatted and scratched behind his ears—or at least where she presumed his ears to be. Ah, yes, there they were. "You're an engaging rake," she told him gently. "You even have nice manners, and I wasn't expecting that from an outdoor dog. I thought you'd be far more aggressive and full of yourself. After all, those sheep certainly jump when you bark. All of them except Cromwell, that is."

"Can I have my dog back?"

Straightening, Esther turned and saw that Craig Nighthawk had appeared on horseback at the fence line. "Certainly," she called to him. "Be my guest."

Craig whistled. Mop lifted his shaggy head and looked toward his master. A whimper escaped him, but he didn't budge.

"Mop, come here."

Mop woofed but remained unmoved.

Craig said something that sounded like an oath, though Esther really couldn't be sure at this distance. He whistled yet again, and when the dog ignored him once again, he dismounted and eased himself through the barbed wire. The man who strode toward her this afternoon had none of the easy manner she'd seen the morning they met. In fact, he looked seriously annoyed.

"What have you done to my dog?" he asked.

"Not a thing, really. I just got home and found him here."

"You've bewitched him, right?" He settled his hands on his hips and looked from her to the dog and back.

"Actually, it was a love potion."

He looked startled. "A what?"

"A love potion."

"Oh, for Pete's sake!"

"I kid you not, Mr. Nighthawk. Mop is smitten."

Realization dawned. "Your dog is in heat?"

"In a manner of speaking. Why do they call it heat, do you suppose?"

He looked at her, as if he couldn't quite believe his ears.

"I can't imagine," he said finally. "Why the hell haven't you had your dog spayed?"

"Why the hell haven't you had yours neutered?"

He scowled. "Because I'm going to need more sheepdogs for the rest of my life, and I can't afford to buy new ones every time I turn around! I have a breeding pair of komondors!"

"You have a female? Really?"

"Yes, I have a female!"

"So Mop isn't deprived as I thought?"

Now he looked thunderstruck. "Deprived? You were worried if the dog was *deprived?*"

"Well, of course I was. Dogs are very social creatures, and sometimes they need the companionship of dogs as well as people. I've been worrying because Guinevere has no one but me. Unfortunately, I can't let her play with Mop because I don't want to have a litter of puppies just now."

"Thank God for small favors. Mop is a working dog. He can't just run off and play any time he feels like it. That's reserved for when work is done."

"That's perfectly fair."

"But *you* need to have your dog spayed."

Esther was offended. "I'll do no such thing! I'll have you know Guinevere has champion bloodlines, and I fully intend to breed her one of these days."

"Good luck. If there's another champion shorthaired Saint Bernard within five hundred miles, I'll eat my hat."

He was very likely right, but that was begging the issue. "When the time comes, that will be the least of my difficulties. For now, she remains as she is!"

"I can't have my dog running off like this!"

"I'm sorry, but there's nothing I can do about what your dog does. Surely other dogs in the vicinity come into heat from time to time. Mop will just have to learn to deal with it. Moreover, you seem to have an unusual amount of trouble keeping your animals on your side of the fence! Maybe you should check for gaping holes. Surely this dog can't have climbed *through* the wire!"

She had a valid point, and it was enough to make him pause before he said something terminally stupid. "He must have jumped."

"And Cromwell, too? If you're having this much trouble with jumping, perhaps you should make your fence higher."

"Maybe," he acknowledged grumpily. The last thing he wanted to do right now was check the fence line again. He'd just done that ten days ago. But the inescapable fact was that he must have wire down somewhere. He'd never known Mop to jump before.

"By the way," Esther said more pleasantly, now that she felt she was winning, "what do you call the other dog?"

"Bucket."

"Mop and Bucket?" And suddenly she couldn't hold it in anymore. The entire thing was too amusing, and laughter spilled out of her helplessly. "Mop and Bucket!"

Slowly, almost reluctantly, a smile dawned on his harsh face. "It was Paula's idea."

All of a sudden she felt deflated, but she couldn't understand why. He must be married. That should have been reassuring, but somehow it wasn't.

He looked down at the dog. "Mop, come."

Mop thumped his tail as if to acknowledge the command, but he didn't move.

"Am I going to have to get a rope and drag you?"

At that, Mop sighed heavily and rose to his feet.

"Now come on!"

Looking as if he were going to execution, the dog obeyed. Craig paused a moment, looking at Esther. "Are the flowers okay?"

She looked down at the beds around the porch, thinking that they looked perfectly healthy to her. And then she understood. "They're beautiful. Thank you so very much for planting them."

He nodded. "Next time just shoo Cromwell off. If you don't want to get close, use a broom. She's scared to death of brooms."

A chuckle escaped Esther. "Really. How did she learn that?"

"From my sister. Paula caught Crom in the kitchen garden last spring and lit into her with a broom. Crom now has the greatest respect for Paula and brooms."

His sister! Relief washed through her in an exhilarating wave. "She sounds like a woman after my own heart."

Craig cocked his head. "Maybe so." He touched the brim of his hat with his forefinger, then started to turn away. He paused, looking at all the sacks in her Jimmy. "Are those groceries? Let me help you get them inside."

"That might be difficult considering we have two lovelorn dogs."

His smile crinkled the corners of his eyes. "I can tie Mop to the fence if you can leash Guinevere."

"Done."

Even in heat Guinevere was a well-behaved dog. She accepted being leashed to the newel post with nothing more than a reproachful look. Mop was less docile, barking a few times after being tied to a fence post. He settled down, though.

Craig's help made quick work of the groceries. It felt strange to have a man in her house, though. Outdoors his presence was commanding, but indoors it was...overwhelming. He seemed to fill rooms in a way that made it impossible to ignore his presence. Her house, which had seemed large to her, now felt full to the rafters. Esther told herself that was simply because she wasn't used to having anyone else there.

"Can I offer you some coffee?" she asked when he set the last bag on the counter.

"Just a glass of ice water, please."

The kitchen was a large room in the style of ranch kitchens, and she hoped someday to put a big table in it. For now she had a small dinette that looked even smaller when Craig folded himself into one of the chairs.

She poured a glass of tea for herself, but as she was debating whether to join Craig at the table or keep a safe distance at the counter, the doorbell rang. "Excuse me."

It was Verna with another letter. "You're getting popular,"

the letter carrier said with a grin. "Two letters in one week. Some kind of record, isn't it?"

"Can you come in for some tea?" She was surprised to feel herself hoping both that Verna would accept and that she would refuse.

"Sorry, I can't. You're not my last stop today. Have a good one."

Esther watched her go, wondering why her life suddenly seemed to be a sea of conflicting emotions. And why had Verna been in such a hurry to leave? Usually she wanted to chat for a couple of minutes.

As the woman drove away, Esther saw Nighthawk's horse and dog, tethered to the fence post, and no Craig in evidence. There were a lot of scenarios that might be drawn, but she had a strong feeling which connection Verna had made. By tomorrow evening it was probably going to be all over Conard County that Craig Nighthawk and Esther Jackson were romancing.

Inwardly Esther shrugged. Considering that she was a recluse, she hardly cared what anyone thought. Then she looked down at the envelope in her hand. It was addressed in a spidery scrawl that she didn't recognize, without a return address.

Suddenly her heart was hammering so loudly that it filled her ears. With shaking hands, she ripped the envelope open and pulled out a yellow sheet of paper. Her eyes skipped over everything, down to the signature.

Dad.

"Esther? Esther, what's wrong?"

She heard Craig Nighthawk's voice. It seemed to come from far away, from an entirely different planet than the one on which she stood holding a letter from the man who had shattered her body and her life.

"Esther?" Tentatively he touched her shoulder.

Jerkily she turned her head to look at him, and felt a shudder pass through her as shock released its grip. She couldn't find her voice, but there was mute appeal in every cell of her body.

He hesitated visibly, then reached out for her, wrapping her tightly in his arms and holding her close to his chest. "What happened?'' he asked gently. ''Did that woman say something to you?''

Some corner of her mind registered that this was the way a man's touch was supposed to feel—safe and caring. Part of her was stunned that she was even allowing herself to be held, but the rest of her reached out for the comfort she had never before known. No one had ever held her caringly. Never.

''Is it the letter?'' Craig asked. ''Is there anything I can do?''

She ought to straighten, ought to pull away. She couldn't afford to depend on anyone, certainly not a man she hardly knew. But she needed what he was offering, and with every fiber of her being she wanted to cling to him.

Holding her tightly with one arm, he took the letter from her hand and read it.

''What's wrong?'' he asked. ''All he says is he wants a chance to apologize to you. Is that what upset you?''

She tried to pull away, but his hold tightened. Her cheek was pressed to his chest and she could hear the steady thud of his heart. He felt so hard, so strong. What could he possibly understand about her terror?

''Esther, please. I can't help if I don't know what's wrong.''

''I don't want his apology!'' Anger was beginning to come to her rescue, swift and hot. She'd cowered enough in her life and despised herself for it. Her entire psyche was a tangled web of scars, shame and guilt. It no longer mattered which scars were rational and which fears were unfounded. It no longer mattered that none of it had really been her fault. She was wounded, permanently warped, and none of those feelings would ever go away. And that made her angry.

''Why not?''

''He killed my mother! He hurt us both for years! And he wants to hurt me again!''

Craig never slackened his hold on her shoulders, keeping her tucked to his chest even though she was trying to yank away. ''That isn't what he says.''

''Well, I don't believe him! I stopped believing him before I was five. He lies about everything.''

"Okay. He lies about everything. Did he really kill your mother?"

This time when she pushed away from him he let her go. With clenched fists she glared up at him. "Do you think I'm lying? The man went to prison for second degree murder! Now he's out and wants to find *me*. He's going to kill me. I know it!"

"But maybe he's learned something, Esther. Maybe he really *is* sorry now."

"No. No way."

"But why would he want to kill you? It's been a long time."

She shook her head almost wildly, her hair flying. "Not long enough. It'll never be long enough. It was my testimony that sent him to prison!"

Chapter 4

Craig forgot about his horse and dog tethered to the fence post. He forgot about sheep and ranching and his sister and her kids and all his financial worries. All that mattered was this small, emotionally battered woman and her fear that her own father wanted to kill her.

He didn't doubt her. The man was a convicted murderer so it was obvious he was capable of it. And if her testimony had been what put the man away, he might well be harboring a grudge.

He coaxed Esther back into the kitchen and got her settled at the table. "I'll put the groceries away while you talk," he told her. "Just tell me where everything goes."

It was nuts, he thought, but it was the only safe thing to do right now because he'd made the mistake of holding her. Now he knew how she felt in his arms—and how very much he wanted to hold her even closer. How very much he wanted to taste her and touch her. His reaction embarrassed him a little because it was so inappropriate. He had thought he'd gotten himself under control a long time ago.

Her directions about where to put things were mechanical,

as if she had withdrawn and only a superficial part of her mind was involved in the task. Guinevere, still hitched to the newel post, whined as if she sensed her mistress's distress, but Esther didn't seem to hear her.

Craig began to feel uneasy. He'd had his share of hard times, but nothing had prepared him to deal with an emotional crisis of this type. There wasn't a thing he could possibly say to her that would ease her fears. All he knew was he couldn't leave her alone.

"I was going to get a gun," Esther said suddenly.

Craig turned from putting the last of the food away and waited expectantly.

"I figured that if I got a gun I could protect myself. Sheriff Tate talked me out of it."

That was probably wise, he thought. He didn't know this woman at all, but somehow he couldn't imagine her as Annie Oakley.

She looked at him from hazel eyes that had gone flat and empty. "So how do I protect myself?" she asked him. "Just what am I supposed to do? Wait for him to show up in the middle of the night and strangle me? Or shove me down the stairs the way he used to?"

"He shoved you down the stairs?"

She nodded. "Once he even threw me." She touched her leg. "That's when my leg got messed up."

"The doctors couldn't do anything?"

"I didn't get to them soon enough. He was on a binge and wouldn't let my mother take me. Or maybe she didn't want to take me." She shrugged. "They didn't have any money, so they probably couldn't afford it."

"And no one investigated? No one tried to take you away from them?"

She shook her head slowly. "This was over twenty years ago. Twenty-five years ago. Nobody interfered in a family. My parents said I fell down the stairs, and I didn't dare say otherwise."

"My God."

"But I remember. I was just four, and he picked me up and

threw me as hard as he could." She shrugged a shoulder. "I was crying about something. I don't remember what. What I *do* remember is him saying he wouldn't have thrown me if I had just shut up."

"So it was *your* fault?"

"It was always my fault." She shook herself then, and some of the life came back to her eyes. "Sorry. You don't want to hear this, and I certainly don't want to repeat it. I must be boring you."

"Boring isn't the word I'd choose." Folding his arms, he looked down at her, taking in the way she was almost huddled as if she expected a blow. "You really think he's after you?"

She bit her lower lip and shook her head. "I can't say for certain. Who could? But...yes, I think it's a definite possibility."

"Are you sure your testimony convicted him?"

"How can I be sure? I was fifteen at the time and I can barely remember getting on the stand. But I know he told the police that he and my mother had gone out to a bar together, that she'd gotten into a fight with someone in the parking lot, and that he'd intervened and brought her home where she tripped and fell down the stairs."

She lifted her head and looked up at him. "They'd gone to a bar all right. But she was fine when they got home. Maybe a little drunk, but not as drunk as he was. They got into a fight, he beat her up pretty bad, then knocked her down the stairs. I saw the whole thing."

"But maybe they had other evidence, too."

"I don't know. I *do* know that he said he'd kill me if I ever told anyone what he'd done."

"But you did anyway."

"He killed my mother!"

He unfolded his arms and spread his hands. "I'm not criticizing you, Esther. I'm just thinking how brave you were."

"I wasn't brave, I was mad. As furious as I've ever been. But I don't want to talk about it. Damn it, I don't even want to think about it! Why couldn't *he* have been the one to fall down the stairs?"

But he hadn't been, and Craig felt a genuine concern for Esther's safety. There was absolutely no way anyone could predict what her father might do. All these years in prison might simply have turned him into a very angry, very vindictive man.

Although the letter didn't sound that way. Of course, it was brief, so brief that it wouldn't be safe to reach any conclusions based on it.

"I'm sorry," she said abruptly. "I shouldn't have said that."

"Why not? I can understand why you wish he'd fallen down those stairs."

"But it's wrong to wish that on anyone."

Craig shook his head and expelled a long breath. "So, let me see. It's not enough that he hurt you and terrorized you throughout your childhood. It's not enough that he's terrifying you right now. You have to feel guilty as well for wanting him out of your life?"

"I don't feel guilty for wanting him out of my life! I just shouldn't wish him dead."

"Why the hell not? It's apparent he won't stay out of your life any other way!"

The stark words hung on the air, and Esther seemed to shrink as if from a blow. He felt like a crud, a complete and total crud. But why should he feel bad for stating an obvious truth? Damn, this woman was an emotional mess. All twisted up in the barbed wire of guilt and fear. He wondered how she managed to laugh as easily as she did. He also wondered how she was going to handle this. And he felt about as useful as teats on a bull.

"Have you talked to the sheriff?"

"He said he'd keep an eye out, but there isn't a whole lot he can do unless my father does something."

"I guess that makes sense. Unfortunately."

She astonished him then with a small smile. "Unfortunately. No, I can understand it. He's served his time. Theoretically he's learned his lesson."

"Rehabilitated unless proved otherwise."

She nodded. "That's it."

"So..." He shook his head again and looked around.

"Would you mind if I made some coffee?"

"I'll do it."

Before he could stop her, she rose and limped toward the coffeepot and sink. He watched her move, taking no pains to conceal his stare, thinking it was a damn shame what people did to each other sometimes. He'd seen plenty of intolerance and hatred in his day, but he figured there ought to be a special place in hell for parents who hurt their kids. After all, a parent was the one person on earth that a kid ought to be able to trust.

"What are you going to do?" he asked her. The breeze must have changed direction because suddenly the yellow café curtains over the sink were billowing as warm, dry air blew into the kitchen, carrying with it the scent of sage and grass.

"I don't know. I'm thinking about moving again."

"Can you afford to?"

"Not really." She finished adding coffee and water to the coffeemaker, turned it on, and limped back to her seat. "Besides, there's no guarantee he wouldn't just find me again. If he's really determined, how could I possibly hide?"

He couldn't imagine that it was impossible to hide. There were a couple of TV shows that wouldn't be on the air if it were all that easy to find an individual. "How did he find you?"

"Through my agent. She has a policy of not releasing addresses or phone numbers, but one of her new employees apparently couldn't see anything wrong with giving my address to my father."

"I guess it never crossed the twerp's mind that if your father didn't already have your address there might be a good reason."

"I guess not."

"Makes you wonder, don't it?"

She smiled then, a more relaxed expression that told him she was beginning to unwind from her fear. That gladdened him more than he wanted to think about. "They say it takes all kinds."

"Yeah, but there oughtta be a special law against turkeys and total idiots."

"I rather like turkey for dinner."

He chuckled, truly liking her and her sense of humor. "It sure beats eating crow."

She laughed, visibly relaxing.

"Don't leave town, lady. I like your sense of humor."

She flushed a little and looked away. "It wouldn't pay to leave, I guess. I have to maintain some kind of contact with the rest of the world—assuming I don't want to give up my career—and as long as I do, sooner or later he'll find me."

The coffee finished brewing and Craig found the cups in the cabinet by the sink, filling one for each of them and joining her at the table. Esther wrapped her hands around her mug as if they were cold, although the day was plenty warm, and the breeze coming through the open windows of the kitchen did little to cool things down.

She spoke. "You know, I never realized how depressing rain is until I got away from it."

"Where are you from?"

"The Pacific Northwest. Portland and Seattle and assorted small towns. We moved a lot, probably because my father was always in trouble. Anyway, it rains a lot there. Most of the time, in fact. There's an old joke that Oregon is thirty-eight million umbrellas with feet."

Obliging her, he cracked a smile. "Not my kind of place."

"I never really thought much about it. That's the way it was. I just pulled on a raincoat or picked up an umbrella and did what I needed to. But since I moved here—one of the very first things I noticed is how dry it is. Believe it or not, the dryness is invigorating. After I'd been here a week, I felt like I was coming out of a long, dark tunnel."

She shrugged, smiling faintly, and turned her head to look out the window as if she couldn't bear to meet his gaze. "Of course, that may have had something to do with a change in circumstances."

"Maybe. But there *is* a difference between dry and humid climates. Now maybe I'm prejudiced because I grew up not too far from here, but I prefer a dry climate."

"Two percent humidity may be a little extreme, though. In the winter my skin cracks."

She was trying to draw the conversation away from her worries, he realized. Maybe that was a good thing, maybe that was even a healthy thing, but it wasn't the way he was programmed. As a rule he didn't like to let go of a problem until he'd come up with some kind of solution—although in this case there didn't appear to be any solution in sight.

Well, if she was going to shore up her defenses and close him out, then she didn't need him anymore, and he might just as well get back to his work. The fence sure as hell had to be down somewhere, and he needed to find it before he lost more than a lovesick sheepdog and a batty ewe. He ought to ride over and check on how the flock was doing, too, before he headed back to the house and got to work on the new flooring for the shearing shed. There was always something that needed doing and he didn't have a whole lot of time to spend gabbing over coffee.

On the other hand, his spirit rebelled at leaving this woman alone with her fear. Her quite justifiable fear. "Listen," he said on impulse, "why don't you come stay at my place. My sister would probably be thrilled to have some company."

She looked startled. "That's...very kind of you. But I'm afraid I can't."

"Why not?"

"I have a deadline to meet. I need to work, and to do that I need my studio. No, I really couldn't stay with you, but thank you for offering."

"Well, it's up to you. If you change your mind, give me a call. I'm in the phone book."

And then he was left with no alternative but to go. He couldn't just plant himself in her kitchen for the rest of the day making aimless conversation, leaving her to wonder if he ever planned to let her get on with her life. And he *did* have things he needed to do. He rose, and she rose with him.

"I can find my way out," he assured her. "If you need anything, just call my place. If I'm not there, Paula or Enoch will be, and they'll be over lickety-split."

"Thank you."

He waved away her thanks. "That's what neighbors are for."

She walked him to the door anyway. "I'll keep Guinevere on a leash until she's out of heat."

He flashed her a sudden grin. "We may not be able to defeat the call of the wild."

She pursed her lips almost primly. "My Guinevere will stay indoors so your Studley Dooright might as well just stay home."

Something crazy must have possessed him then, because just before he stepped out onto the porch he turned to face her, looking straight down into her wide, beautiful hazel eyes. "He may not be the only Studley who comes calling. Have a nice day."

He touched a finger to the brim of his hat and hightailed it out of there before she could reply. He was definitely losing his marbles, but man, it sure felt good. It had been too damn long since he'd done something outrageous just for the sheer fun of it.

But nothing was ever that easy or uncomplicated. Nope. That night while everyone watched TV, Craig found himself standing out on the porch looking up at the stars like some lonesome coyote. If he'd had the vocal cords for it, he would probably have howled at the moon.

He'd always thought of himself as a loner, believing himself to be content. Sometimes he got downright chapped when he spent too much time with people. But here he was, walking around and feeling lonely all the time.

Of course, it could be because he'd had to give up so much in the last few years. Even his war gaming had gone by the wayside, his carefully painted miniatures put away so that children couldn't break them, his sand table dismantled so that Mary and Bill would have a bedroom. Nor could he even cast any new figures to occupy himself with painting and mounting them. The materials were expensive, and besides, he didn't want molten lead around the children. Hell, he didn't want lead around Mary and Billy period.

Not that he regretted it. He believed in taking care of kin and to hell with the cost. But he missed his hobby.

He missed being on the road. He missed his trucker friends who'd kept in touch for a while but, face it, he was off the beaten track and their loads were taking them elsewhere.

The house that had once seemed ample now seemed crowded and noisy, but that was okay, except when he was feeling melancholy and lonely and wanted something that he couldn't quite name. All the life and liveliness inside only made him feel even lonelier.

But this feeling had been coming over him periodically ever since he could remember. What he ought to do was go back inside and watch that murder mystery with Paula and Enoch instead of standing out here looking up at the Big Dipper and feeling smaller than a flyspeck.

Instead he kept right on staring up into the infinite vastness of the night, feeling as if he might spin away into nothingness.

Back when he'd lived on the reservation, finding a woman he was allowed to date had been quite a challenge. Kinship had reached out among ranks of cousins to the extent that he could travel twenty-five or thirty miles, cast his eye on a waitress he'd never seen before in some diner, and be told she was related to him in some way that put her off-limits. It had been a relief when he got out into the larger world and discovered that he was free to ask just about anybody for a date.

Until he learned he was often being used. It was his being Indian that attracted most non-Indian women, not his personality or character. He had begun to feel like a scalp on somebody's coup belt. Several unpleasant experiences had made him extremely cautious, but not even caution could fully protect him. It certainly couldn't protect him from the hurt he saw in a woman's eyes when her family objected to him. Or when her friends walked away. Or when total strangers said something on the street.

That kind of treatment killed a relationship sooner or later. It had sure ended his. He had felt guilty all the damn time about the price a woman was paying to be with him, and guilt had made him resent her. In the end he was never sure if she left because he drove her off or because she got tired of being shunned by her family and friends.

Nor did it matter which it was. Either way it spelled disaster.

So what the hell was he doing getting the hots for a white woman? Because he *was* getting the hots for Esther Jackson. So far, each time he'd felt a flicker of it, he'd managed to smother it before he was forced to really notice it. Today something had shifted and now he was deeper in manure than the grass under the compost heap.

She had beautiful auburn hair, dark and rich with red. Her unusual hazel eyes, framed in thick, dark lashes, almost seemed to be lit from within. He didn't know why, but a woman's hair and eyes were the two features that most attracted him. In Esther's case, she was so busy trying to hide that leg brace that she managed to conceal any other attractive attributes she might have—except that day he'd found her wearing jeans. There was no mistaking then the gentle curve of her hips and the slender length of her legs. But it was her hair and eyes that had begun to haunt his dreams.

Like lovesick Mop who'd spent most of the remainder of the day sending soulful looks in the general direction of Esther's house, he found himself mooning about yards of silky hair trailing over his skin, about laughter flashing like sunlight in a pair of hazel eyes, about a laugh that was as refreshing and gentle as the bubbling of a lazy brook on a summer's afternoon.

Damn, he had a case of it, worse than any since his early twenties. He could almost have laughed at himself, except that the yearning was so powerful.

It didn't matter anyway. He'd never seen a woman who was looking any less for a relationship. She was plainly self-reliant, and not by word or gesture had she betrayed even the remotest interest in him as a man.

And even if she had, it would have been a recipe for heartache.

Hell, it was nothing to get all worked up about anyway. He just needed to get laid. All of this mooning was merely a function of protracted celibacy. There was nothing special about Esther Jackson except that she was an unattached female. Any unattached female would have the same effect on him.

Yeah. Right.

Laughing quietly at himself, he decided to drive into town and get some ice cream. The kids would be thrilled tomorrow and it would give him something to do besides mope.

The stairs mocked her. Esther stared at them with sudden loathing and considered sleeping on the couch in the study rather than climbing them. It wasn't that they were difficult to climb or descend—although they were—but suddenly she was awash in memories of the role stairs had played in her life.

Stairs were everywhere, and she'd never developed a phobia about them. They hadn't been responsible for her own injuries or her mother's death, after all. Her father bore the entire, unmitigated blame for that. Other than a qualm about the difficulty she would have mounting them because of her leg, she hadn't been put off by the stairs in her house.

Until tonight. Until she had to sit up with her insides roiling in fear over Richard Jackson's return to her life. *Dad.* How could he dare sign himself that after all he'd done? There wasn't a man on the planet less deserving of that title.

She had turned off all the lights again because the darkness seemed safer, the action a definite throwback to her childhood. When Richard had been on a drunken tear, she and her mother had tried desperately to stay out of the way and to avoid attracting his notice. One of the ways they had done that was to turn out all the lights and hide. Among her earliest memories was hiding in closets with her mother.

There was a sliver of moon tonight, and its light fell through the uncurtained window at the landing where the stairs switched back, and fell in a silver cascade toward Esther's feet.

It could have been beautiful, moonlight gleaming on polished wood. Instead it looked eerie, a stage set for a play that hadn't yet happened, a stage awaiting the arrival of the actors.

She shuddered and forced herself to turn away. If she ever bought another house she was going to buy one without stairs. Ridiculous or not, she didn't need unnecessary reminders of her past.

That was one of the reasons she didn't even keep a photograph of her mother out where she could see it. Not that there were many pictures. Family photos had consisted of the occasional snapshot taken by a friend or neighbor.

And that was another thing. Her parents had had a lot of friends, especially in earlier years, while Esther was still small. Neither of them had been such heavy drinkers back then, and had gone through long periods where they didn't drink much at all. There had been friends who came over in the evening to play cards and friends who had lived next door. There had been laughter and even some love.

She could remember it, if she tried very hard, although she usually tried to avoid it because it hurt so much. But there had been a time when her father hadn't been so angry very often, a time when she had felt secure in his arms and love.

Then had come the drunken rage when he threw her down the stairs. After that...well, after that things had steadily deteriorated. His drinking had increased, and so had her mother's. And sometimes Esther had felt that the very sight of her and her useless leg had repulsed them so much that they had hidden in booze.

Maybe. Her analyst had suggested that Richard Jackson had felt so guilty for hurting his daughter that he had sought forgetfulness in his drinking.

Esther wasn't prepared to be that generous. After all, saying the man drank out of guilt almost sounded like a valid excuse. But there wasn't any excuse. None at all. And in the end she had come to believe that her father hated her, that he had never really loved her at all.

Now he wanted to talk to her, and here she was in the middle of nowhere with a staircase that might prove to be the perfect weapon for him. After all, he'd managed to kill her mother by knocking her down the stairs. Out here with no witnesses, and with Esther's bad leg, he could probably make it look like an accident.

God! Couldn't she stop thinking about this? She was going to go nuts and all the man had done was write to her! He hadn't even said anything about showing up; he'd just written a letter.

But she hadn't written back to the address printed beneath his signature, nor was she going to. What then? If he got no answer would he call? Or would he just show up on her door-step?

Feeling disgusted with the way her mind kept worrying the problem, like a rat on an exercise wheel, she ordered herself to go into the kitchen, turn on the lights and make a cup of tea.

She turned on the overhead light, but its brilliance was far from reassuring. The brightness inside made the darkness beyond the window opaque. No longer could she see the moonlit countryside and that made her even more uneasy.

She forced herself to ignore the feeling while she put the kettle on and tried to decide between her various teas. Green tea, she decided at last. It had been a long time since she'd made herself a cup.

And this had to stop, she told herself. Her father had consumed the entire first fifteen years of her life with fear, and she wasn't about to let him consume any more.

But how could she stop this obsessive cycling of her thoughts? She was scared, the man posed a threat, and until something concrete happened to settle the issue, she could hardly just stop being afraid, right?

When the tea was ready and she poured herself a cup, she had to fight the urge to turn out the light once again, thus making herself safe in the dark. She believed that if she didn't give in to the fear, perhaps she could conquer it.

But it wasn't easy, especially when it occurred to her that someone could come right up to the window, look into the brightly lit room and see her clearly. But the café curtains were drawn, she assured herself. Somebody would need a ladder to see over them.

Was that a car engine? Her heart slammed into overdrive as she strained her ears to hear. The wind here never seemed to stop, and even now it was making little sounds, rattling the power and phone lines against the eaves, making the dryer vent clatter. Maybe...but no. At some level just below the audible, she detected it, a faint rumbling vibration.

Then it stopped and she heard the distinct *thunk* of a car door slamming. Panic ripped through her in a searing wave, then subsided as adrenaline took over. Moving swiftly, she grabbed a butcher knife from the block on the counter and headed for the front door.

No one, absolutely no one, was going to beat her up ever again.

She left the light on in the kitchen, not wanting to alert the person outside to the fact that she was aware of him. Golden light fell through the door into the foyer, illuminating it. She hesitated only a moment before stepping out there, taking care not to cast any shadows across the windows on either side of the front door.

Someone was outside. She could see the dark shadow on the porch through the sheer curtains on the window beside the door. Gripping the knife tighter, she took a deep breath and moved another step closer to the door.

Her heart was hammering so loudly that it was a moment before she realized that the person outside was knocking gently on the door. *Knocking?* She froze, confused. Her father wouldn't knock, would he?

"Esther?"

She recognized the voice, and in an instant relief poured through her, leaving her feeling weak. Craig Nighthawk. What was he doing here after midnight?

She walked toward the door, and with each step the confusion of the previous moments when past and present had somehow mingled to create a nightmare slipped away, leaving her firmly centered in the now.

Opening the door, she found Craig Nighthawk standing on

her porch holding a foil bag and two plastic spoons. He held them up. "Ice cream? I just bought some in town and thought you might like to share."

Then his eyes fell to the butcher knife in her hand. "Did something happen?"

She looked down at the knife and felt horror creep through her. She'd been carrying a knife with the intention of inflicting serious injury, possibly even fatal harm. That wasn't her, was it? She didn't do things like that.

"Esther? Is something wrong?"

She looked up at Craig, wondering how someone she hardly knew could be so welcome. "I... No. No, nothing's wrong. I just..." For some reason it seemed impossible to explain that she had been terrified of nothing at all except her own fears. "I... was nervous, worrying about my father, and when I heard your engine..."

He looked embarrassed. "I guess I take the jerk of the year award. I should have thought about how it would make you feel when you heard me drive up in the middle of the night. I was on the way back from town with the ice cream when I saw your light was on—"

"My light?" she interrupted. "But the highway is a mile from here."

"There's nothing else out there to get in the way. I could see your light easily from the highway."

It had never occurred to her that her house lights would be visible that far away. Now how was she going to deal with that?

He shifted a little and lifted the bag. "I'm sorry I scared you. Would you like to share some ice cream with me or should I just go home before it melts?"

He asked the question gently, as if he realized he was not the foremost thing on her mind. She hesitated, not because she was uncertain, but because she seemed to be unable to drag herself out of the morass of her own confusion and concern.

"Come on," he coaxed. "Just sit out here with me on the porch. I have a spoon for each of us and we'll eat out of the carton."

She started to step out with him when she realized she was still carrying the butcher knife. "I— Just a minute. I'll be right back."

When she returned without the knife, they sat together on the top step and ate from the carton like a couple of kids. Moment by moment her fears receded until they seemed like a bad dream she had had long ago. The night became once again beautiful, the Milky Way a misty, sparkling spray across the heavens.

The ice cream was one of the better brands, rich and creamy, and she savored it slowly on her tongue.

"This is my favorite time of day," Craig remarked. "When I was trucking it was the best time for driving. Now it's just a quiet time when the work is done. I've spent a lot of hours looking up at the stars."

"I prefer the dawn."

He looked at her. In the faint silver light of the sliver moon, his face was unreadable. "Any particular reason?"

"It means the night is over."

He didn't reply, just waited for her to continue. Something about his silence made her feel safe, as if she could be sure he would not judge her.

"It's ridiculously obvious," she said deprecatingly. "My father always got drunk at night. Never in the morning or the afternoon. So the nights were scary. Full of threat."

"Makes sense. That's why you were holding the knife when I got here."

She nodded. "I'd worked myself up into a fine state."

"Don't say it like that," he chided. "Don't say it as if you have anything to apologize for, because you don't. Anyone in your position would be uneasy. Isn't there someone you can get to stay with you until you're sure there isn't any danger?"

Esther shook her head. "I don't really know anyone around here." She smiled wryly. "I'm a recluse, you see."

Just then, headlights turned off the highway and began to head up the driveway toward them. Esther gasped. Her stomach rolled over uneasily as fear speared through her. Her father!

Craig watched the lights for a couple of seconds then turned to Esther. Even in the dim moonlight she could see that his face had gone hard. "Go inside," he said flatly. "Get the hell out of sight."

With one more wild look at the approaching headlights, Esther obeyed.

Chapter 5

Craig stood on the top step, waiting as the car approached. From inside the house, Guinevere barked, and he heard Esther shush her.

He was bound and determined that no one was going to hurt Esther Jackson while he was near enough to do anything about it. He'd gotten only the sketchiest glimpse of what her childhood must have been like, but he had no trouble filling in the blanks.

Nobody, absolutely *nobody*, deserved the kind of treatment she'd had from her parents, and by God he was going to make sure that her father didn't hurt her again.

A corner of his mind insisted on reminding him that he didn't know this woman, that her problems were really none of his concern, but he paid it no heed. For even though he'd always been a loner, he'd also felt it was the obligation of a human being to get involved when someone needed help, and Esther Jackson plainly needed help. It was a purely humanitarian gesture, he told himself. There was nothing at all personal in it.

His hands clenched and unclenched as adrenaline began to

pump through his veins. That damn car was sure taking its own sweet time getting here. He watched the headlights wind their way up the narrow dirt track, knowing full well no one was driving this way by accident. Whoever it was better have a damn good excuse.

As the vehicle drew close, he saw the silhouette of a rack of lights on top of it. A cop. That didn't make him feel any easier. While a cop wouldn't pose any threat to Esther, he was never going to forget being carted off to jail for a crime he hadn't committed. If hell froze over and demons played with snowballs, he would never again feel easy around the police.

The sheriff's Blazer pulled to a stop in front of him. The spotlight flashed on, nearly blinding him. He heard the car door open, then Virgil Beauregard's voice reached him.

"Where's Miss Esther, Mr. Nighthawk?"

"Inside. We didn't know who was coming up the road, so she's waiting inside."

"Ask her to step out, please."

Slow anger burned in the pit of Craig's stomach. He understood perfectly that the cop was only doing his job, making sure that Esther was all right, but he didn't like the assumptions behind it.

Esther had apparently been listening, because she stepped out onto the porch before Craig even turned to come get her. Behind her, through the screen door, Guinevere chuffed.

"I'm all right, Beau," she told him. "Mr. Nighthawk and I were just having some ice cream together. I'd offer you some, but I suspect it's all melted by now."

The spotlight snapped off and Virgil Beauregard became visible. He approached them. "Sorry for the scare, Mr. Nighthawk, but we've been alerted to keep an extra sharp eye on Miss Esther, and I've never noticed her lights being on this late before. And I didn't expect to find anyone here."

Craig nodded, understanding but still irritated. There was no way he was going to tell anyone it was okay, not after his life had been destroyed by suspicions.

"Thanks, Beau," Esther said. "I really appreciate you going to the trouble."

"It's no trouble, Miss Esther. Living this far away from everyone, you got no one to depend on except us."

"And my neighbors," Esther said warmly, resting her hand lightly on Craig's forearm. "Would you like to come in for some iced tea? Or I could make coffee?"

Beauregard hesitated only an instant before accepting. Watching the other man climb the steps, Craig suddenly realized that Deputy Virgil Beauregard was sweet on Esther Jackson and she didn't even realize it. And what he felt then was a hot surge of jealousy, fueled by her familiar use of his nickname. His jealousy heated up another notch when Guinevere greeted Beau as a long lost friend, and Beau returned the greeting with familiarity.

Beauregard had it all going for him, Craig thought as he followed the two of them to the kitchen. He was a good-looking white man in his late thirties with a steady, respectable job.

Not that it mattered. There was no possible way it could matter. Esther Jackson plainly wasn't looking for a man, and Craig Nighthawk knew for certain that he wasn't looking to get hitched, only to get laid, and Esther wasn't that kind of woman.

Esther poured iced tea for all of them while Craig rinsed the melted ice cream out of the carton and tossed it. "Never ceases to amaze me how fast that stuff melts to nothing," he remarked.

"It was already a little soft by the time you got here." She gave him a smile. "I've been considering getting an ice-cream freezer."

"I've got a really good one," Beau volunteered. "My mother gave it to me for my birthday a couple of years ago, and I don't think I've used it but twice. You're welcome to borrow it, if you like. I mean, it makes sense to try it out before you buy one. Make sure you like it."

"Thank you. That's very kind of you."

He shrugged and colored faintly. "I'm glad to do it."

Well, Craig thought with sour humor, he supposed he could offer to lend "Miss Esther" a pair of sheepshearing scissors.

Or some wire cutters, or some of the paper twine he used to bale wool.

Conversation languished for a few minutes, as if nobody really had much of anything to say. Finally Beau rose and carried his glass to the sink.

"I need to get back on patrol," he said. "Thanks for the tea, Miss Esther."

"My pleasure, Beau."

He smiled down at her. "I'll be back by a couple of times tonight, so rest easy." Then he nodded to Craig. "Good night."

Esther walked Beau to the door and watched him drive away into the night. It was good to know the sheriff was beefing up the patrols, good to know that men like Virgil Beauregard were watching over her.

Not that they would be able to do much good if Richard Jackson showed up. Her first instinct had been to turn to the police when she learned that he knew where she was, but the more she thought about it, the more she realized how useless police protection would be.

"Are you okay?"

Craig had come up beside her, and was looking down at her with concern.

"They'll drive by here five or six times a day, maybe more, but it won't do any good."

"Why not?"

"Because they can't watch me every minute. Because it never did any good in the past. They were never able to keep him away, or keep him from hurting us. He always came in the dark and—" She broke off sharply. "It doesn't matter. If he's made up his mind to get me, he'll get me."

She said it in a bleak way that ripped at his heart.

"No, he won't," Craig said flatly, his mind made up before he even knew it.

"What do you mean?"

"Just that you're not going to be alone at night. I can sleep on your porch as well as I can sleep out in the pasture or at home. If you can handle the daytime, I'll handle the night-time."

She looked at him with an almost painful swelling of emotion. Her breathing accelerated and her heart seemed to squeeze with yearning—yearning for the safety and caring she had never had. "I—I'm...I can't ask that of you."

"You didn't. I offered. Like I said, I can spread my bedroll as easily here as anywhere. Now you just trot yourself inside and go to bed. Don't worry about a thing. Anybody comes near this place, I'll hear him long before he gets here."

"Guin will bark."

The dog, recognizing her name, whined through the screen door.

"Sure she will. But you won't have to face it alone."

She looked down for a few seconds, as if she might find an answer to the puzzle written on the planks at her feet. Then she nodded, giving him a shy smile, and reached out to touch his arm lightly. "Thank you. I feel awful about letting you do this but..."

"But you're afraid," he completed. "You certainly have reason to be. And until we scope this out and have a better idea of what your father intends to do, I'm willing to do anything I can to help out." Taking a chance, he covered her hand with his as it lay on his arm. She didn't pull away.

"If I could trust him—" She broke off again and sighed, lifting her head to look out over the moon-washed landscape. "If I could trust him, I could believe his letter. But he always lied. He was always promising Mom that he wouldn't hit her any more, or that he wouldn't hit me any more, or that he'd never take another drink—the list was endless. He broke every promise he ever made."

"Not a good guy to trust."

She looked at him, wondering if he was being sarcastic, then laughed as she realized he was trying to lighten the mood. "No, he never was a good guy to trust."

Then, with no more warning than a strange light in his dark eyes, he slipped an arm around her shoulders and drew her gently against his chest. For an instant she thought she would lose her balance as her full weight came to rest unexpectedly on her weak leg, but then she was steadied against his chest.

"Relax," he said huskily. "I won't hurt you."

Funny, but that had never occurred to her. Any other thought she might have had was swept away by astonishing sensations. He was so...hard. She had never imagined that the feeling of her breasts being pressed to the hard wall of a man's chest would feel so...good. Or that she would be so aware of his hardness. As if she were leaning against a wall of steel. A *warm* wall.

Impossibly, he was still smiling, looking down at her with that strange fire in his eyes as he said, "If you want to squawk, do it right now, Esther. Otherwise I think I'm going to have to kiss you."

"Why?" Her entire vocabulary seemed to have shrunk to that one word. She couldn't gather her thoughts to say another thing. Besides, there was only one thing in the world that she wanted to know, and that was why, for the first time at this late stage of her life, a man wanted to kiss her.

His smile broadened. "Count on you to ask. Because you laughed."

She blinked, her astonishment growing. "Because I *laughed?*"

"You have an irresistible laugh. Because you were scared and you laughed anyway. That's special."

And suddenly she felt special standing there in the circle of his arms, pressed to his chest, while his exotic face lowered toward hers. Special, and warm, and...tingly in a way she had seldom felt in her life.

And then his mouth settled over hers, warm and surprisingly gentle. It wasn't the kind of kiss she'd seen in movies, the openmouthed gulping kisses that had always looked repulsive to her. It was a soft touching of lips that somehow coaxed her to tip her head back and welcome him.

His lips moved against hers and she responded, trying to give him the same feeling he was giving her. The softest, lightest of caresses, like a butterfly's wings, or the brush of flower petals. So soft she leaned closer, needing something more....

He gave it to her, a gentle, teasing touch of his tongue over her lower lip. It tickled and she pressed her mouth harder against his, wanting the tickle to go away, to never end...and as she pressed harder her mouth opened, inviting him inside.

His tongue slipped past her teeth, finding hers and frolicking. She had never before thought of her tongue as an erotic organ, but then she had never thought she would actually want an openmouthed kiss. A French kiss, the girls in high school had called it. But whatever it was called, she found herself thrilling to the wondrous sensations his caresses evoked.

Oh my! The brush of his tongue against the inside of her cheek danced along her nerve endings, spreading to the farthest points of her body. Another touch against the inside of her lip and she quivered, sensing that there was something even more powerful than these touches just ahead, something she needed and wanted more and more as he drew her deeper into the kiss.

But just as she was about to sag against him, he lifted his mouth and looked down at her. He was shaking. She could feel it. And panting as if he had just run a great distance.

But so was she. With dim amazement she listened to her own rapid breaths.

"You're so sweet," he whispered. "You don't just have an addictive laugh, you've got an addictive mouth."

Then he swooped on her again, taking her back into the pleasurable hinterlands of his kiss, drawing her deeper into the circle of passion. His arms tightened and she let go, trusting him to hold her, trusting him to take care of her.

It felt so good to finally just let go!

Her arms slipped up, and her hands gripped his shoulders as if she might drown if she didn't hang on. His hands began to rub circles on her back, a sensation that at once soothed her and aroused her even more. Her blood seemed to be turning warm and heavy, like molasses, and in the pit of her stomach there was a fluttery sensation, like nervousness only it felt so much better.

When he lifted his mouth from hers again, she followed him like a flower seeking the sun, wanting so much more than these brief, fleeting touches. And there was more. Her entire body shrieked it.

Instead of giving her another kiss, he cupped the back of her head in one big palm and drew her head onto his shoulder. "I don't...I don't think we ought to keep this up," he said breathlessly. "We might go somewhere we're not ready for."

She rested against him for a long time, fighting a wave of disappointment that threatened to make her weep. This was the first time in her entire life a man had kissed her, and she didn't want him to stop, especially since this might be the last kiss she would ever get.

But she had too much pride to force the issue, and it was as plain as day to her that Craig Nighthawk wasn't really interested in her as a woman anyway. How could he be, when she was defective. God, she was nearly thirty years old and she knew perfectly well how put off men were by her brace and limp. Not once in her entire life had anyone even asked her for a date, and the way she figured it, there was only one reason for that. She just didn't have any sex appeal. Zip, zero, zilch, *nada*. It was as plain as the nose on her face.

Craig Nighthawk had kissed her because...because...oh, it was just because he felt sorry for her. Not because she had an "irresistible" laugh. Not because he was drawn to her. That just didn't happen.

But heavens, was she attracted to him. Just the mental vision of him could make her knees turn to jelly. Long legs encased in worn denim, a tight butt, hard chest, broad shoulders...and his face, so sharply chiseled with high cheekbones, and those dark eyes that were surprisingly expressive. Dark pools into which she would joyously have leapt.

Except that he didn't really want her. He was just trying to take care of her.

"You'd better go on up to bed, Esther," he said huskily. "Don't worry about anything. I'll be right here all night."

She nodded and drew away, wishing that those words meant a whole lot more.

* * *

Mop woke him in the morning. It wasn't an unusual experience when he slept outside, so it was a few minutes before he remembered that he was sleeping on Esther's porch and that Mop was supposed to be at home.

He opened one eye and looked at the dog. "What are you doing here?" Dawn was barely a faint glow in the east, and dew had formed during the night, leaving his clothes feeling cold and damp. The last thing he needed was to be dragged out of bed at an ungodly hour by a lovesick dog. "You're supposed to be at home."

Mop groaned and licked his chin.

"I don't want to get up, dawg." What he wanted was never to move again. The worst part of being on the wrong side of thirty was that you began to notice that every broken bone, torn ligament or sprain you'd ever had really hadn't healed. No, they'd only pretended to. On a damp, chilly morning like this every one of those old injuries lodged a protest.

Mop moaned and lapped his cheek. One big brown eye peered out between thick cords of fur.

"All right, all right." He sat up slowly, easing his way back into his body. Morning stiffness was no big deal and he refused to give in to it—except for moving a little gingerly until the kinks worked out.

Apparently Mop didn't think that sitting up was enough. He licked Craig's cheek again and whined impatiently.

"Okay, okay. I'm coming. Slowly."

The dog sat on his haunches and waited expectantly. Craig stretched widely, then rose to his feet. Cripes, even his ankles felt stiff this morning.

But, oh, what a beautiful morning it was going to be. The dim light of the dawning day flowed across the breeze-tossed grasses, making them look like a dark, mysterious sea. The mountains, rising up out of the blackness of night, were already rosy at their tops, kissed by the light of the sun he could not yet see. As he watched, the pink slowly descended the mountain slopes, vanquishing the darkness until the sun at last rose above the horizon and bathed the entire world in its warm glow.

"Good morning."

He turned to find that Esther stood just inside the screen door, and suddenly he was glad he had dawdled to watch the day's beginning. She looked adorable, he thought, her face still soft and flushed from sleep. Her hair was twisted into a single long braid that draped over her shoulder, but tendrils had escaped to create a soft nimbus around her face. In this light, her eyes looked soft and mysterious.

He wanted to kiss her. Instead he said, "I need to be going."

"I just started a pot of coffee, and I bought some doughnuts in town yesterday. Can you stay just a few minutes more?"

"For coffee? You bet." His lips stretched into a smile he didn't really feel, because there was something about that woman and this morning that made him yearn—positively *ache*—to be in bed with her, holding her. Exploring her. Loving her.

Oh, man, he had lost his mind!

Esther looked at Mop. "How'd he get here?"

"I suspect he flew on the wings of love."

Esther grinned, then chuckled delightedly. "Do you have *any* animals that behave normally?"

"That depends on what you mean by normal."

"Well, you have a sheep that seems to be able to teleport through the fence. And now you have a dog that flies...."

His own smile relaxed. "There has to be a hole in the fence somewhere. I just haven't found it."

"Of course you haven't. Both Mop and Cromwell have learned to fly. It's quite obvious that there can be no other explanation."

"But how did they learn to fly?"

She cocked her head pensively. "Clearly a wizard must have passed through the county at some time, and cast a spell of enchantment over your dog and your ewe."

"But why not *every* dog? Or *all* my sheep?"

"Oh, that's obvious! He only had enough magic powder to

sprinkle two animals, and he quite naturally picked the two most enterprising animals he could find.''

"Makes sense to me, if by enterprising you mean that they're pains in the doofus.''

She giggled. "Please, let's be kind in our descriptions. I certainly don't want Cromwell angry with me. She might devour something really important, like my paintings or that beautiful old cottonwood.''

"Please, she's a sheep, not a goat. She has better taste.''

"I guess marigolds and geraniums qualify as better.''

"They're certainly more expensive.''

Another gurgle of laughter escaped her. "Some people *do* seem to use cost as a measuring stick.'' She looked down at Mop. "I feel awful about leaving you outside, Mop, but really, you can't come in while Guinevere is confined to quarters. It would defeat the entire purpose.''

Mop wagged his tail then lay down with a "humph.''

Craig stepped into the house with Esther, half expecting Mop to slip right by him, or Guinevere to come charging out around his legs. But Mop kept his post on the porch, and Guinevere was once again leashed to the newel post.

"I hate to do that to her,'' Esther remarked, "but it's the only way I can be absolutely certain she won't dash out the instant I open the door—even though she's ordinarily a very well-behaved dog. I'm afraid some impulses are stronger than training.''

He glanced down at her, wondering if she meant anything by that, but the hazel eyes that met his were clear and without guile. No double entendre meant, he decided. Esther Jackson was apparently incapable of it.

He watched her limp ahead of him into the kitchen, and found himself wishing there was something that could be done about her leg. Not for himself, but for her. She couldn't possibly like having to wear that brace.

The coffee was ready, and she poured two steaming mugs full. He carried them to the table while she retrieved the box of doughnuts.

"These are my worst vice,'' she confided as she set out

plates and napkins. "Every so often I just *have* to have a doughnut. A chocolate one with icing. Or one filled with strawberry jam. Or a blueberry one."

A laugh burst out of him as she opened the box and revealed a full dozen doughnuts. "You were going to eat all those?"

She flushed and nodded. "I told you, it's my worst vice. Once or twice a year I go crazy on doughnuts and don't eat anything else for a couple of days."

He couldn't say why, but that touched him. "Then I shouldn't eat any. I don't want to shortchange you."

She pushed the box toward him with a laugh. "Please. I'd be very grateful if you'd keep me from overdosing."

"If I try real hard, I might be able to eat three."

"Then by all means try very hard." For herself she took only one, a chocolate doughnut with chocolate icing. "The bakery in town makes incredible doughnuts. And bread. I love their sourdough rye."

"I'll have to try them sometime." Sometime when he could afford to buy bread, instead of Paula having to make it several times a week. "Are you going to be all right today?"

She colored faintly. "Yes, I'll be fine. It's…only at night that I have a problem. It was the only time I really had to be afraid of him. In the daytime he was either at work or sleeping it off." She shook her head. "I guess it's silly to feel that I have nothing to fear from him now in the daylight. I mean, if he wants to hurt me it's because I put him in jail, and I don't think that'll change according to whether it's day or night."

"Probably not. If revenge is what he really wants. But have you considered that his time in prison probably dried him out pretty thoroughly?"

"I hear they make some kind of rotgut in prison."

"I hear that, too. But that doesn't mean anyone was making it in the prison he was in. Or that he got any even if they were. For all you know, he may have been on the wagon all this time. And he may have done some serious thinking."

"That's what I'm afraid of, that he's spent the last fifteen years thinking seriously about how to get even with me."

Craig backed off, biting into a blueberry doughnut to keep

from pressing the issue. Esther wasn't being perfectly rational about this, but there was no good reason why she ought to be. The bottom line was that the man had beaten her and her mother for years, and that he had killed her mother and crippled her. If Richard Jackson had turned into some kind of saint and did penance for the rest of his life, he doubted that Esther would ever be able to trust him again.

"Okay," she said finally. "Maybe he's quit drinking. Maybe he had even figured out that what he did was wrong. Maybe his apology is sincere. I still don't want to see him. And I'm still going to be scared to death at night because he might get drunk again and come looking for me."

She pushed her plate aside and looked at him. "He used to come looking for me, you know. There wasn't any place I could hide. If I went to a friend's house to spend the night, he'd call and order me to come home. I mean...when he wanted to beat me, nothing stopped him."

His gut twisted with pain and sympathy for her. He'd thought he had it rough being a reservation Indian who like as not would get clobbered really good if he wandered into white folks' territory after dark. Or if he had the nerve to ask a white girl out. Well, none of that amounted to a hill of beans beside being beaten again and again by your own drunken father.

Damn, maybe it was time he got off his own pity pot.

Instinctively he reached out and covered one of her hands with his. Immediately she turned her hand over and clasped his.

"I'm sorry," she said. "You don't want to hear this."

"Cut it out. I wouldn't be sitting here if I didn't want to hear whatever you have to say. So just say it, Esther. Tell me how you *really* feel about the bastard."

She surprised him then with a forlorn little laugh. "You know, Craig, I don't think there are *words* for how I feel about him. He's been the bogeyman in my nightmares all my life. Other kids worried about the bear in the closet. I worried about the man who'd come through my bedroom door."

Craig had a sudden horrible thought. "He didn't... I mean... Did he ever sexually assault you?"

Esther gasped. "No! Oh, no! Oh, I think I would have killed myself if he had ever.... No. Absolutely not."

Craig felt an incredible sense of relief. At least there was one injury she hadn't suffered.

"No," Esther said again. "That would have been...I don't think I would have been strong enough to survive that. I'm basically a very weak person."

"Weak?" He was astonished that she could think any such thing. "If there's one thing you're not, it's weak."

But Esther knew better, and as she watched Craig drive away a little while later with Mop sitting on the seat beside him, she thought about just how very weak she was.

It wasn't strength that caused her to keep trying to hide from her father. It wasn't strength that had made her hide in closets and under beds, or that had made her testify against him. Hell, no! Terror had motivated her and was still motivating her. It had driven her to testify against him, for fear that he would kill her next. It had driven her all the way out into this underpopulated part of the country in the vain hope of evading him.

Oh, she was weak, all right. If she had any gumption she wouldn't be quailing in the dark at night, she would be making some kind of plan to deal with her father.

Instead of leaving the front door open as she usually did when the weather was warm, she locked it. Guinevere eyed her hopefully from where she was leashed to the newel post.

"Come on, girl, let's get your breakfast. Then we'll go out to paint."

Guin appeared to like that idea, thumping her tail eagerly. She always liked to go out to the studio. Evidently, from its days as a barn, the building contained a great many delightful odors. Guin never tired of nosing around.

The phone rang while Guinevere was still eating. Esther answered it, for some reason expecting it to be Craig Nighthawk. The voice she heard chilled her to the bone.

"Hello, Esther. It's Dad."

Chapter 6

Sweat was rolling down Craig Nighthawk's brow, running into his eyes and burning, despite the bandanna he had knotted around his head. The August day had soared above ninety, and even though it was dry heat, it was damned uncomfortable for heavy work. The sun was beating mercilessly down, frying his neck. Finally he gave up and put his hat on again.

There was a pile of sheep manure nearby, fresh enough to draw nasty, stinging flies. Cromwell, the only one of the sheep curious enough to pay him any mind, stood a few feet away, contentedly munching on greenery, and watching Craig work.

Some days, Craig thought, that damn ewe would look a whole sight better roasting over a big fire. Or stewing in a pot. There were limits, and that damn ewe was pushing them.

He hadn't a doubt in his mind that Cromwell had something to do with the fence being down. In fact, he was getting paranoid enough to think she might have just leaned on it and rolled over, pulling it down with her. Theoretically her wool ought to be stuck all over the barbs, and she ought to have a cut or two to show for the encounter, but there was nothing.

Okay, so she knew better than to press right where the barbs were....

The sun was frying his brain. It was far more likely that something besides Cromwell had taken down the fence, though he damn well couldn't figure what. This section wasn't anywhere near a road and there was no sign a truck had come this way recently. So maybe it was a UFO.

Or some kids. Yeah, it was probably kids. School didn't start until next week, and by this point in the summer they were probably bored enough to do just about anything.

Anything was likelier than Cromwell doing this herself. Although... He looked at her as she stood placidly chewing greenery, and thought that she looked a damn sight more intelligent than most people would credit a sheep.

Craig snorted at himself and returned his attention to stretching the barbed wire from post to post. It was easier to concentrate on the difficult task of repairing the fencing than to think about what Cromwell might or might not be capable of.

It was his damn upbringing rearing its head again. Fact was, he'd had a traditional upbringing, steeped in the magic and mysticism of his people. It wasn't that he scorned it, but he had come to think it had very little bearing on the world in which he had chosen to live: the white man's world.

It was as if there were two entirely different realities coexisting side by side, and the rules were different in each one. In his childhood he had come to respect the world and all its denizens from the rocks beneath his feet to the birds winging through the sky. He never cut a tree without thanking it for its sacrifice, and when he looked at Cromwell he saw another intelligent resident of this planet, one worthy of respect.

But this was the white man's world, and here the rock was cold and without life, and the birds and sheep were merely dumb animals to be used. It was sometimes a struggle to keep that in mind. And sometimes he didn't even try.

But the fact was, he had to function in this world, and the ways of his people didn't fit here. He'd figured that out a long time ago, and while on the road as a trucker he lived according to the white man's rules and beliefs.

So he ignored the feeling that Cromwell was playing a game with him, and tried to ignore a niggling feeling of worry about Esther Jackson.

But finally he couldn't ignore it anymore. It distracted him more and more until the wire he was stretching snapped back on him and ripped the sleeve of his shirt and the skin beneath. He swore and threw down his pliers. Mop, who had been dozing in the bed of the pickup, sat up and looked inquisitively at him.

Yanking at the bandanna around his head, he pulled it off and scoured his hot, sweaty face with it. If his thoughts didn't quit wandering over to Esther's place, he was apt to cut his throat on this stuff. Barbed wire was nasty, and it couldn't be strung loosely if it was to do its job, which was to keep the sheep inside the pasture without them getting all tangled up in the stuff. But he needed to pay attention, and paying attention was growing increasingly difficult.

Swearing again, he wrung out the bandanna, twisted it and tied it around his head again. If he did nothing else today, he had to finish repairing this section of fence. It wouldn't be safe to leave the sheep here otherwise, not only because they might stray but because predators would find it easier to get to them. His worry about Esther was just going to have to wait.

But as his worry increased, so did his speed. Impelled by need, his hands grew swifter and stronger. He nicked himself a few extra times on the wire, but he got it strung in record time nonetheless.

This break was a new one, and it worried him considerably. He still hadn't found the break where Cromwell had initially escaped to eat Esther's flowers, and that worried him even more. He'd been over the whole damn fence line since then. Was somebody playing some kind of game with his fence and his sheep?

Well, it wouldn't do any good to fuss about it until he could be sure something was being done deliberately. After all, fencing did manage to come down all on its own.

He threw his tools into the back of the truck, along with the roll of wire, and took Mop into the cab with him. Before he did anything else, he was going over to see Esther and make sure she was okay.

Damn his mystical soul anyway.

His truck bucked wildly over the open ground until he reached the fence-line road he and Enoch had been working steadily on extending. Some day they were going to have a graded road around every inch of the fence, but for now they could work on it only as time permitted—like so much in their lives. It would sure be a whole lot more efficient to keep up with the fence if they could do it in a truck, though.

Maybe by the end of next summer.

When he reached the front gate he didn't even head up to the house to change, just hit the road and drove around to Esther's house. Although their houses weren't all that far apart, it wound up being about five miles by car. He lived off Willis road, and her driveway was off county road 93.

Nothing appeared to be amiss when he pulled up to her house. Her car was parked in front of the garage, as if she had just come back from somewhere. The mail truck was pulled up outside the barn, and he figured that must be where Esther was.

He left Mop sitting in the truck and went to find out. Just before he reached the barn, the side door opened and Verna Wilcox stepped out. When she saw him, she nodded. "Afternoon."

"Afternoon, Verna. How's it going?"

"Not bad, not bad at all. Ain't seen you much lately. Paula says you been out herding them sheep."

"And mending fences."

She grinned. "Always some of that to be done."

"Isn't that the truth. Is Esther in?"

"Busy painting." She hesitated. "You know her real well?"

"I'm getting to." Which he didn't think was stretching it a

bit. Hell, he'd slept on the woman's porch last night and was still aching this afternoon as a result. Someday maybe he would figure out how a plank floor could be harder than the lumpy ground.

"Well, something has her upset if you ask me. She won't tell me nothin', and it's none of my business, but she's real upset."

He nodded. "I'll see what I can do."

Verna nodded, wagging a finger at him. "See that you do. She's got a lot of painting to do before her show next month and she doesn't have time for this." She cocked a brow. "Maybe you did something?"

"Couldn't have."

Apparently satisfied, Verna drove away.

Craig hesitated then knocked on the door and stepped into the studio.

He was surprised by the amount of light that flooded the old barn. He hadn't known that she had replaced so much of the roof with skylights turning this musty old place into a bright work space.

But he was even more surprised by the picture Esther was painting. From the top down, in washes of blue, lavender and gold, mountains were appearing on a huge sheet of white paper. Colors at once vivid and translucent caught his eye and filled him with wonder.

"That's gorgeous," he blurted.

Startled, Esther whirled around. "Oh! I thought it was just Verna coming back because she'd forgotten to give me something."

"I'm sorry I disturbed you."

"No, no, it's all right. I'm beginning to lose the best light and I'd need to stop soon anyway." She dropped her brush in a jar of water and set her palette aside on a sawhorse table. "Is something wrong?"

"I've been worrying about you all day. Just couldn't shake the feeling that something was wrong with you." And now she would laugh at him and make him feel like an utter fool, he thought.

She looked down and tugged at a paint-splattered towel she had tucked into the waistband of her jeans. It came free and she held it in one hand while she reached for the brush she had dumped in the jar of water. Gently she swished the brush in the water, rinsing it. Finally, apparently satisfied, she began to dry it gently with the towel, twirling it so the bristles came to a point.

Just as Craig was about to apologize again for bothering her, she looked at him.

"My father called this morning."

He felt his heart thud. "What did he want?"

"To see me."

"What did you say?"

"That I never, ever want to see him again. That I wanted him to just leave me alone. Then I hung up on him." She grimaced. "It wasn't a very adult conversation."

"What the hell difference does it make?"

"None, I guess." She shrugged one shoulder and set the brush down along with the stained towel.

She looked so tired, he found himself thinking. Utterly exhausted as if life had completely worn her out. She took a step toward him and winced, betraying the fact that her leg hurt.

"What's wrong?" he asked.

"Nothing, really." She smiled wanly. "I'm just tired. I've been painting like a demon, trying to forget that damn phone call, and I guess I've been standing too long—"

Before she finished, he swept her right off her feet into his arms. Instinctively she grabbed for his shoulders. "Craig..."

"How about I carry you to the house, set you on one of your kitchen chairs, and make you something to drink? You look hot and tired."

"No!" In a rush, unreasoning fear rose inside her, causing her to pummel his shoulders with her hands and try to wriggle free.

"Esther..." Stunned, afraid she would hurt herself, he tightened his grip. In her current position if she fell to the hard floor, she might get seriously injured. "Esther, stop...."

"Let me go! Damn it, let me go now!"

She was fighting wildly, hitting and scratching, and at any moment he was going to lose his grip on her. Having no other choice, he dropped to his knees, wincing a little as they cracked against the hard wood floor. At least he was able to set her down.

She twisted away, sobbing, crying out as her injured leg protested, her brace scraping as she dragged herself across the floor away from him. "Don't," she gasped. "Don't ever…don't.…"

He stayed where he was, kneeling, ignoring the stinging of his right cheek where she must have scratched him, ignoring the dull ache of one of his shoulders where she had punched him, ignoring the sharp pain in his kneecaps. He watched her, at once cautious and concerned as she continued to struggle across the floor to get away from him. God, what had he unleashed?

Suddenly she collapsed facedown on the floor, burying her face in her hands and crying so hard that her shoulders shook.

He hesitated, reluctant to approach her again in her present state, but genuinely worried about her. It would have taken a much duller man not to realize that lifting her into his arms had triggered this terror, and that it must have something to do with the horrors of her childhood.

God, he felt so helpless! He was afraid that if he touched her again he would just scare her more, but she was so upset he felt an urgent desire to comfort her somehow. Finally, when her sobs seemed to be easing, he took a chance and stretched out beside her on the floor. Gently he laid a hand on her shoulder.

"Esther? Esther, I'm sorry. As God is my witness, I didn't mean to scare you."

Another hiccuping sob escaped her. "I—I know. I know."

He squeezed her shoulder, wishing he dared to turn her over and pull her into his arms. In the last few minutes, however, he had learned that Esther Jackson wasn't very different from a vial of nitroglycerin. A wrong shake could cause an explosion.

So he waited patiently, with his hand on her shoulder, hoping she would eventually feel comfortable enough to turn to him. Although why should she? As far as he could tell, little in life had given her cause to trust anyone at all.

God, something inside him curdled when he thought of her not even being able to turn to her mother for security. On top of that, society had turned a blind eye to the mistreatment she had received.

It wasn't that his own childhood had been sheltered. Living on an impoverished reservation as he had, he'd seen the evils of alcohol and child neglect and abuse, though he'd been spared himself. He'd also seen plenty of other evils, having largely to do with poverty and racism. But none of that meant he couldn't still hurt for a little girl who'd once been abused by the two people in the world she should have been able to trust absolutely.

Nor did it mean he couldn't hurt for this isolated woman with her deep scars and still-tender wounds. In his own life he'd managed to make peace with most things in his past, but that was just his nature. For him it was easier to shed hurtful things than to let them keep torturing him. For some people, though, shedding those things could be next to impossible.

Finally, taking a huge chance, he gripped her other shoulder and drew her into his arms. He was tensed in expectation of another explosion, but instead she settled against him, even as she gave in to another burst of sobs.

But her sobs quickly eased, and finally she lay exhausted against him. She was soft and warm, and he had to resist an urge to pull her closer. He'd forgotten how good it felt to hold a woman, and for some reason Esther felt especially good.

Her head rested on his forearm and her face was pressed into his chest. Her small but strong hands clutched at his shirt-front as if it were a lifeline. He reached down and covered one of her hands with his, squeezing gently, trying to let her know that he gave a damn.

Which was little enough to give when faced with this kind of grief. But she needed to cry, he thought. Maybe she'd been needing to cry for a long time.

"I—I'm sorry," she said brokenly.

"It's okay."

"No…" Her voice broke, still full of tears. "No, I hit you. I shouldn't have…."

"It's okay," he said again, giving her a gentle squeeze. "You were scared."

"Hitting is wrong." Her voice strengthened a little and began to rise. "Hitting is *wrong*. I know that! My God, I saw enough of it in my childhood. There's never any excuse! Oh, God, I'm just like my parents…."

"Esther…Esther, stop. It's not the same thing at all."

Slowly, so very slowly, she raised her tear-stained face. "What do you mean?"

"You weren't hitting me because you were mad at me or because I wouldn't listen to you, or even because you were just frustrated. Were you?"

"No." She closed her eyes and drew a long, steadying breath. "I was…I was…"

"Trying to protect yourself."

She nodded miserably. "It was— I was suddenly— My father used to pick me up like that and throw me. I just—"

"You just had a flashback, that's all. It's okay. It's okay to hit in self-defense."

"But you weren't…you wouldn't hurt me."

He didn't answer immediately, just stared down at her until finally her eyes opened. "You don't know that," he said. "Not really. How could you? We just met." He hesitated. "Did he pick you up like that when he threw you down the stairs?"

She nodded, her hazel eyes huge in her face.

"Hardly surprising you went ballistic." He shook his head and dared another squeeze.

"You're very understanding."

He shrugged a shoulder. "Just calling it like I see it."

"I'm still sorry I hit you."

"Apology accepted. Not necessary, though."

At that a small smile peeped through and her expression became almost shy. "You're stubborn, aren't you?"

"So I hear from time to time."

He looked so exotic, and suddenly awareness pierced Esther, driving out all the confusion of her earlier feelings. Fear, sorrow, embarrassment, even old hurts seemed to recede into the background of a sudden, astonishing awareness of Craig Nighthawk.

His dark eyes looked down at her, holding her gaze steadily. A strand of his long, black hair lay across his cheek and she wanted desperately to reach up and brush it gently aside. She wanted to run her fingertips all over his face, learning the texture of his skin, memorizing the plains, hollows and hills. What had come over her?

But her heart skipped a couple of beats, then settled into a faster rhythm, signaling her acute awareness of him. Deep inside, her womb began to feel heavy and she found herself wishing for touches she could scarcely imagine. Instinctively, she pressed her knees together, a movement that at once eased and worsened the ache.

It was as if his gaze held her, forbidding her to look away. Tears were drying on her face, leaving her skin feeling sticky and tight, but she couldn't even move a hand to wipe them from her cheeks. All she could do was look deep into his dark eyes and feel herself falling...

Craig knew the exact instant he lost the battle. The sensation of her fingers rubbing absently against his chest hadn't been enough, nor had her parted lips, or even the yearning that seemed to glow in her hazel eyes. No, it was the instant he felt her knees clamp together, signaling exactly what she was feeling.

He knew he shouldn't do this. A voice in his mind was barking protests, but he didn't heed them. His heart sank a little, recognizing that he was setting himself up for exactly the kind of misery he'd sworn he would never allow to happen again. Nothing else seemed to matter when every cell in his body was straining for a closeness he hadn't had in a very long time.

If he didn't shoot himself over this, she was probably going to do it for him. But even that realization didn't stop him. He was caught in a force as old as the planet, and like a whirlpool it was dragging him down.

Gently, with exquisite care, he tipped her chin up a little more, then lowered his mouth to hers. They had kissed before; she wouldn't be upset by a kiss. And to him it felt as if she melted right into him, welcoming him gladly. Instinctively, he drew her closer, cradling her shoulders and her hips as near as he could get them. He needed more, so much more, but for now he had to be content with merely tasting the heady brew of his desire for her.

Anything more was out of the question.

When he lifted his mouth from hers, her eyes fluttered open, looking dazedly up at him. She wanted more; the wish was plainly written in her eyes. He wanted more, too, damn it.

He tried to speak, but his voice seemed to have fled. He cleared his throat, and managed a husky croak. "Are you afraid?"

She looked startled, then color flooded her cheeks and rose to the roots of her hair. "No," she whispered, her voice sounding almost strangled. "Should I be?"

Should she be? What a hell of a question to ask *him*. There was no reason on earth she ought to be afraid. All he wanted to do was give her all the pleasure he possibly could.

And that was why *he* was afraid of *her*.

Sanity reared its ugly head. If he gave this woman everything he wanted to, he would be walking into a situation he didn't want to be in. Nothing but heartache lay down that road.

Of course she wasn't afraid. She didn't have any idea of where they were heading. But he did, and for both their sakes he gathered his self-control and wrapped it around him like a suit of armor.

Esther saw and felt the change. Knew in her heart the instant he withdrew from her. In that instant he abandoned her on the edge of a steep precipice, leaving her feeling as cold, exposed and abandoned as she had ever felt in her life. In that instant she hated him.

She rolled away from him swiftly, and tried to struggle to her feet, made awkward by her brace. Her awkwardness only made her angrier at him, because it was all his fault she was lying on the floor of her studio trying to get to her feet and feeling so damn embarrassed by her responses to him—responses which he had deliberately drawn from her.

Oh, she could kill him!

"Esther. Esther, look, I'm sorry...."

She made it to her feet and glared down at him. "Just leave," she said sharply. "Just go."

He felt like an ass reclining on the floor while she stood over him, but decided it was wisest to remain where he was. The lady was a powder keg right now.

"I'm sorry," he said, though for once he didn't mean it the way it probably sounded. He wasn't sorry as much for her sake as for his own. Tasting forbidden fruit was always a mistake, especially when it turned out to be sweet.

"I—" She broke off, looking suddenly confused, as if his apology had prematurely interrupted her anger. "Look, you'd better just go."

"I was planning on sleeping here tonight." As soon as the words were out, he wanted to kick his own butt. Given the circumstances, they sounded all wrong. Quickly he tried to forestall her fury. "I mean, in case your father shows up."

Conflicting needs collided head-on, leaving her torn by her desire to be left alone and her fear of being alone. Damn him for putting her on the horns of this dilemma.

Taking a chance, Craig sat up, then pushed himself slowly to his feet. "Look," he said. "I got carried away and I apologize. It won't happen again."

Of course it wouldn't, Esther thought miserably. Why should it? Never in her entire life had a man wanted her for anything at all.

She looked down at her brace, feeling her eyes puff with tears she refused to shed. God, she hated that thing. It was a badge of her shame, one she couldn't even hide. Her own personal version of the scarlet letter.

"Please leave," she said again, then turned and limped away with as much dignity as she could muster. When she reached Guinevere, she bent to scratch the dog's head and untie her leash from the hook in the wall. Then, head high, she walked out of her studio.

Behind her she heard Craig say, "I'll be back." She ignored him and just kept walking.

She needed to eat, but could hardly bring herself to. Not even pasta primavera could tempt her appetite. With the bowl of pasta in front of her on the table, she stared out the kitchen window and watched the daylight fade from the sky.

Night seemed to seep out of the nooks and crannies where it had hidden all day, spreading slowly to the shadowed places and across the ground to climb the walls of the barn. She watched it slide stealthily across the window ledge beside her, a conquest so gradual that it was impossible to say when day became dusk and dusk became dark.

Ordinarily she would have been enthralled by the gradual changes of hue as night slowly leached all the color from the world, but tonight she was locked in a misery so deep that not even the beauty of nightfall could pierce it.

Her cocoon, carefully spun of isolation, was beginning to unravel. She wasn't really isolated. How could she be isolated when she had an agent out in the big bad world, when sheriff's deputies dropped by, when her next-door neighbor could turn her life on its ear any time he chose? When her father could find her.

She'd been deluding herself, wearing blinders and focusing on just one thing: putting a huge distance between herself and Richard Jackson. But it hadn't done her any good.

God, she felt bruised and battered. Not physically. No physical bruise could hurt the way emotional ones did. She had spent her entire childhood feeling this way, so sore inside that the passage of her own thoughts was painful, like a breath of cold air over a sensitive tooth.

She had thought, though, that all that pain was behind her. Had honestly believed that with her father out of her life, she would never feel this way again.

God, how mistaken she had been. But how could she have

imagined that in a matter of just a few minutes Craig Night-hawk could make her feel every bit as bad?

She had to stay away from him. At all costs. Never again would she let anyone into her life who could make her feel like this.

God, why had she ever let him touch her? Why had she been asinine enough to curl into his embrace as if he offered some kind of shelter or protection? And him! Why had he kissed her when it was so clear he didn't want her? The instant her brace had touched his leg he'd lost all interest.

And why shouldn't he? She was defective and she damn well knew it. No man wanted a woman who limped around with a steel brace strapped to her leg, and all he'd done was react the way she had always expected: with revulsion.

But this was all her own fault. She, and no one else, had let down her guard enough for Craig Nighthawk to slip past her barriers. She had let him inside where he could wound her, and he had done precisely that.

Not because he was a cruel or evil man, but just because he was a man. Just for a minute there he'd forgotten that she had a bad leg and he'd kissed her. He hadn't meant to leave her feeling like this, she knew.

But he had.

A cloud scudded across the crescent moon and Craig watched it with glum resignation. It was going to rain before morning. He would have to make a shelter out of the tarp wrapped around his bedroll and hope it didn't rain too hard. Not that it really mattered. He'd been soaked before and would be soaked again before his time was done. It kind of went with ranching.

It also kind of went with sitting up all night to keep watch over one slightly crazy woman. He sat on his side of the fence, refusing to even consider the possibility of crossing over to sleep on her front porch again. He wouldn't put it past Esther Jackson to call the cops if she found him trespassing, and his reputation was bad enough around here since his arrest for the little Dunbar girl's kidnapping.

He supposed if he had a grain of the common sense a man ought to have, he would just march away and sleep in his own damn bed.

But he was worried about her, especially since her father had called only that morning. The man was beginning to strike him as just a little too persistent for comfort. He wouldn't sleep a wink if he wasn't close enough to keep an eye on her.

But hell, what a fiasco in the studio that afternoon! Damn, first he scared her half to death by picking her up, then he had given her entirely the wrong idea by holding her and kissing her. He wondered how she would react if she even guessed a tenth of what he would like to do to her. It took no great leap of the imagination to envision himself kissing her in all kinds of intimate places. Tasting her. Touching her. Burying himself deep inside her.

Not that it was ever going to happen. It was probably for the best that she was mad at him. It would help keep him in line so he didn't make a great big mistake by getting involved where there could only be sorrow.

Closing his eyes, he tilted his head back and turned his face up to the sky. The wind caught his hair, whipping it around his face, but he ignored it.

He never felt as centered as he did when he was sitting on solid ground beneath the night sky. It was as if he tapped into some flow of power between the earth and the heavens. He could almost hear the whispers of the stone people in the ground beneath him, could almost feel the spirit in the wind that rippled the grass like waves on a sea.

In that instant he felt more connected with himself and with his roots than he had in a very long time. It was as if all his years in the Anglo world washed away, leaving him cleansed. Leaving him as he had been so long ago, sitting around a fire with his father and grandfather, with his uncles and cousins, listening to stories that made him swell with pride and eagerness. Stories that had made him forget the ugliness of his daily life.

Although that ugliness had been relative, he supposed. His people were often hungry because they could no longer hunt as they once had. The land to which they had been confined was too small to support enough deer for hunting, and the buffalo were gone. They had been told to become farmers, but the land was poor and too dry. So they had often gone hungry.

There had been the curse of alcohol, too, and the curse of having no jobs, and the curse of being treated like scum when they left the res.

But the earth had still been beautiful, and the sky had still been blue, and when a man was blessed with the opportunity to sit a few moments beside a stream, however muddy and small, he knew that not everything was bad.

And tonight, sitting beneath the clouding sky with the wind whispering secrets to the night, he found himself remembering the stories his father and grandfather had told of the days when his people had been great warriors. The days when they had been blessed by the bounty of the earth.

They had been blessed, his father had said, because they had honored the earth. But too many of them had forgotten how to do that, had become distracted by the material things the white men brought.

Craig supposed he was one of them, living cut off from everyone and everything except his ranch and his sister's family. But that had been a conscious choice, because on the res there were almost no choices left. You couldn't put a people in a prison and rip away their religion and culture and expect them to be anything other than dependent.

But he hated dependency, and had moved out to escape it. And in moving far enough away, he had discovered that it was possible to live in this world that had seemed so forbidding when he had been a child.

But now, having succeeded in escaping, he wondered what he had escaped. Not only was he feeling lonely all the time, but he was beginning to feel rootless as well. Nothing on earth would induce him to return to the hopelessness of reservation life, but he somehow had to make a peace within himself if he was to continue in any kind of life.

That peace whispered around him now, hinting at ways that would keep him in touch with the earth while he lived apart.

Encouraging him to reach out for the power that filled the air around him and claim it as his birthright.

And that was the surprising blessing he was beginning to discover in his life as a rancher. Perhaps in the end it would prove to be for the best that he had had to give up trucking. Sometimes he almost hurt when he thought about what he had given up, but then he would get on his horse and ride with the sheep for a while, or take the pickup and drive around the fence line, and he would discover this incredible sense of...rightness. As if when his feet touched the soil, his soul found its source.

So he continued to sit, his arms wrapped around his knees, his head tipped back to the heavens. Watching over Esther Jackson was going to be good for his soul.

At ten-thirty, he watched a deputy drive up to her place and step out. Esther came to the door to greet him and they chatted for several minutes before he drove away. It looked like Beau Beauregard, but he didn't stay all that long so he was probably not making any better time with Esther than Craig was. Not that Craig cared.

The clouds overhead thickened, and lightning began to fork across the sky. The wind kicked up until the rustle it made in the grass was loud enough to sound like the chirping of a million crickets.

All of a sudden he found himself remembering a stormy afternoon as he'd driven across eastern Montana. The day had started brilliant and clear, but as he drove east, he watched a storm build behind him.

At first the puffs of cloud had been innocent enough, white and fluffy like cotton balls. But as he'd watched in his rear-view mirrors, their number had grown and they had begun to come together, their undersides growing darker as their burden of water had grown.

Finally, from north to south as far as the eye could see had stretched the black wall of a squall line. It had still been behind him, though, and as he drove ahead of it, drenched in the sunlight, he played a game of tag with nature.

Eventually he lost. One moment he had been in sunlight, and the next he had been in the dark gray-green of a stormy world. He could still see the sunlight on the road ahead of him and on the open land to either side, but now he watched as the storm's shadow gradually swallowed the rest of the world.

Before the easternmost ribbon of highway had fallen into shadow, the rain had caught up with him, a heavy, gusting downpour that had sometimes made the trailer behind him feel more like a sail than a loaded van.

He still remembered the exact instant when he had realized how small and powerless he was. Ordinarily, he had felt big and powerful, driving a loaded eighteen-wheeler and looking down on other cars and trucks as they passed by, taking great care because of his huge size and weight. But when that storm had blown across him and pulled at his trailer, he'd known just how puny he really was. How big the powers of nature were.

He got some of that same feeling now sitting beneath a stormy night sky with the wind whipping about him. Puny. Insignificant.

Maybe he was having a megalomaniacal delusion here, thinking he needed to watch over Esther Jackson, believing he might be of any help at all if her father showed up. Maybe he was just being a fool.

But power flowed through him, rising from the earth and arcing down from the clouds, meeting in the wind.

He stayed.

Chapter 7

The storm was making Esther edgy. Ordinarily she loved the raw power of the elements, but tonight the flash of lightning and crack of thunder seemed threatening. Even pulling her pillow over her head didn't help.

Guinevere was restless, too, moving from spot to spot around the bedroom and whining occasionally as if the floor were too hard and the night was too loud.

Finally, giving up, Esther switched on the light and climbed out of bed. Guinevere sat up and looked at her expectantly.

"Yes, I give up," she told her dog. "Absolutely and completely. Although, perhaps I ought to see about getting some sleeping pills, because if I don't start to get a decent night's sleep I'm never going to finish all those paintings for the show."

Guin chuffed.

"Terrible, isn't it? I may ruin my career because I can't get my nerves to settle down. I mean…really, Guin, why should this storm bother me?"

The Saint Bernard woofed.

"So, you don't think it's the storm that's bothering me?

You're very likely correct. Craig Nighthawk is bothering me. Now how do you suppose he can do that when he's miles away?'' She refused to mention her father because she didn't want to bring his image into this already disturbing night.

But Nighthawk... Sighing, she looked toward the window where lightning was flashing at an astonishingly rapid rate. The thunder never stopped rolling. Nighthawk could move to the opposite end of the country, but he still wouldn't leave her alone.

Enough of this mooning around. What she needed was a nice cup of tea, or a glass of milk. The storm would probably lessen by the time she finished drinking one or the other, and she would be able to go to sleep.

She hesitated only a moment before deciding to put her brace on beneath her nightgown. She couldn't exactly explain why, even to herself, just that somehow, tonight, she didn't want to be at a disadvantage, and being utterly alone had nothing to do with it.

In the kitchen she refilled Guin's bowl with fresh water and offered her a doggie biscuit. For herself she settled on a glass of milk.

The phone rang. For an endless minute, she almost didn't answer it, sure it would be her father again. But why should he call when she'd already hung up on him once? On the other hand, who else would call at nearly midnight?

The phone hung on the wall within reach, and she stared at it as if it were a ticking bomb. No. Yes. Finally, unable to stand her own dithering, she reached for the receiver. What could Richard Jackson do to her over the phone?

"Esther, it's Jo. I know it's late where you are, but I'm in Europe and it's the only opportunity I've got to call you."

Esther listened to the rush of words her agent spewed from thousands of miles away and let relief wash over her.

"First, did you get my letter about your father getting your address and number?"

"Yes, yes I did. He's written me and called me, Jo." She waited patiently, knowing there would be a detectable lag between her statement and Jo's response thanks to the great distance over which they were speaking.

"He did? That son of a bitch! Oh, Esther! You must be terrified! Tell me you're not alone. You've hired somebody, haven't you?"

"Hired someone?"

"A bodyguard! Don't tell me you haven't considered it. Esther, this man is dangerous. He killed your mother, for God's sake, and you helped put him behind bars. You need protection."

Esther thought of Craig Nighthawk and how much safer she had felt with him sleeping on her porch. A bodyguard hadn't occurred to her, though. Nor did she really like the idea of being watched over by a total stranger—even assuming she could afford such a thing. "I'll be fine," she heard herself say. "The sheriff is keeping an eye out."

"Oh, well that really makes me feel good," Jo said sarcastically. "You're counting on some backwoods hick to keep you safe?"

"I wouldn't describe the local sheriff that way, Jo. He's really a very caring man."

Jo apparently used the transatlantic delay to calm herself, because her next statement sounded more reasonable. "Well, you'd know better than I would, since you're there. But really, Esther, no police force can provide the kind of protection you need. At least get someone to stay with you. That might be enough to keep that SOB away."

"I'll see what I can do about it."

"Promise?"

"Promise."

"I feel better. Now we can talk about business. After your show closes in London, I think I'm going to be able to arrange for a showing in Paris. You're on the way up, my girl! Oh, yes, you're rocketing straight to the top, so keep painting your little fingers off. How is the big one coming, by the way? Everyone here is excited to see it."

They talked for a few more minutes about the paintings Esther was hoping to complete in time for the London show, chatted a couple more minutes about mutual acquaintances, then said goodbye.

Guin had finished her biscuit long since, and had come to rest her head on her mistress's knee. Esther scratched behind her ears and tried not to notice that the storm hadn't abated one little bit. In fact, the violence outside seemed to have escalated, which oddly reassured her. It was doubtful that her father would come looking for her in the midst of a storm this severe.

But even as the thought crossed her mind, there was a heavy hammering at her front door. For an instant her heart stopped dead and the room seemed to spin before her eyes. Then common sense reared its head. Her father wouldn't hammer on the door like that. He would take a softer approach, not wanting to scare her into flight. Maybe.

Guin barked and took off toward the door. Esther followed hesitantly, sure it wasn't her father yet fearing that her instinct was wrong. He'd always come by night in the past, hadn't he?

But Guin sat down at the door and began thumping her tail emphatically. Whoever was on the other side of that door, the dog was happy about it. Maybe it was Micah Parish—yes, it must be Micah, checking up on her again.

Guin barked again, looking back at her as if to say, "What's the problem? Hurry and open the door."

Esther looked down at herself in her ankle-length white cotton gown and robe set and decided she was decent enough for anything except church.

And somehow, when she threw the door open, she was not surprised to find Craig Nighthawk there. It was as if her thoughts had conjured him out of the night, and she was in no mood to question the magic or the powers of the universe.

But he was soaked to the bone.

"What happened to you?" she asked.

He looked almost embarrassed to tell her. "I've been sitting on that hill over there watching your house to make sure nothing happened to you."

"You didn't need to do that!"

He shrugged. "Whatever. Fact is I did it. Anyway, it's pouring cats and dogs out there so when I saw your light come on I figured I'd beg to come in out of the cold.''

She looked down at the saddle he'd set on the porch beside him. "What happened to your horse?"

"She took off." He shook his head. "Damn storm. The lightning scared her, I guess. She'll turn up at the barn tomorrow. But in the meantime..." He looked down at himself.

"You shouldn't have been out there," Esther scolded him. "Whatever were you thinking? Did I ask you to do any such insane thing?"

"No." He settled his hands on his hips and canted his pelvis to one side in a way that drew her gaze and caused her to lose her breath. This man was deadly in a pair of jeans, she thought stupidly. Especially in *wet* jeans.

"No," he said again, sounding impatient. "You didn't ask me to do any such damn fool thing, but I went and did it anyway like the damn fool I am. This hero business is for the birds! *Now* can I come in and get warm, or do you want me to die of hypothermia out here? The temperature must have fallen thirty degrees...."

Not thirty degrees, Esther thought automatically as she stepped back to let him in. Maybe fifteen. Or twenty. But of course it would feel much colder to him since he was soaked. She closed the door behind him, shutting out the fury of the storm.

"You could have been hit by lightning," she scolded, needing to stay annoyed with him because if she started thinking about just what it meant to her to know he'd been sitting out there watching over her, particularly after the scene they'd had that afternoon...well, she would be lost. And she couldn't afford to allow herself to be lost because he would only reject her eventually, and a rejection of that magnitude would probably kill her.

She realized abruptly that her thoughts were babbling in utter confusion. Drawing a deep breath, she squeezed her eyes closed and fought for equanimity.

"You okay?" Craig asked. His voice held a note of impatience, but when she didn't answer he said more gently, "Esther? Are you all right?"

Her eyes snapped open in time to see Guin rise on her hind legs and plant her forepaws firmly on Craig's shoulders. She was horrified. "Guin! Off! Now! Oh, you know better than that." She looked up at Craig apologetically. "I think she's glad to see you."

"I kinda got that feeling." Gently he took Guinevere's paws and lowered her back to the floor. He gave her a pat and a scratch before he straightened to confront Esther again. "Would it be too much trouble to give me a towel?"

Painful color flooded her cheeks. "Oh, I'm sorry! Yes, of course. The bathroom's down that hallway on the left. There should be plenty of fresh towels."

He paused long enough to pull off his boots and socks and set them beside the door, then on bare feet he padded down her hallway and disappeared.

What now, idiot? she asked herself. She certainly couldn't send him back out into the storm—nor did she want to—but she didn't have anything to offer him to wear, and he certainly couldn't sit around in those wet clothes all night.

A blanket, she decided. He could wrap up in a blanket while she threw his clothes in the dryer. Then she could go upstairs and leave him the freedom of the house. Not that she would sleep. How on earth could she sleep while he was under the same roof?

A loud crack and roll of thunder shook the house to its foundations. The lights flickered ominously, then steadied. Guin looked at Esther, then trotted down the hall after Craig. The dog probably felt safer with him, too, she thought.

In the study she had a quilt that she'd bought at the county fair earlier that summer. She went to get it and left it outside the bathroom door. "There's a quilt on the floor out here," she called in to him. "Bring your clothes to the kitchen and I'll throw them in the dryer."

There, she thought with satisfaction, she'd managed to sound cool about the whole thing. He would never guess that inside her were jittery longings she could hardly bear to admit to herself.

It was embarrassing, she thought as she went to the kitchen, to be having urges and fantasies that she had so firmly stifled many years ago. Embarrassing to feel herself reacting as if she were fifteen instead of thirty. She had a crush, pure and simple.

She'd had a crush on Lance Morcombe, too, and had thought she'd learned her lesson. Lance had been the editor-in-chief of her high school paper, and she had been feature editor. He'd called her nearly every evening to talk about the paper, and they'd invariably wound up laughing and talking about personal things. She could still remember the way his brilliant blue eyes had smiled at her. She could also recall exactly how she had felt when she had discovered that he was crazy about her best friend.

Which just went to prove that men were interested in bodies more than personality. Lance had spent hours on the phone with her every night, but she wasn't good enough for him to date. Nor had Lance been an exception.

So what the hell was she doing going ga-ga over a guy who could have his pick of able-bodied beauties?

How many times did she have to be humiliated before she would read the writing on the wall? Damn, sometimes her own stupidity appalled her.

Sighing, she paused by the kitchen window and pulled back the curtain so she could look out into the stormy night. Lightning was flashing so rapidly it kept the world almost continuously illuminated. It seemed highly unlikely that even a thirst for revenge would bring Richard Jackson to her door tonight.

A sound behind her caused her to turn. Craig Nighthawk stood in the kitchen doorway wearing the colorful quilt like a toga. He carried an armload of sodden clothes. Beside him stood an adoring Guinevere.

"I think she smells Mop on me," he said.

"Where *is* Mop?"

"I left him at home."

She glanced toward the window. "The sheep must be miserable out there tonight."

He shrugged a shoulder. "I don't think they evaluate things the same way we do. Besides, they've got good wool coats to keep 'em warm, and plenty of lanolin to keep 'em dry."

She felt herself smile. "That's true. They couldn't ask for better protection."

He lifted the bundle of clothes. "Dryer?"

"Oh!" God, she felt like such a fool the way she kept overlooking the obvious. This man rattled her nerves entirely too much. She pointed. "Behind those folding doors."

Then she looked swiftly away because her nerves couldn't handle much more of the sight of him wrapped in nothing but that quilt. Oh, it was perfectly decent, but knowing he wore nothing under it was...seductive.

"Would you like a hot drink?" she asked, grasping desperately for her composure. Oh, this was terrible. Her life had been so devoid of men since she had grown up and had something to say in the matter, that she could be rattled by something as simple as this. How pathetic.

"Whatever you have would be great."

"Tea? Hot chocolate?"

"Hot chocolate, please."

It gave her something to do with her hands and kept her back to the room as he closed the dryer door, switched it on, and sat at the table. Amazing how much you could tell just by listening, she thought.

She started a pan of water boiling, and spooned instant cocoa mix into two mugs. A low rumble of thunder shook the house again, causing the mugs to rattle on the counter.

"Damn, it's some wicked night out there," Craig remarked. "We'll have tornadoes for sure."

"I hope not. I'm in a state of blissful ignorance and I'd like to stay that way."

He laughed, a warm deep sound that seemed to touch her very heart. The man didn't laugh easily; she'd learned that about him already.

"We get 'em occasionally hereabouts," he told her. "Of course, that doesn't mean you'll ever actually see one."

"Have you?"

"Once, when I was driving. I was on the highway, driving a truck, and I watched a funnel cloud for about twenty minutes before it dissipated. Damn, it was beautiful. Scarily beautiful. Other times I've seen 'em start. That's usually a good time to find cover, which is why I don't have a dozen stories about seeing 'em touch down."

The lights flickered again, in company with another roll of thunder. The water on the stove was beginning to steam. Slowly, knowing that her refusal to face him was becoming painfully apparent, she turned around, trying to think of something light and amusing to say.

Before she could open her mouth, however, Guinevere rose to her feet, lowered her head and began to make the sounds that suggested she was about to vomit.

"Oh, Guin, no!"

But Guinevere had considerably more urgent matters on her mind. Lowering her head even further, she dumped the contents of her stomach. It wasn't very much, though, and that made Esther uneasy.

She grabbed a towel and threw it over the mess, then knelt beside Guin and hugged her. "What's wrong? Did you eat something you shouldn't have?"

Guin gave a whimper, then vomited again. Once again there was almost nothing.

"I don't like the looks of this," Craig said. "If there's nothing in her stomach she shouldn't be vomiting."

"That's what I think." She looked over her shoulder at him, forgetting her embarrassment in her concern for the dog, and got a full-on view of broad, bronzed shoulders. Some corner of her mind took note of the beauty of the man, even as the rest of her scurried around looking for some way to help the dog.

Forcing herself to look away from Craig, she stroked Guinevere's back. "What's the matter, sweetie? Hmm? Did you eat something outside?"

Guin looked mournfully at her mistress, then heaved again.

"I think I'd better take her to the doctor," Esther said. Her vet back in Seattle had told her never to ignore it when a dog vomited and there were no discernible pieces of food or bone in it. "You won't mind if I leave you here alone?"

"You're not going to leave me here," he said. "I'm going with you. I don't want you out on these roads in this weather, especially not in the middle of the night. Go get dressed while I look after Guinevere."

Esther hurried upstairs as fast as she could to change into a skirt and blouse. Damning her brace for a nuisance, she worked with impatient, fumbling hands to remove it so she could put on underwear. When she went to put it back on, she hesitated, thinking it might be easier to just forgo it, but then she decided not to be stupid about it. Without the brace to stabilize her leg, she was truly handicapped, and apt to fall flat on her face, something she didn't care to do at any time, but especially *not* in front of other people.

Her hands fumbled again as she considered the particular other person involved in tonight's misadventure and realized that she *really* didn't want to fall down in front of *him.*

God, Esther, your life is getting to be so limited! Why are you worrying about stupid things like that?

When she limped back into the kitchen, the mess on the floor had been cleaned up, Craig had dressed again in his wet clothes and Guin was huddled under the table looking as miserable as Esther had ever seen her.

"I called the vet," Craig said. "He'll be waiting for us."

She looked at him, astonished he had gone to so much trouble. This wasn't his concern and she certainly wouldn't have expected a man to get involved at all. "Thank you."

He shrugged. "Jake always appreciates a few minutes to make himself a cup of coffee and get his pants on."

"Do you have to go to him often?"

"Usually he comes to me. Or rather my sheep."

"Do you know him well?"

"I don't know that I'd say that."

Guinevere was reluctant to step out into the stormy night, so Craig picked her up and carried her to Esther's Jimmy.

"You'll hurt yourself!" Esther protested as she trotted after him into the windy, wet night. Twice she nearly lost her balance and had to slow down.

He put the dog into her cage in the back of the car then faced Esther. "She weighs about the same as one of my sheep."

Which probably explained the breadth and strength of the bare shoulders she had seen just a short while ago in her kitchen.

She was glad to pass him the car keys when he offered to drive, and soon they were bucking their way down her rutted driveway to the highway. Guin whimpered occasionally from the rear.

The rain had let up a little, but the lightning was still flickering nonstop, and the rumble of the thunder drowned the roar of the engine.

"Jake Llewellyn is a very nice man," Esther remarked. "Guinevere just loves him."

"Everything with four legs loves that man. And most of the two-legged critters like him just as well."

Given that it was the middle of the night, it was hardly surprising that she couldn't think of a thing to say. The silence initially felt awkward to her, but Craig didn't seem to mind it, so finally she relaxed. With her head slightly turned, she watched him drive. His hands looked strong and capable on the steering wheel.

Out of nowhere she was shocked by an image of those hands on her flesh. Hot color flared instantly in her cheeks, but her mind wouldn't let go of the image. An ache began low inside her, and she closed her eyes, caught in the sway of urges too strong to stifle.

For years she had refused to indulge such fantasies because they only made her miserable, but now she seemed unable to stop them. As clear as if it were happening that very instant, she could see his dark hands against the pale flesh of her breasts, and with the image came an unmistakable spear of arousal.

She wanted this man. In the privacy of her heart and mind, she admitted how much she wanted him to hold her and touch her. She knew it wasn't possible, that he would never want her in such a way, but part of her rebelled against that reality. Part of her demanded to know why not. Part of her wondered why once, just once, she couldn't know the delight of love-making. And another part of her, a scarier part, was prepared to sacrifice pride and good sense in order to have her way.

Guinevere whimpered, yanking Esther out of her dangerous thoughts. Her concern for her dog overrode everything else, and she felt ashamed for having let her thoughts wander even a little bit. Poor Guin!

She even felt a little bit of panic. Guin had been her closest friend and companion for six years now, and Esther just didn't know how she would manage if anything happened to the dog. A large chunk of her heart had belonged to Guinevere since her puppyhood, and life without her was impossible to con-template.

"We'll be there soon," Craig announced as if he felt her increasing worry.

"I'm so scared," Esther admitted to him. "I'm probably making entirely too much out of this, but...I'm scared any-way."

"You don't have to apologize for caring about your dog, Esther. And you don't have to apologize for being worried about her. I'd be worried sick if it were Mop or Bucket."

She liked him for being able to admit that so easily. But then Craig wasn't much like the men she had known in the past. He seemed comfortable with himself, as if he didn't need to prove anything. It was surprisingly relaxing and comforting.

"I was never allowed to have a dog as a child," Esther found herself confiding. "I always wanted one, but I waited until I felt I had a good enough home for one, and could be sure that I could take care of her if she got sick or anything."

"So Guin is your first dog ever?"

"Yes. I've spoiled her rotten, and I've gotten ridiculously goofy about her."

"Why ridiculous? Esther, believe me, Guin doesn't think she's been ridiculous to think the sun rises and sets on you. Why should you feel silly for feeling the same?"

"Because she's just a dog?" She said it tentatively, because that was what she'd so often heard, but she didn't quite believe it.

"*Just* a dog? What does *just* a dog mean? Pardon me, but I think dogs, cats and every other living thing are worthy of respect, the same respect we'd give to another human being. The inability to speak English is hardly the measure of a being's worth. Or at least it shouldn't be, although I've known quite a few people who thought it was. My point is, humans have a tendency to consider every other species inferior, and therefore less worthy of love and respect. That's ridiculous. *Difference* doesn't necessarily imply inferiority."

Once again he had surprised her. "You've thought a lot about these things."

"Driving a truck, there isn't much to do except think." He tossed her a smile just before he negotiated the turn into the veterinary clinic's parking lot. "But I think my upbringing had a lot to do with my feelings on the subject. All life is sacred, not just human life."

Jake Llewellyn was waiting for them, and opened the front door as soon as he saw their headlights. He held the door open while Craig carried Guinevere inside.

"Down the hall, first door on the left," he said. "Just put her on the table."

Esther hurried after them, and when Guin was on the table, she put her hand on the dog's neck to comfort her. Guin seemed more interested, however, in licking Dr. Llewellyn's hand.

"How you doing, girl?" the vet asked her as he scratched her behind the ears and checked her eyes at the same time.

Guin whined briefly.

"That's what I hear," Jake replied. "An upset tummy with nothing in it. So what did you get into, sweetheart? Hmm? A nasty old spider?"

He made Craig and Esther wait outside while he examined Guin. The next ten minutes of Esther's life were some of the longest she'd ever known. It reminded her, in fact, of the night her mother died, when she had paced a hospital waiting room wondering what was to become of her now.

"God, that's terrible!"

She wasn't aware she had spoken out loud until Craig said, "What's wrong? What's terrible?"

"Oh, I was just remembering..." She hesitated and then decided she might as well face up to it. "I was remembering the night my mother died. I spent an hour pacing a hospital waiting room just like this, worrying and impatient. But what suddenly struck me was that I was more worried for myself than I was for my mother. I couldn't imagine what was going to happen to me if she died."

"What's so awful about that? Given the kind of mother she apparently was, I wouldn't hold it against you if you'd felt like cheering."

Almost in spite of herself, Esther chuckled. "It's hard to cheer about being put in a foster home. Are you always so understanding of human weakness?"

He shrugged and gave her a crooked smile. "I'm just as human as the next guy. Who am I to judge? So, what were the foster homes like?"

"Adequate." Now it was her turn to shrug. It wasn't a period of life she liked to remember.

"You weren't mistreated or anything?"

"No, not at all. It was just...I couldn't make the connections I needed to make for it to feel like home. They were all really nice people, though. It isn't as if they didn't want me to feel at home."

His dark gaze was suddenly penetrating. "Have you ever felt at home anywhere?"

In an instant she went on the defensive. "Of course! I feel perfectly at home wherever I live." But was that true? Suddenly uncomfortable with the realization that she might not really know what it meant to feel at home, she didn't want to look too closely at the matter.

Before Craig could press her any further, Jake joined them. "I want to keep Guinevere until late this afternoon, Esther. I can't find anything obviously wrong, but I don't want you to take her home on the off chance that she'll start vomiting again. It doesn't take much to put a dog into acidosis, and if she vomits again I'd rather have her here where I can do something right away. Okay?"

"Yes, of course, but…is she going to be all right?"

Jake smiled. "I really think she will. But vomiting of this nature is serious in a dog, and if I need to take steps, the sooner the better. I'll call you if she worsens, otherwise you can come get her at four this afternoon."

Leaving Guinevere behind was awful. Esther couldn't remember when her heart had ever felt so empty.

Craig reached out and took her hand as they crossed the parking lot to the car. "She's going to be fine. I'm sure of it."

"But Jake didn't want to take any chances."

"That's just good policy. Honestly, Esther, I think if he thought that Guinevere was in serious danger he wouldn't have told you to go home."

She nodded, needing to believe he was right. But it sure didn't seem right to go home without Guinevere.

Craig helped her up into the Jimmy, a courtesy she wasn't accustomed to, then climbed behind the wheel and exited the parking lot.

"I'd suggest a sandwich or coffee somewhere," he said, "but this place closes up tight by ten o'clock."

"I can make us something when we get home." The idea of a cozy middle-of-the-night meal with him actually sounded good. Sleepiness had fled when he had arrived earlier, and it didn't appear to be interested in returning.

"I don't want you to go to any trouble."

Did that mean he didn't want to spend any time alone with her? Or did he mean exactly what he said? She hesitated, trapped in her insecurities.

And then, as if her guardian angel suddenly decided to intervene, a voice in her head whispered, *What have you got to lose?*

Good question, she realized. What did she have to lose? Nothing ventured, nothing gained, as the saying went. If she didn't invite him to have a sandwich with her, he never would. And if he declined, was she any worse off?

Emboldened, she said, "It's no trouble, really. I have some turkey breast that will make wonderful sandwiches."

"You're on," he said promptly. "I love turkey."

So they rode on into the night while she wondered wryly if all she needed to do to attract a man was keep plenty of turkey on hand.

By the time they got home, the rain had stopped but the yard in front of her house was a great big mud puddle with the forlorn heads of flowers sticking out of it. In the distance thunder still growled and lightning still flickered, giving the night a restless, uneasy feeling.

Esther climbed out of the Jimmy, nearly losing her footing on the wet, slippery ground. She steadied herself against the door, then hurried up onto the porch, suddenly afraid that Craig would offer to help her. She didn't want him to help her. She didn't want him to see her as someone who *needed* help.

All of a sudden she froze. On her door a white piece of paper fluttered, seeming to almost glow in the darkness.

Craig's voice came from behind her. "Looks like someone was here."

Esther didn't want to take another step. She was as afraid of that sheet of paper as if it were a doorway to hell.

Craig stepped up beside her. "Maybe one of the deputies was by and left a note so you'd know he was here."

Esther suddenly realized that she'd been holding her breath. Letting go of it in a great gust, she seized the possibility he offered. "Yes! That has to be it. Beau must have stopped by again."

Stepping forward, she took the paper down, unlocked the door and stepped inside. The house felt chilly and damp, and so very empty without Guinevere. A pang of renewed loneliness struck her as she limped through the house to the kitchen, switching on lights as she went.

"Why don't you throw your clothes in the dryer again," she suggested to Craig. "You're still wet."

"Thanks, I will."

But he didn't move and she realized that he was waiting for her to read the note in her hand. His questioning glance in the direction of the paper and her reluctance to even look at it spoke volumes. Slowly, fearfully, she raised it.

It was from her father.

Chapter 8

Craig built a fire in the living room fireplace while Esther huddled under the quilt on the couch, her braced leg stuck out in front of her. She couldn't seem to get warm, and she shivered even inside the cocoon of the quilt.

The fire was soon burning brightly, and Craig disappeared down the hallway. Before long she heard things rattling in the kitchen. He was probably making them something hot to drink, she thought.

Like a drowning victim clinging to a straw, she was trying to focus on the ordinary and mundane. Anything except the note from her father that said he had been there.

Craig returned eventually with a plate of turkey sandwiches and two mugs of hot chocolate. He held the sandwiches toward her. "Help yourself."

"I'm not hungry. Thank you."

"Try to eat something anyway, Esther. Put some fuel in the system. You'll think more clearly and you'll probably warm up."

Obediently she took half a sandwich and bit into it. Much to her surprise, when the delicious flavors of turkey and tomato touched her tongue they awakened her appetite. She devoured what she had in her hand and reached for another half sandwich.

Craig watched her with smiling eyes. "Are you always difficult?"

She looked up, surprised. "What do you mean?"

"I sometimes get the feeling that if I said the sky was blue you'd argue that it was green."

Color heated her cheeks. "I'm not contrary."

"No, but you sure as hell don't want me to do anything for you. Even something as small as making a sandwich. Why? Are you afraid it'll give me power over you?"

She was embarrassed to realize that his assessment was quite close to the truth...and equally embarrassed to realize that his having power over her sounded...intriguing. Tempting. What would it be like to be totally at the mercy of Craig Nighthawk? Not that she would ever find out.

"Is it just me?" he asked her. "Is it something about me? Maybe those stories you've been hearing about my checkered past? I didn't hurt that little girl, you know. I never laid a finger on her."

Horror washed over her. "I know that! Do you think I'd have ever let you into my house if I hadn't known that?"

They stared at each other from opposite ends of the couch, and Esther suddenly felt as if they were at opposite ends of the world.

And that was her fault, she realized. She'd been so preoccupied with her own problems, with the scars from her own past, that she had never once considered that Craig Nighthawk might have some problems of his own. That he might have some tender scars of his own.

"Forget it," he said before she could think of anything to say that would close the gap between them. "I'm just getting edgy because I'm so tired. You must be exhausted, too. Finish that sandwich, then curl up and go to sleep."

But now she really had lost her appetite and put the sandwich back on the plate. "You go ahead and sleep," she said. "I don't know if I can."

"There was nothing threatening in that note, Esther. All he said was he was sorry he missed you and would call you."

"But he put it out there sometime between one and three in the morning! That's hardly unthreatening. Would you go to visit someone at that time of night?"

"I might if they were family and I'd just pulled into the area after a long drive."

She stared at him with utter hopelessness, feeling that she was losing her only ally in a hostile world.

He shook his head finally. "I'm not saying you aren't right to be afraid. I'm just trying to put it in the best light possible. Don't worry, you aren't going to be alone at night until this is settled one way or another. I plan on staying here every night."

She ought to protest. Some corner of her weary mind recognized that this was a terrible imposition to make on this man, and that she had no right to such concern from him, but she simply couldn't bring herself to refuse his help. Not now that she knew that Richard Jackson was here and knew where her house was.

"You come with me in the morning when I get my things," he continued. "I want you to meet Paula, so you'll be able to call her during the day if you get scared. I also want you to feel comfortable about running over there any time you feel a need for company."

He patted the sofa beside him. "Now curl up and sleep. Or go upstairs if you'd rather. I'll be here." She hesitated and finally he opened his arm. "C'mere," he said softly.

And for some reason she did precisely that, crawling down the sofa until he could tuck her against his side and cradle her head on his shoulder. He made her feel warm and safe, and something deep inside her relaxed that had never relaxed before.

Sleep crept up gently. At some point she became aware that her head was now resting on his lap, and that he was stroking her hair with gentle fingers.

"You have to face him sometime, Esther," Craig said quietly. "Sooner or later you have to face the bogeyman just so he can't scare you anymore."

Sleep captured her then, carrying her away to sunny dreams of a man with long, dark hair and eyes the color of the night sky.

It was nearly noon when Esther opened her eyes. She was alone on the couch, the fire had burned down, and there was no sign of Craig anywhere.

She sat up slowly, reluctant to let go of the cozy warmth of sleep and face the harsh reality of day. Sunlight poured through the windows, almost clear enough to hurt after the cleansing rain.

She'd kept her brace on all night and now her leg felt chafed and sore from the straps. In fact, she felt stiff all over, probably because she hadn't twitched a muscle since she had closed her eyes. If she had turned over during the night, she couldn't tell.

But she felt rested despite the grittiness of her eyes and the stiffness of her body. Her first thought was to wonder what had become of Craig. Her second was to check her answering machine and see if Dr. Llewellyn had called with news about Guinevere.

Smothering a groan, she stood up, adjusted her clothes and limped to the kitchen. The note from her father still lay crumpled on the table where she had left it. She stared at it with loathing, wishing she had never seen it. With one stroke the man had stolen the last vestige of her security from her all over again.

Reaching for the paper, she shredded it into tiny pieces and dumped it in the trash can. She just wished she could get rid of her father as easily.

On the counter was a note from Craig saying he would be back sometime in the early evening, but to call his sister if she needed anything.

That was all right, Esther thought. By the time she bathed, dressed and straightened up the house from last night, it would be time to drive into town to get Guinevere. Not enough time to get nervous and edgy.

Just the same she checked to make sure all the doors and windows were locked before she went upstairs to bathe. Bath salts and hot water went a long way to improving her mood, and she decided to treat herself by wearing her favorite lavender broomstick skirt and matching peasant blouse with a silver concho belt.

A little talc helped with the chafing from her brace and made her feel so feminine that she indulged in makeup, a rarity for her.

Downstairs she threw the towels from last night—thoughtfully rinsed out by Craig, apparently—into the washer, then made herself a quick breakfast of an English muffin and strawberry jam.

By that point she was ready to venture outside. It was only as she began to unlock the kitchen door that she realized how much metaphorical girding she had just done, bathing and dressing to the hilt as if that would help her face the day better.

Well, maybe it would, she thought with a shrug. Did it matter? It was nice to feel that she looked her best for a change.

Outside the day was significantly cooler, as if with the passing of the storm last night had come a hint of approaching autumn. The breeze had that cool dryness that contrasted so wonderfully with the heat of the sun. Enthralled by it, Esther paused in the middle of her back yard, closed her eyes and just soaked it up.

Finally, heedful of time, she continued to the studio, wanting to check whether the storm had done any damage. The air inside the barn was unusually damp but there didn't seem to be any flooding. The large painting of the mountains was still stretched tautly on the frame, although given the dampness in the air she decided to let it dry for a couple of days before she tried painting on it again. In the meantime she could work on one of the small still lifes that she planned.

She took the time to check all the paintings she was keeping carefully pressed in a portfolio, but they were fine, too. It wouldn't be long before she would be shipping them to Jo who would take care of the rest of the process for her. Esther did nothing but paint. She refused even to concern herself with framing. Others, she believed, were better at those things than she, and to this day her belief had never been tested because she had never set foot in a gallery to see one of her paintings on display.

Another one of her personality quirks. She vastly preferred anonymity, and her fame as a painter interested her only in that it made it possible for her to keep painting.

All of that, she knew, could be traced back to her self-consciousness about her limp and the basic insecurity a person developed when she felt unloved by her parents. Whatever the reason, she was happy with the way things were and couldn't imagine anything more horrifying than having to meet the world at large.

Satisfied with the condition of things in her studio, she locked up and headed toward town. She needed a few odds and ends from the grocery store, so she decided to go shopping before she picked up Guinevere. Thinking of her dog, she pressed a little harder on the accelerator.

What she didn't want to think about were Craig's last words to her. Ever since she awoke they'd been trying to wedge their way into her thoughts. *Sooner or later you have to face the bogeyman just so he can't scare you anymore.*

Her hands tightened on the wheel as she tried to force the words away once more. He didn't know, she told herself. He couldn't possibly understand. Richard Jackson was more than a bogeyman. He was the man who had crippled her and killed her mother.

There was no way to equate that with the fear of a monster in the closet. No way at all.

Face him so he couldn't scare her anymore? Not likely. There was only one reason he could want to see her after all this time, and that was to kill her. Just because he was too canny to threaten her on the phone or in writing didn't mean he was harmless.

And she was so very disappointed that Craig couldn't see that.

* * *

She thought she saw her father as she was loading her groceries into the Jimmy. A gray-haired man stood across the street, smoking a cigarette as he leaned against the lamppost. It was him. It had to be. God, he was following her!

Her heart climbed into her throat, and her hands began to tremble violently. She had to get out of here now!

Swiftly she walked around the Jimmy and climbed in behind the wheel. When she looked again, the man was gone. Shaking, the sour taste of fear filling her mouth, she sat motionlessly, trying to figure it out, but her thoughts were scrambling around like terrified mice.

Maybe that man hadn't been Richard at all. It could have been almost anyone. After all this time she really didn't know for sure if she could recognize him. Maybe her imagination was running wild.

And maybe he had seen her getting into her car and had gone to get into his so he could follow her. It was a distinct possibility, and one that did nothing to comfort her.

She needed to go to the sheriff, she decided finally. She should have called him first thing this morning and told him about the note Richard had left. There had to be something he could do now that it was apparent that Richard was here.

She nearly dropped the keys first, but finally managed to get them into the ignition and turn the engine over. Then, watching her rearview mirror almost as much as the street ahead of her, she drove to the sheriff's office. There didn't seem to be anyone following her.

The Fates must have been favoring her, because there was a parking place right in front of the sheriff's building. She steered straight into it and parked, then waited a minute or two to see if she saw the man again. But he wouldn't show himself this close to the sheriff, would he?

Inside, she found Nate Tate in the front office talking to Velma about some vandalism at the high school. As soon as he saw Esther he turned to her with a smile. "Sweetie, you look gorgeous this afternoon. You better stay off the streets or I'll have to cite you for disturbing the peace."

She couldn't even bring herself to smile, and in an instant

he was across the room, taking her elbow gently. "What happened?"

Velma stood up at her desk and leaned toward her. "Esther? You okay, girl?"

"I...I'm fine, really. Just scared."

Nate looked straight down into her eyes. "Your father?"

She nodded. "I had to bring Guin to the vet around one this morning. When I got home there was a note from him taped to my front door. He said he was sorry he missed me, and that he'd call."

"But you didn't see him?"

"No...but I..." She trailed off and looked beseechingly at him. "I think I may have seen him when I came out of the supermarket, but I'm not sure. It's been so many years, but a man was standing across the street, smoking a cigarette, and something reminded me so strongly of him that I came straight here."

"You did the right thing," Nate told her. "Exactly the right thing. Do you have the note you found on the door?"

Suddenly feeling stupid and miserable, she shook her head. "I ripped it up. I ripped it up into the tiniest pieces I could manage. I'm sorry—"

He silenced her with a shake of his head and a smile. "I probably would have done the same thing. Don't worry about it, sweet cakes. Now, do you think you can draw me a picture of this guy you saw?"

Esther felt a burst of hope. Why hadn't she thought of that? "Of course I can!" She glanced at her watch. "But I'm supposed to pick up Guin at four."

Nate turned to Velma. "Give Jake a call, will you? Tell him I need Esther for a little while so she'll be late. If that's a problem, I can send a deputy to get the dog. Whichever is better for him."

Then he turned back to Esther. "Now you come back to my office. I'll get you some paper and pencils and we'll see what you can do to help us find this guy, okay?"

She smiled then, feeling a whole lot better. "Okay."

As she sat at Nate's desk with the blank sheet of paper

before her, she found herself wishing she had taken a better look at the guy. Now she had only the vaguest recollection, broad brush strokes of impression that her mind was undoubtedly going to try to fill in.

Closing her eyes briefly, she reached for the snapshot that her brain had taken in the first instant she had seen the man. Then, working swiftly, she began to make pencil strokes on the paper before her.

Twenty minutes later she handed the paper to Nate. He studied it intently, then nodded.

"We'll be able to identify him from this," he told her. "But you have to understand, legally I can't touch the guy. I can have my men keep an eye out for him, and I can have them keep a sharper eye on you, but I can't do anything about this man until he does something illegal. Fact is, I can't even ask him what he's doing in these parts. Well, I can ask, but he doesn't have to answer. Legally, my hands are tied until he actually does something wrong."

Esther nodded, feeling apprehensive again.

"Of course," Nate continued, "I could always have a personal word with him, something to the effect that he'd better hope you don't stumble and sprain your ankle while he's around, because if anything, however minor, happens to you, we're going to be looking really hard at him."

"Thank you." It wasn't all that she could have wished for, but even Richard Jackson might take pause if Nate Tate spoke to him that way. Most mortals would.

"Now," Nate said, perching on the corner of his desk and looking down at her, "why don't you consider coming to stay with Marge and me? Just until this guy moves on. We've got a spare room and you'd be more than welcome."

The offer touched Esther deeply. Tears prickled her eyes and she had to blink rapidly. "Thank you, Nate. I appreciate that more than I can say."

"Nothing to thank me for. What good is a neighbor if he's not willing to help out when you need him?"

"Well, I thank you anyway, but I'm afraid I can't accept.

I've got so much work to do to prepare for my next exhibition. I can't afford to let my father interfere with it, Nate.''

He cocked his head to one side and frowned. ''Your life is the important thing.''

''My career *is* my life. Without it, I'm nothing. I'm not going to let him destroy me through fear.''

The sheriff nodded, managing to look at once resigned and understanding. ''Sounds exactly like some damn fool thing I'd say myself. Okay, have it your way. I'll just make sure the patrols run by your place more frequently now, and that everybody's on the lookout for this man.''

Rising, Esther looked at the sketch he was still holding. ''The more I look at it, the more convinced I am that it's my father.''

''Well, it's sure not anyone local. I'd recognize him if he were.''

That sent another chill skittering along her spine. That was when she realized just how much she'd been hoping she'd mistaken someone local for her father. ''I'd better go get Guin,'' she said finally.

''Check with Velma first. Somebody may have already gone to get her.''

When she stopped at the dispatcher's desk, Velma shook her head. ''Jake said you come by whenever. It's no problem. He also said to tell you Guin's just fine.''

''Thanks, Velma.''

''No problem. Anything else I can do, you just holler, hear?''

When Esther stepped back out onto the sunny street, she felt considerably better, as if discovering how much support she had strengthened her somehow. Her head was up and her step was light. And quite consciously, she refused to look around to see if she saw the man again. She didn't want to know if he was there. Sooner or later, it seemed she was going to have to deal with him. Until that time she wasn't going to cower.

Her newfound courage lasted all the way to the vet's where Jake told her that Guin was just fine.

"I don't know what was wrong," he told her. "She vomited once more after you left her, but she didn't go into acidosis. When she woke up this morning she was bright-eyed and energetic. She ate a full breakfast and pretty much downed a whole bowl of water. Since then she's been sleeping, but that's her normal schedule, isn't it?"

Esther nodded. "She sleeps through most of the day while I work. Her most active time is in the evening."

"Well, then, she's just fine. I can only speculate that she ate something she shouldn't have, something that was a little toxic to her."

Guin was thrilled to see her, wagging her entire body with delight and clearly resisting the urge to jump up on Esther only with the greatest difficulty. She leapt into her transport case with undisguised eagerness, and woofed a friendly farewell to Jake Llewellyn.

Jake waved as they drove away. He was, Esther thought, a remarkably warm and friendly man. In fact, now that she thought about it, she'd met a number of very nice, very friendly men since moving here. Back in Seattle she'd avoided men completely, talking to them only when business demanded it. Since coming here, though, she hadn't been able to get away with that. The men of the sheriff's department were rather persistent about looking after her, and now her neighbor was thrusting himself into her affairs with all the determination of a knight-errant.

Isolated? Had she really believed herself to be isolated? She suddenly felt an urge to laugh out loud. Since coming to Conard County she was less isolated than she had been at any time in her life. The people here just wouldn't let her be, and she apparently hadn't felt any desperate need to insist upon it. The daily visits from deputies had become a welcome part of her life, along with Verna's arrival with the mail. And it felt damn good to be headed home knowing that deputies would be stopping by frequently, and that in a few hours Craig would arrive.

No, her isolation had been a state of mind, and now that it was shattered, she was incredibly relieved. How absolutely appallingly awful this situation would have been without all this support!

When she pulled up to her house and saw that a deputy was already waiting, she could almost have kissed Nate. Micah Parish stepped down from her porch and came around to speak to her through the driver's window.

"Nate didn't want you arriving home alone," he told her. "Seems you saw your father in town?"

"I think so."

He nodded. "Well, then, just give me the house key. I'll go inside and check things out. On the off chance there's someone in there, you and Guinevere stay right here. If I'm not back out in five minutes, get the hell out of here, okay?"

Just like that, all the sunshine was gone from the world again. The threat had never seemed more real or more hideous. There was something so stark about his order for her to drive away if he didn't come back out.

Another shiver trickled down her spine and she looked away from the house, out over the prairie toward the mountains. They were late-afternoon dark now, almost slate gray. The air was still so crystalline from the night's rain that the mountains seemed almost magnified, with every detail standing out clearly. She wondered if she could accomplish that effect with her watercolors.

Guin groaned a happy sound from the back, as if she knew she was home and that at any moment she was going to be allowed to run free. Which, of course, she wouldn't until she was out of heat.

God, had five minutes ever dragged so slowly? Esther found herself drumming her fingers on the steering wheel and tapping her toe. If something happened to Micah Parish...

But nothing did. He stepped out the front door eons later—or so it seemed—and waved that it was all clear. Then he headed toward the barn. Esther considered getting out of the Jimmy, then decided to wait. Someone could be hiding in the barn just as well.

But no one was. When Micah came striding back across the

hard-packed earth toward her, she climbed down from the Jimmy and went around back to let Guinevere out.

Guin was apparently waiting for this opportunity. Rather than sit patiently to be leashed as she usually did, she leapt right by Esther, nearly knocking her over, and ran for the open fields.

"Guin! No! Guin, come!"

But the dog barely halted to glance back at her before she dashed even farther away. Esther stared after her in despair, knowing there was no way on earth she could catch the Saint Bernard.

Micah came up beside her. "She'll come back, Esther. She always has."

"But she's in heat!"

"Well, hell." He looked after the rapidly vanishing dog, then chuckled. "Guess my kids'll get those pups sooner than I thought."

Almost in spite of herself, Esther felt her natural good humor reasserting itself. "They'll be mutts. Most likely half komondor."

He arched a dark brow. "She's got a thing for Nighthawk's dog, huh?"

Esther chuckled. "The two of them appear to be madly in love. For the moment at least."

Micah shook his head. "Well, that ought to make one hell of an interesting cross. Then again, maybe the two of them won't get together."

"I've got my fingers crossed, but I wouldn't put any money on it."

Micah reached inside the Jimmy and pulled out the grocery bags. "I'll carry these inside for you, then I've got to be heading home. Faith always worries when I'm late. Say, would you like to come have dinner with us?"

Again she felt tempted, a desire that surprised her.

Ordinarily she backed away from such invitations without the least regret. "Thank you. May I have a rain check? I need to be here when Guin gets back."

Ten minutes later she watched from the front porch as

Micah Parish drove away. With his departure, her unease returned, but there wasn't a damn thing she could do about it except go inside and lock the door behind her.

Come home, Guin, she thought. Come home soon. I don't need to be worrying about you, too.

"Oh, hell!" Craig looked at the two dogs out by the shearing barn and wanted to groan. Esther was going to be furious.

"Where'd that Saint Bernard come from?" Enoch asked.

"She belongs to Esther Jackson."

"The woman you're spending the night with?"

"The *lady* on whose porch I'm sleeping," Craig corrected him quickly.

Enoch flashed a very male grin. "Yeah. Right."

"Believe what you want. But I know better than to get mixed up with another white woman. They're nothing but trouble."

Enoch's smile faded. "Yeah," he said finally. "It can be a real pain." Craig suddenly remembered how badly beaten Enoch had been in high school when he dared to ask a white girl out. Her brother and his friends had made sure that Enoch never got so far above himself again.

Craig looked at the two dogs who were quite happily mating and wondered what the hell he was going to tell Esther. Not that there was much he could have done. Mop was plainly in his own yard, and Guin was just as plainly trespassing.

"Oh, hell," he said again as it struck him that something might be wrong with Esther. The dog had gotten away from her somehow. What if she was hurt? "I need to get over to Esther's place pronto. If Guin's running loose something's wrong."

Enoch gave him another irritating smile. "Yeah. Okay, go see what's up. I'll bring her dog over when they're done."

Craig hesitated, knowing that if the dog had merely gotten away from Esther somehow, she was probably going to be upset with him for not bringing Guin. On the other hand, given what the two dogs were doing right now, it might be forty-five minutes before they could be separated. And, damn, didn't the two of them look pleased as punch? He nodded to Enoch. "Thanks."

He trotted across the yard to his pickup, then took off like a bat out of hell. It was entirely possible he was overreacting, he knew, but he was suddenly unable to think of anything except the note that had been on her door last night. That fluttering white sheet of paper saying the bastard had been there in the dead of night.

And for all he passed it off as nothing unusual to Esther, he felt every bit as disturbed by the timing of that note as she did. He just hadn't wanted to add to her anxiety by agreeing with her—although in retrospect maybe he had been treating her like a child. Esther certainly didn't deserve that from him.

The long summer evening was just drawing to a close as he pulled up in front of her house. The Jimmy was parked out front where she usually left it, and lights were blazing throughout the first floor of the house. She was growing uneasy as night descended, he realized. She didn't even have Guinevere to keep her company now.

Unless something was wrong. Fear gripped him by the throat as he trotted up the steps and hammered on her door.

A minute crept by, and then another. He hammered again, shouting her name, and wondering if he ought to break the door down.

"Craig?"

He swung around and found Esther standing in the yard to his left.

"Craig, what on earth...?"

He bounded down the porch, leapt the rail, and picked her right up off her feet. "God, woman, you scared me half to death! Your dog is over at my place, all your lights are on but you didn't answer your door...."

"I was out looking for Guin." She sounded breathless and was looking at him uncertainly. Her hands were braced on his shoulders as she dangled helplessly in his arms. "Craig, I don't like to be...picked up...."

He could hear the note of panic beginning to rise in her voice, and he quickly set her on her feet. "Sorry," he said swiftly, stepping back. "Sorry. I was just so glad to see you okay...." He didn't want to admit any more than that, either to himself or her. "I didn't mean to overwhelm you."

She astonished him with a wry smile. "I think you're overwhelming by nature. So Guin is at your place? Can one hope she isn't busy making herself a mommy?"

He spread his hands. "I cannot tell a lie. I would have brought her but I was worried about you and there was no way just then to separate the dogs..." He shook his head. "I'll help pay for whatever costs there are from this."

Esther couldn't allow it. "Absolutely not. Guin set off on this misadventure all on her own. She's *my* responsibility and I won't have you paying for her misconduct." She shook her head and tsked. "I was afraid she was going to get to Mop. Do you suppose dogs fall madly in love?"

"Those two seemed to have. Mop's never gotten this excited or mopey over Bucket."

"Poor Bucket," Esther said whimsically. "Her husband has been unfaithful. Whatever will she do now?"

Craig stared at her then let out the heartiest laugh he had in years. "What will she do? She'll keep on herding sheep with Enoch, and at some future date she'll make puppies with Mop. He may be wild about Guin, but he'll probably find Bucket's blandishments too much to resist when the time comes."

"Just like a man."

His smile faded. "I hope you're joking about that."

"Should I be?" She tried to take the sting out of the words with a smile but failed.

"I realize your father formed your impression of men, Esther, but some of us are okay, you know? We don't believe in cheating, we don't beat women, we don't get drunk, and we love our kids. Some of us belong to a very different class of person."

She instinctively reached a hand toward him, but didn't touch him. "I know that," she said quietly. "I didn't mean to insult you."

"I wasn't insulted. I'm just tired of being lumped into

groups without regard to the kind of person I really am. Lazy, drunken Indian is another category where I don't fit, but lately I seem to be getting lumped into the 'men are rotten' category even more often.''

"Trust me, I wasn't lumping you into any category at all, Craig. If I had been, I'd never have said those things."

"Now how am I supposed to take that? That as far as you're concerned, I'm not a man?"

She took a quick step back, obviously frightened by his vehemence. That made him even madder, but before he could act like an absolute jerk, he caught himself. She had good reason to think poorly of men, he reminded himself. Plenty of reason. He had no business getting on her case about it, and when it came right down to it, maybe he did belong in that Rotten Men category. Just look at how he was haranguing her over a stupid, perfectly innocent remark. The kind of remark people—both men and women—made a thousand times a day.

The real problem, he realized unhappily, was that he didn't want Esther to lump him in with her father. In her eyes, he wanted to be as far removed from that man as possible. She was hardly likely to do that if he kept jumping on her.

"Sorry," he said. "I guess I'm getting too sensitive."

Her expression softened and she stepped closer. "I can understand that. Male bashing seems to have become a national pastime."

"Bashing *anything* seems to have become a national pastime."

They looked at each other for several moments, as if allowing themselves time to regain their balance and absorb their new perceptions of one another. Esther spoke first.

"Is there…any chance that Guin will come home tonight?"

"Oh! Sure. I should have mentioned, my brother-in-law is going to bring her over as soon as—well, you know."

Dusk had grown too deep for him to be sure, but he thought she blushed. He liked that about her, that she could still blush. He was all for women's equality, but he didn't see why that had to mean that women became as tough as men. Of course, to be fair, he still held some old-fashioned, pigheaded notions. Esther was exactly his kind of woman in a lot of ways.

Except, he reminded himself, that she was rather prickly and a little too emotionally wounded. God, how he hated knowing that he was always being judged according to what her father had done. Every time she got that scared-rabbit look in her eyes he wanted to shake her and shout, "Look, I'm not your father!" Which of course would have proved he was no better than Richard Jackson. Regardless, he wouldn't do such a Neanderthal thing anyway. But sometimes he sure as hell wanted to.

"It's nice of your brother-in-law to offer to bring Guin back," Esther said uncertainly.

"Oh, I think he just wants an excuse to meet you."

"Meet me? Why?"

"Because I'm spending so much time over here." Now he was sure she blushed.

"Oh."

She looked down at her toes and Craig became suddenly aware of how dressed up she was today, and how pretty she looked. "You look nice," he heard himself blurt.

Esther's blush deepened and she looked shyly up at him.

"Thank you. Would you like to come inside? I can make us something to drink."

Grabbing at anything that might set the world back onto an even keel, he said, "I could kill for a glass of orange juice right now. You wouldn't happen to have any?"

"I have some frozen concentrate. I'd be happy to make that if you like."

"I'd like it very much."

She had to unlock the door to let them in.

"I got worried when I saw all these lights on," he told her. "You don't ever have your place lit up like this."

She gave him a wry smile. "It was a totally childish impulse on my part. Without Guin I started to get really uneasy, and when I finally decided to go out and look for her a bit, I realized the last thing I wanted to do was come back to a dark house. Of course I understand perfectly that light is no pro-

tection, and that an intruder could have hidden just as well
with all the lights on but—'' She shrugged and gave a self-
deprecating laugh.

"I might have done the same thing."

"You?" She laughed again. "Oh, I don't believe you're
ever scared."

He watched her pull a can of orange juice from the freezer,
open it and dump it into a blender with water. "I've been
scared."

She turned to look at him, the blender whirring behind her,
and he could tell from her expression that she realized she had
said the wrong thing. It was no big deal, he told himself. What
did it matter if she thought that he was never afraid. They
were just neighbors and she could believe anything she wanted
about him.

But somehow it was important to correct the record. "I was
scared to death when I was in jail for a crime I didn't commit.
I could hardly sleep most nights, and sometimes I thought I
couldn't stand another minute of it. I get scared sometimes
when I walk down the street and I realize some people are
staring at me like I'm going to pounce and kill one of them
at any minute. I get scared that some night some of them might
decide to take the law into their own hands."

"Craig!" Her voice was full of horrified sympathy.

He shrugged. "It hasn't been that long since this area was
settled. Some folks around here still think Indians are ver-
min."

"But—"

He interrupted her. "Most people here don't feel that way.
I know that. That's one of the reasons I settled here and
brought my sister's family here. But how many people does
it take to form a lynch mob?"

Her hand flew to her mouth. Behind her the blender labored
on.

"I realize that those things aren't supposed to happen anymore, but there are a lot of ways to kill a man without making
it look like vigilantes did it. I've been beaten bloody for no
reason other than I'm an Indian, so it isn't hard for me to

believe that somebody might take that extra step, especially when they still think I hurt that little girl.''

He shrugged, looking straight at her. ''I've been scared lots of times, Esther. But I still live here, and look those people right in the eye. That's what I was trying to tell you last night.''

She shook her head as if she could forestall what was coming.

''You have to face what you fear, Esther. Honest to God, if you keep running, the bogeyman just gets more powerful. Spit in the devil's eye. Meet him head-on.''

''He could kill me!''

''I'm not suggesting you meet him alone. Just that you set up a meeting with him at a safe place. I'll be there. Hell, half the Conard County Sheriff's Department would be there if you asked. Meet him and face him. Take his power away from him!''

Chapter 9

Esther stared at Craig with huge, horrified eyes. "I can't," she whispered. "I can't."

He thought he'd never heard sadder, more hopeless words. He rose from the table and crossed the kitchen to her, reaching around behind her to shut off the blender. "I know," he said finally, a sense of hopelessness bleeding into his own words. "I know you can't. But it would still be the best thing you could do."

She looked up at him, her hazel eyes beseeching him. Damned if he knew what she wanted, but he knew what *he* wanted. His whole damn body was screaming at him to just lean against her so he could feel her womanly softness.

But he wasn't going to do that. Standing before him looking as enticing as a tall glass of icy water on a hot summer day was the biggest trouble a man could walk into. Never mind that she was white and he wasn't and that the racial purists would have a field day trying to make her miserable. Never mind that the looks and stares would finally be more than she could handle. Never mind any of that hogwash he usually used as an excuse to keep his distance.

No, the real problem here was that this woman was wounded in a very essential way, and that she didn't have the inner fortitude to face her demon. As long as her life was being controlled by fear, she wouldn't have room in it for much else.

He kind of wished that wasn't so, because it would be the easiest thing in the world to just lean into her right now and drive all her fearful thoughts away with the heat that was pounding in his loins. He was hot and heavy and aching so fiercely he could hardly believe he had gotten to this state just from being in the same room with her.

"Face him, Esther," he heard himself say hoarsely. Then with more self-control than he thought he had, he turned away and resumed his seat at the table.

Esther stared after him, feeling frightened and disappointed all at once. Something had happened in the last few moments. She had seen it in the sudden fire of his gaze, in the way he had loomed over her as if she were prey and he the hunter, as if she were all that existed in the universe.

The moment had passed quickly, but she knew she hadn't imagined it. The air was almost too thick to breathe, and her body was responding to something powerful. Deep down inside, where her womb throbbed yearningly, she knew she wanted his possession and damn the consequences.

Just once, whispered some pleading voice in her mind, just this once. Let me know. Let him teach me. Take me. She was willing to give herself completely if only she could have one taste of the forbidden fruit.

But he had turned away just as she had almost fallen into his arms. He had turned away as so many before him had, but this time she didn't think it was because of her brace. This time, even worse, she felt he turned away because he found *her* lacking in some essential way that had nothing to do with her injury.

Face him, Esther.

She turned her back to Craig and with shaking hands finished mixing the orange juice. It was ridiculous of him to expect that of her, she told herself. He didn't know anything about her father, about the vicious, deadly kind of man he was. Face him? She would be facing her own executioner.

She placed a glass of orange juice in front of him, but as she started to turn away, he gently caught her wrist.

"Esther."

She looked down at him, resentment, fear and anger all warring within her. "You don't know," she said thinly.

"No. You're right. I don't know."

She jerked her wrist out of his grip and stepped back. "I don't like to be grabbed. I don't like to be picked up. Don't touch me like that again."

A knock sounded on the door before either of them could say another word.

"That must be Enoch," Craig said. "I'll get it."

She let him because of course it might not be Enoch. It might be Richard Jackson. Fear was a worse prison than iron bars, she thought bitterly. Far worse.

She heard voices from the front of the house. The next thing she knew her kitchen was suddenly filled to overflowing with two ecstatic dogs. Guinevere and Mop ran in circles chasing each other joyously. They managed to knock over a chair, and nearly knocked Esther over, too.

"Hey," said Craig from the doorway. "Mop, cut it out." The komondor let out a joyous groan and skidded to a halt right in front of him. Guinevere skittered across the linoleum, bumped into the cabinets and stopped beside Esther. She looked up at her mistress with a big grin, her tongue lolling to one side.

"That good, huh?" Esther asked her. "Well, I hope you're prepared for the consequences, Guin. There are *always* consequences."

"Esther," Craig said, "this is my sister's husband, Enoch Small Elk."

Esther found herself looking at a man who was considerably shorter than Craig but with a strong, stocky build that reminded her somehow of a workhorse. His hair wasn't quite as dark as Craig's, and it was worn short. He also had a pair of friendly brown eyes that made Esther feel immediately at ease.

"Sorry," Enoch said, "but Mop just wouldn't let your dog go. I finally decided to bring them both because I sure couldn't see any other way to get your dog home."

"Oh, that's perfectly all right," Esther assured him. "But will Mop go home with you? What are you going to do without your sheepdog?"

"Oh, he'll come with us all right," Craig said, an amused glint in his eye. "He just doesn't listen to Enoch."

"Why ever not?"

Enoch smiled. "It's just that I work with Bucket and Craig works with Mop. Believe me, Bucket doesn't listen any better to Craig than Mop does to me."

"But they both listen to Paula," Craig said.

"They listen to her *broom*," Enoch corrected.

"Wouldn't you?"

"Of course."

Esther found herself laughing at the men's repartee, forgetting all the dark things that had been making her so miserable only minutes before. "May I offer you orange juice, Enoch? I just made it."

"Actually, Paula and the kids are out in the truck so I'd better be going. But thanks."

Hardly even hesitating, Esther said, "Why don't you ask them if they'd like to come in, too? I'm sure I have cookies somewhere for the children, and I can certainly make more orange juice...."

Paula Small Elk was a beautiful woman with a round, friendly face and her brother's hair and eyes. The children were adorable, although Esther had little experience of young children and didn't quite know what to say to them. They seemed perfectly happy to sit at the table with juice and cookies, though.

"It's about time we met," Paula told her warmly. "I know we haven't been the best neighbors, but that's only because we've been so busy trying to get the sheep operation up and running."

"I've been busy, too."

"Oh, I know! Craig says you're a painter. Do you have anything hanging in the house that I could see?"

Esther always got a little embarrassed when anyone wanted to see her work, but Paula's smile was so open and friendly, and so eager, that she answered, "Well, I *do* have one hanging in the living room."

She took Paula to see the picture while the men watched the children. Craig's sister was instantly appreciative of the painting of seagulls above the gray waters of Puget Sound.

"You have a love for nature."

Esther nodded. "It's so...perfect, in its own way. Oh, I'm not saying there's no ugliness in it, but it's just...I guess what I'm getting at is that there's no malice."

"I wouldn't be too sure of that," Paula argued seriously. "I've watched a cat play with a mouse it caught. Is that really so very different from when a human bully picks on a weakling?"

"But cats are only obeying their instincts."

"So, unfortunately, are bullies."

Esther started to argue, but then thought better of it. It didn't matter. Besides, maybe *bully* was the best description for men like her father who picked on women and children. She willingly would have bet that her father never beat up another man his size in his entire life.

"I think there's an instinct," Paula said, "to kill those who are smaller and weaker. Or to drive them away. You see it in a lot of animals when the runt of the litter is pushed out of the nest and not allowed to nurse. Unfortunately, I think the instinct sometimes goes a little out of whack in humans."

Esther nodded. "And of course, we're supposed to be civilized."

Paula laughed at that. "Civilized? If you ask me, that's very superficial. It sure disappears quickly enough when people get upset about something." She turned her attention once again to the painting. "You find peace in nature. That must be what Craig is drawn to."

Esther felt her heart skip two beats in rapid succession. Craig was drawn to her?

"Oh, you're very pretty," Paula hastened to say. "Don't misunderstand, please. But Craig avoids women, even pretty women, and I was wondering what made you so different." She indicated the painting with a jerk of her chin. "Now I know. Do you have many more?"

"Oh, they're all out in my studio in the barn. I'm getting them ready for an exhibition in London."

"London? You must be a big deal."

Esther quickly shook her head. She didn't like to think of herself that way. "It's just that my paintings sell better in Europe than in the States."

Paula smiled. "You're a big deal. I can tell. Well, sometime you come over and have dinner with us, okay? And sometime I'll come over here and you can show me some more of your paintings."

They returned to the kitchen to find that the children had finished their cookies. Craig was washing Mary's hands at the sink, and Enoch was using a damp paper towel to clean Billy up.

"There's a beautiful painting of seagulls in the living room," Paula told her husband. "Go look at it while I finish cleaning Billy."

"It's a beautiful painting," Craig offered. "I was admiring it last night."

"Thank you," Esther said, feeling embarrassed. As her paintings went, it was not one of her best executed, nor one of her most brilliant. She kept it simply because she needed to be reminded that even on the grayest of days gulls soared freely.

A short time later the Small Elks departed, explaining that the children needed to go to bed. That left the two dogs and Craig, and the dogs didn't seem interested in anything but one another. They lay side by side on the cool tile floor of the kitchen and watched the world from sleepy eyes.

Feeling suddenly awkward, Esther looked at Craig. He was staring at her, his gaze resting at a lower point on her body. Instinctively she looked down and saw that the swelling of her nipples plainly showed through the layers of her bra and her blouse.

All of a sudden she couldn't breathe. She knew what he was thinking and she was paralyzed, torn between conflicting fears. She was terrified he would touch her and terrified he wouldn't, and she didn't know which possibility scared her more.

He apparently had no qualms. In three strides he was across the kitchen and standing right in front of her. She backed up a half step and came up hard against the counter. There was nowhere to go.

He could have trapped her with his body against the counter, but he didn't. Instead he trapped her another, easier way, by the simple expedient of reaching out and running his index finger in a small circle around her nipple.

It was the lightest of touches, but the effect was electric. She gasped and let out a small whimper as arcs of pure delight shot through her.

Never had she dreamed that a touch could bring such pleasure. Walls almost as old as she was began to crumble as she realized that a man's touch could be gentle and giving. As she realized how much she could want it and more.

He smiled at the sound of her whimper, not a satisfied or triumphant expression, but one that suggested he was enjoying her pleasure as much as she. His finger continued to trace tight little circles around the hardening bud of her nipple until she thought her knees were going to give out.

As if he sensed it, he lifted her onto the counter and stepped between her legs. She didn't have time to panic over being lifted, and now that her insides were turning into warm syrup, she didn't especially care that she was trapped. Just please don't let him stop!

Now he traced both nipples in the same maddening way, his brow furrowed as if he were concentrating intensely. As her womanhood began to dampen and throb, it was at once frustrating and seductive the way his hips held her legs open. She wanted, needed, to bring her knees together, but his body prevented her. The openness of her position, though, made her feel more incredibly soft and feminine than she would have imagined possible.

More! Oh, please, more! her mind cried out.

But he continued to taunt her with those maddening little circles, until of their own volition her hips began to rock gently, almost imperceptibly. She needed something more and she hardly knew what.

"God, you're so responsive!" he said huskily. "So warm and willing and..." He trailed off.

The brace, she thought with a sudden burst of panic. He's thinking about my brace!

But no such thought had entered his head. Instead he reached for the concho belt around her waist and released it. It fell to the counter with a clatter that seemed unnaturally loud. Esther stopped breathing.

Slowly, slowly, he lifted the hem of her peasant blouse.

"Lift your arms," he demanded huskily.

She couldn't have protested to save her life. Something magical was happening here and she didn't want to miss it. Once, just once, and damn the consequences. Slowly, wondering how she managed it when her muscles felt like thick syrup, she raised her arms.

He continued to lift the hem of her blouse slowly, and it was the most exquisite sensation she had ever known to feel the fabric whisper across her skin, revealing her secrets.

She had always believed that if this moment ever happened, she would be mortified by her own nakedness. Mortification, or even mild embarrassment, never entered her head. Instead she was filled with impatience, wishing he would hurry and show her all the delights that awaited beyond the threshold she had never crossed.

But he was in no hurry. He whispered softly to her, as if his voice had deserted him and speech required almost more breath than he had. "I won't hurt you," he said. "Trust me, Esther...trust me...."

She was rapidly getting past the point where trust mattered. She just wanted that damn blouse over her head *now!* It covered her face briefly, concealing him from her, but even as it did she knew that her breasts in their lacy bra were revealed. The knowledge sent a sharp spear of pleasure straight to her core, causing her womb to clench almost unbearably.

Then the blouse was gone and she could see him looking at her breasts. With helpless fascination, she looked down and watched as his fingers brushed over the lacy cups of her bra, exciting her. Enticing her. She caught her breath in anticipation, wanting more, so much more....

Suddenly he tucked the first two fingers of both hands inside her bra. They felt scalding hot and she gasped at this new sensation against her virgin flesh. Grasping her bra, he leaned forward, gave the clasp an intent look, then released it.

Her breasts spilled free, and in that instant she became an absolute wanton. Arching her back, she offered herself to him, eager for the mysteries she had only read about.

"Esther..." he whispered raggedly. "Esther..." His dark eyes lifted to hers, holding her gaze as if seeking some kind of answer there. At the same time, he lifted his hands and cupped her in heat.

She drew a sharp breath and felt another wave of delight wash over her. So intimate, so...good. When his finger brushed across her nipple, the sensation was so sharply exquisite that she arched sharply and a soft whimper escaped her.

"Oh, it's good isn't it," he murmured huskily. "So good to be touched like this..."

His thumbs played with both nipples now, suspending her in a pleasure like none she had ever known. She wanted it to go on and on and never stop...except that she began to feel other needs, needs for harder, deeper touches in other, even more intimate places.

"Put your hands on me, Esther," Craig asked huskily. "Touch me, too...."

Her eyes were heavy-lidded with desire, her thoughts scattered to the four winds. A moment passed before she comprehended what he wanted, and when she did, a sudden shyness overtook her.

"It's okay," he coaxed when she hesitated. "I like to be touched, too."

Finally, finding her courage, she lifted her hands to his shoulders and slipped them within the collar of his shirt.

"Open my shirt," he demanded hoarsely.

The snaps ripped open with a loud popping noise, baring his chest to her. And suddenly she didn't need courage, because she wanted nothing more than to touch his smooth coppery skin and learn its contours and textures.

Oh, he felt so good! And the freedom to caress him felt even better. He leaned into her tentative touches as if they felt as good to him as his felt to her. Esther was transported, caught on a wave of pleasure that seemed to come from both what he was doing to her and what she was doing to him.

Then, oh then he drew her close to him, so that her breasts met his hard chest—such a wonderful feeling—and he bent his head to take her mouth in a kiss so deep she felt she was drowning in him.

She shifted, trying to get closer, and pinched the skin of her thigh between the strap of her brace and the counter. It was a sharp pain, out of place, and it jerked her back to reality as abruptly as if she had been dunked in ice water.

Suddenly she was pushing desperately at him, needing to be free of his hold, afraid of what she was doing and where it might lead. Oh, God, she couldn't allow any man to have control over her ever again! Not even control of this sweet kind!

"Esther…Esther, what… Honey, what's wrong?"

He backed up quickly and watched with concern as she burst into sobs and tried to cover herself with her hands.

"Here," he said hoarsely, yanking off his shirt and draping it around her. "It's okay. Sweetie, I'd never hurt you. It's okay."

But she could hardly hear him. Her mind was suddenly full of memories of her mother and how she had given her life into the hands of a man only to wind up dead at the foot of a staircase. Maria Jackson had made the mistake of trusting a man's hands to be gentle, but they were only gentle when they wanted to be. Other times they wanted to be hard and hurting. Buried deep in her mind in a place no reason could reach was the memory of the sickening sound of a fist hitting human flesh hard, and of a woman's keening cry.

"Esther...Esther..."

Gradually she became aware that Craig was calling her name and that Guinevere was whimpering nervously. Returning to herself she wanted to die with humiliation.

"Oh, God! Oh, God, I'm so sorry!"

"It's okay," he said soothingly. In fact, he had a pretty good idea that some memory of hers had been triggered and sent her into a panic, because there had been no mistaking her enjoyment of their mutual exploration. He had to confess, though, that he didn't know what in the hell he was going to do about it—if anything. It wasn't his problem, after all. At least as long as he didn't make it his problem.

And damn, what was he doing getting himself tangled up with this woman anyway? For the love of Mike, he ought to know better.

But his heart twisted with sympathy for her. She looked so damn miserable huddled there on the counter trying to hide in his shirt—which she actually could almost do. When had she become so tiny, and why hadn't he noticed it before?

Because she was so straightforward. Because she stood tall and never let the world see the frightened woman inside her. Well, not precisely. There wasn't any way to explain it. Esther Jackson just somehow seemed like a woman who could handle damn near anything. Only she couldn't. Some things could sneak up on her and overwhelm her before she had a chance to stiffen her spine and rally her defenses.

Like now. Whatever had just happened had occurred without warning. It had come up and latched on to her like a shark out of the deep. That was the only reason it had gotten the upper hand, of that he was sure. If she had known it was coming, it never would have overwhelmed her.

Now she was probably more embarrassed by her reaction than upset at whatever had caused it. He had the worst urge to reach out and wrap her in his arms, but he knew from experience that wouldn't be wise.

Damn, he felt so helpless, and there was nothing he hated more than feeling helpless. Finally, not knowing what else to do, he pulled out a chair and sat at the table. The two dogs, fully sensing the tension, looked from him to her in a quandary.

"Oh, hell," Craig finally said, tired of soulful brown eyes accusing him. "Get out of here, you two." He opened the back door and let both dogs run out. They went with evident relief.

"You shouldn't have done that," Esther sniffled.

"Why the hell not? I don't think Mop is going to make her any more pregnant than he already has. Besides, they won't go far. Mop'll bring her back soon."

She kept her head bowed. "How can you be sure of that?"

"Because he's a sheepdog. He'll herd her." Thank God she was talking again.

She looked up, and a fugitive smile tugged at the corners of her mouth. "As well as he herds Cromwell?"

"Cromwell is an exception to every rule." He felt his heart twist again as he looked at her. Her eyes were puffy and red, and her nose was swollen. She looked perfectly miserable, but like some warrior princess she was trying to put the best face on it. Trying to move past it bravely. He admired the hell out of her.

"Yes, I suppose she is." Clutching the shirt around her, she looked miserably around as if she wanted to find a way out.

He hesitated, not understanding, then realized, she couldn't get down from the counter without using her hands, which were fully occupied trying to keep her covered with the shirt.

He stood up quickly. "I'll just...go into the next room while you, uh, get your shirt on."

The look she gave him was unabashedly grateful. "Thank you. My legs are going numb up here."

He waited in the living room until she called out, "Okay." Then he hurried back wondering what the next stage in this fiasco was going to be. Surely it couldn't be simple.

She stood uncertainly in the middle of the kitchen, fully clothed again, and offered him his shirt. "Thank you," she said.

"Nothing to thank me for." He pulled on the shirt and snapped it quickly, wanting to put her at ease.

"Yes, there is. You've been very patient with what can only be described as lunatic behavior on my part. I can't imagine what you must think of me."

He cocked his head to one side and told her. "That you're a woman who's been hurt very badly. That you can't trust easily, which is hardly surprising. I can certainly understand why you're leery of men."

She looked astonished, and finally another small smile peeped through. "You're damn good, Nighthawk."

"No, I just pay attention. My gift is to listen."

That gave her pause. She hadn't thought of it that way before. "Your *gift?*"

"Each one of us has an ability of some kind that is a gift to others. Mine is listening."

"And mine is painting."

He shook his head slowly. "No, I think yours is laughing."

"Laughing? Me?"

"You laugh a lot. You're very humorous. You sure know how to make me smile. Your painting is a talent, but your laughter is a gift."

Intuitively she understood what he was getting at. She liked the way he looked at things. There were times in her life when she felt the only thing about her that mattered to the rest of the world was that she could paint a decent still life. "Well, I wasn't laughing a few minutes ago, and I want to apologize for the way I, um...you know."

He smiled then. In fact, she had a sneaking suspicion that he almost laughed. "Apology accepted."

"Thank you. It must have been unnerving for you."

"Unnerving isn't the word I'd choose."

She blushed scarlet then and looked away. "Well, enough of that. I wonder what the dogs are up to."

"Let's go out and see."

The night was chilly, kissed with the first breath of autumn. Craig had been right, the dogs hadn't wandered far from the house. In fact, they were both frolicking in the yard, rolling with one another as happily as puppies.

Esther suddenly had a pang that Guin had never before known doggy companionship. Apparently she'd been missing it. And certainly Esther couldn't roll around with her like that.

"I feel so guilty," she said aloud. "I ought to get another dog for Guin to be friends with."

"I think Mop has already taken care of the need for another dog," he reminded her.

"That's true. Heavens! What will their puppies look like?"

"I'm kinda curious myself."

Esther giggled. "Oh, I can just see it! Imagine a komondor with spots like Guin's. Or an all-white Saint Bernard."

"How about a puppy with a mixture of short and shaggy hair?"

"Oh, no! No, that couldn't possibly happen...could it?"

Craig smiled, wondering why everything should suddenly feel all right just because Esther Jackson was feeling humorous again. "Are you ready to put money on it?"

"No. Absolutely not! I'm not a betting woman."

"Then maybe we'll have a puppy that looks a little bit like both."

Esther liked the way he included them both in that statement, as if they were having the puppies together. Which, she guessed, they were. Assuming, of course, that Guin was pregnant.

But looking at the big but gentle komondor, she somehow felt certain that he was as virile as he was big and shaggy. There would be puppies all right. And they would probably be as surprising as their parents.

Chapter 10

Craig had been sleeping on her couch for a week. Esther paused in the doorway of the living room and looked at his pile of neatly folded blankets and pillow. She could have offered him a bedroom upstairs, but somehow she couldn't bring herself to do it. That seemed way too intimate, and she wasn't prepared for intimacy with him.

Oh, heck, why not be honest about it? She was uneasy sharing a roof with a man, any man. She could argue with herself until she was blue in the face, but the fact was, men just simply made her nervous.

Intellectually she understood that not all of them were abusive, but emotionally she was like a puppy that had been kicked one too many times. The conditioned reaction was there regardless. Foot means kick. Man means pain.

Sighing, she turned toward the stairs and began to limp her way up them. Guinevere darted ahead of her. Time for a shower. Her day's work was done, the light was gone, and she was tired. A good hot shower would not only wash off the remaining pigment from her paints, but it would unknot muscles tight with tension and relax her. She could hardly wait.

She was halfway up the stairs when she heard a car engine out front. Verna, she thought. Must be some bill that hadn't come with the rest of them last week. Guinevere, already waiting impatiently at the top of the stairs, dashed right down, taking care not to knock over her mistress.

Suppressing a wince, Esther turned around and headed wearily down the stairs, too. For some reason her leg was acting up today, feeling as if it were unbearably weary even though she hadn't done anything unusual. She might have overtaxed it without realizing it, but the muscular weakness that had resulted from nerve damage could be unpredictable in its effect.

She reached the bottom of the stairs just as someone started knocking on her door. Guin woofed deep in her throat and nosed the door. Well, that certainly wasn't Verna out there. After all this time she and the dog both recognized the letter carrier's distinctive rap.

Caution gripped her and she tried to move silently as she crossed the foyer to the door. It had to be one of the sheriff's deputies, she reasoned. They were coming so often now...but not at this time of day. Never at this time of day. Of course that didn't mean they couldn't be doing something different today.

When she reached the door, she checked to make sure it was locked. It was. Then she peered around the edge of the frame out the window and found herself staring straight into the face of her father.

"Esther!"

The nightmare had come true. Even through the glass she could hear his voice. She began backing up, lost her balance and fell. Panic clawed at her, causing her heart to pound thunderously in her ears as she dragged herself across the floor to the newel post. Behind her, Guin growled deeply.

"Esther! I know you're there!"

Yes, he knew she was there. She'd looked right into his

eyes and suddenly she was a small child again, utterly at his mercy.

Sobbing for air she reached the foot of the stairs and grabbed the newel post for balance as she pulled herself to her feet. Guin barked warningly at the door.

"Esther, please…"

Please? Was that really him saying please? Never…not once… Gasping, she achieved her feet and looked wildly around. All the windows were locked. They had to be. She'd locked them herself and hadn't opened any of them since.

The kitchen door! Moving as swiftly as she dared, terrified of falling again, she headed for the kitchen. Behind her her father hammered on the door and called her name while Guinevere's barks grew in volume and frequency.

"Just listen to me!"

When had he ever listened to her? Suddenly she was four again, looking up at the huge, angry man who towered over her, crying, "Daddy, no! No! Please, Daddy no!"

Never had he once listened to her, not once in fifteen years, and then he'd had to sit in court and listen to her accuse him of murder. If he'd been willing to hurl her down the stairs because she had cried when she slammed her finger in the door, then he was willing to kill her for sending him to prison.

The logic was as inescapable as her panic.

She reached the kitchen at last and took what comfort she could from the fact that Richard was still hammering at the front door and calling her. Sobbing, she reached the back door and found that it was locked. With shaking hands, she drew the cafe curtains closed so that he couldn't look in and see her, then she grabbed the phone, dialing Craig's number. Paula answered.

"It's my father," Esther gasped. "Paula, my father's here, beating on my door.…"

"I'll get Craig over there," Paula said quickly. "Did you call the sheriff?"

"Not yet."

"Call. I'll call, too. Now just hang up and call the sheriff—"

Esther slammed the phone into the cradle, then hit the memory button for the Sheriff's office. Velma's familiar voice answered her.

"Conard County Sheriff's Office. State your name and address, please."

"Esther Jackson. I'm at—"

"Esther!" Velma interrupted. "What's wrong?"

"My father's here, banging on the front door. He won't go away...."

"Hang on. I'll send someone right away. Don't hang up, Esther, hear?"

"Yes...yes..." She could hear him calling her from the front, but that was nowhere near as scary as what she felt when he stopped calling her at all. Then Guin stopped barking. From the front of the house came only a diminishing growl. Moments later she heard the *tick* of Guin's claws on the wood floor. It sounded as if the dog were checking out other rooms. Other windows.

Oh, God, she thought, he's coming around the house to find another way in. And then a worse thought struck her. What if he went out to the barn and destroyed her studio?

Dropping the phone, she hurried to the window and peeked out. She couldn't see him. Couldn't hear him. He could come at her from almost anywhere.

Trapped! She felt so trapped! Time. She needed time. If she could just keep him from reaching her until help arrived, she would be okay. Maybe if she hid upstairs it would take him longer to find her.

But the instant she thought of climbing those stairs, her blood froze. What if he got inside while she was climbing the stairs? With her brace she would be at a distinct disadvantage. But worse—oh, God, the thought of encountering him on the stairs was more than she could stand. She might die for it, but she was not going to give him another chance to throw her down the stairs, the way he had thrown her when she was little. The way he had thrown her mother.

Shuddering, she grabbed her biggest butcher knife and tried to decide where the best place was to conceal herself. It never entered her mind to face him down. He had always been bigger and stronger and she had always been at his mercy. In her mind nothing had changed.

The closet seemed too obvious, but she didn't want to crouch down behind furniture because in a crouch she was at a serious disadvantage since it was awkward for her to get up. Where then? There was no place that seemed good enough....

Minutes ticked by in utter silence while she dithered, trying to figure out where to hide. All the while her ears strained desperately, searching for any sound at all.

Guin chuffed from somewhere out front, the sound followed by the lazy *tick-tick* of her claws on the wood floor as she wandered back down the hallway. When she reached the kitchen, the dog sat down and regarded Esther from quizzical eyes.

Esther stared back at her for an interminable moment, wondering what this meant. Had Richard somehow managed to sneak so quietly around the house that he'd eluded the dog's senses?

Suddenly there was another hammering on the door. Guin tore down the hall and started barking wildly.

Oh, my God, he was still there!

Craig was in the barn when Paula found him, laying another few yards of the plank floor they were replacing the old floor with as they could. The planks, separated by a small distance, would allow the sheep manure to fall through into the space beneath, and give the sheep a healthier environment for their hooves. Since he was planning to bring in all his pregnant ewes and keep them in here for lambing, it was going to be essential to get as much of this floor as possible done before spring. Although if Cromwell kept eating the neighbors' flowers, things could get delayed.

"Craig?"

Paula's voice conveyed enough worry that he sat up immediately and looked at her. "What is it?"

"Esther just called. Her father's beating on her door. I called the sheriff—"

But he was already on his feet, dropping his hammer, shucking his tool belt, grabbing for his shirt. "I'm going."

"I told her you were coming."

Shoving his fingers into his front pocket, he dug out his truck keys. "I'll call and let you know."

"Please." She looked up at him from dark worried eyes. "Hurry."

But he was already out the door, loping across the yard to his pickup. Adrenaline was pumping through his veins, slowing down time, making everything seem to take too damn long. He might have been running through molasses.

He cursed every inch of county road between his place and Esther's but finally he was at the entrance to her driveway. He screeched into the turn but had to pull swiftly to one side to avoid a car that was tearing back up the driveway.

Richard Jackson! Craig was sure the gray-haired man behind the wheel of the old Chevy couldn't be anyone else. He hesitated, wondering if he should follow the man. No, Esther had to be his first priority. If she was hurt...

He turned into the driveway and raced down it, nearly flying over the ruts and bottoming out in the potholes. Damn, her driveway must have gotten miles longer since the last time he'd driven it.

But at last he roared into her yard and jammed his truck to a halt. He jumped out without even taking his keys out of the ignition and ran up the steps to the door. It was locked. God! He started hammering as loud as he could. "Esther! Esther, for God's sake, open up!"

He could hear Guin barking, but nothing else.

"Esther! Open up or I'm gonna break this lock!"

Suddenly the door flew wide open and Esther fell sobbing into his arms. He clutched her to him, holding her tightly around the waist, pressing her face to his shoulder.

"Thank God," he said raggedly. "Thank God. When I saw him tearing out of here I thought—" He broke off sharply, unable to complete the sentence. Squeezing his eyes tightly shut, he held her as close as he could get her. "Are you all right?"

"I'm fine, I'm fine," she sobbed. "He was here. Oh, Craig, he was here and he wouldn't go away...."

"I saw him. He was driving away.... Esther, he didn't hurt you?"

"No! No! I never opened the door. He just kept hammering on it and shouting my name...."

He heard another engine behind him. Cuddling her close, he turned a little so he could see the sheriff's Blazer come tearing up the drive.

"The sheriff's here," he told Esther, who was still weeping on his shoulder.

She held her breath and looked up, dashing away her tears with the back of her hand. At her feet, Guinevere chuffed uneasily, and whimpered happily when her mistress scratched the top of her head. "It's okay, Guin," she assured the dog tearily. "It's okay now."

Beau Beauregard stepped out of his vehicle and approached. "I take it he's gone?"

"He was pulling out of the driveway just as I pulled in," Craig told him.

Beau looked at Esther. "Did he hurt you?"

"No. Really. The doors were locked and I didn't open them. He just stood out here hammering and calling me."

Beau pulled out a pad and began writing. "Did you happen to see his car?"

"I did," Craig answered. "A 1986 Chevy Nova, metallic blue, needs a new paint job. Sorry, I didn't get the license number."

"Did you notice if it was a Wyoming plate?"

"Out of state. Blue, I think, but I don't remember for sure."

"Well, out of state is almost as good as the number around here," Beau said with one of his slow smiles.

"Can you keep him away from me?" Esther demanded. "Is there anything you can do?"

"I'll talk to the sheriff about it, Miss Esther, but I honestly don't know. Your property isn't posted, so he wasn't rightly trespassing. He didn't hurt you or anything else, so I really don't see what we can do. I expect the sheriff'll want a word with him, though.''

Esther felt a frustration that bordered on rage. "This isn't fair! He shouldn't be able to terrorize me this way!''

Beau looked as if he were about to agree, then thought better of it. "I'll talk to the sheriff about it, ma'am. I'll let you know what he says.'' Then he cleared his throat, looked down at the toe of his boot, and said, "Unofficially, the son of a gun better not cross my path. You want me to stay out here with you, Miss Esther?''

Esther looked at him in wonderment, then looked up at Craig. He didn't look at all pleased by the deputy's offer. "Uh...thank you, Beau. That's very kind of you. But I'll be okay. Really.'' Craig's arm seemed to tighten around her shoulders, and she found the touch surprisingly comforting.

"Okay, then,'' said Beau. "I wouldn't be surprised if the sheriff calls you later, Miss Esther. Have a good one.''

Esther didn't feel much like going back inside after the deputy left, so she and Craig sat on the porch and watched the late-afternoon wind blow across the prairie. The mountains looked almost black this afternoon, against a sky that was washed out with dust. Esther absently picked at the flecks of pigment that were still stuck to her hands and tried to imagine how she would capture the not-quite-monochrome effect of the pale sky, black mountains and gray-green grasses. The world almost looked as if the sun had bleached it out.

Yet it wasn't hot today. It was a surprisingly comfortable and dry eighty degrees. Perfect. Almost.

"I can't believe it,'' she said finally. "That man is terrorizing me and there's nothing they can do.''

"They have to follow the law.''

"Well, the law is useless! There ought to be *something* they can do!''

Craig hesitated, but decided to go ahead and lay it out anyway. "Fact is, the law is the only thing that kept me from being lynched when they found the Dunbar girl's clothes buried on my property.''

Esther's head swung around and she looked at him with something like horror.

"The law wants to be *really* sure before it acts, Esther. That's the only reason I'm here talking to you now."

She nodded. "And I'm grateful for that. But this—"

"This," he interrupted, "is a case of a man trying to see his daughter. He hasn't made one threat against you. Today he knocked on your door and called your name but he didn't try to break in, and he didn't shout any threats. When you refused to answer the door, he drove away. Esther, if they start arresting people for that, we're going to be in serious trouble in this country."

"You don't understand!"

"I understand perfectly. I understand so well that I broke a bunch of traffic laws racing over here at ninety miles an hour with my heart in my throat, scared to death you'd been hurt!" Damn it, he shouldn't have admitted that, either to her or to himself. He didn't want to care. Caring was just another way to get tied down in responsibilities. To become a captive.

Her hazel eyes were wide, wounded. "I didn't mean..."

"No, I know you didn't." He sighed and tried to calm down. His emotions had been unsettled ever since he'd met Esther Jackson, but hearing that her father was beating on her door had tipped him into an emotional maelstrom. *Get a grip, guy.* "It's just that I can see both sides of this problem very clearly. The hands of the law are tied, for good reasons. But mine aren't, okay? I'll just tell my family that I need to stay here until your father takes the hint and crawls back under whatever rock he slithered out from under."

"You can't do that! You have other things to do, a life of your own. Craig, I won't permit it!" Mainly she didn't think she could stand having him around all the time. Men made her constantly uneasy, although this one more than most—and for a very different reason. She lay awake at night burning, with thoughts running through her mind that ought to be illegal. Unfortunately, she didn't even know enough about the subject to build a good fantasy for herself. She could only remember that time he had lifted her onto the counter and kissed her...and touched her....

A blush heated her cheeks as she realized the direction her thoughts had taken. And at a time like this!

"I'll stay," he said. "The barn floor can wait a few days, and I'm pretty sure that Sheriff Tate and company are going to figure out some way to run this guy off." He shook his head. "I wouldn't care to be in Richard Jackson's shoes if he so much as spits on a sidewalk in this county."

Esther shuddered, feeling suddenly cold as the reality of it all crashed in on her. "He was here," she whispered. "Oh, my God, he was really here." She turned toward him with terrified eyes. "It happened."

Craig hesitated, then reached out and clasped her hand. "Yeah, it happened," he agreed bluntly. "It really happened."

"No...no...I meant...my worst nightmare. That he'd find me. That he'd track me down and come to my home and.... It happened, Craig. It all happened!"

"Except that he didn't hurt you," he reminded her.

She shook her head slowly. "That doesn't mean a damn thing. It's not over yet."

He sighed and squeezed her hand. "If you look at it that way, Esther, it's never going to be over until one of you is dead."

She jerked and pulled her hand free. "What do you mean?"

"Just that if you're going to live in terror of what he *might* do, it'll never be over. Not ever. If Sheriff Tate throws the man out of the county for some reason, what's to prevent him from coming back next week? Or next year? I've said this before and I'll say it again—there's only one way out of this prison of fear."

This time Esther didn't raise her voice to argue with him. She didn't even look mutinous. Instead she stared out over the prairie and admitted to herself that there was no foreseeable end to this.

When Sheriff Tate called, she didn't even bother arguing with him about the appalling state of the law.

*   *   *

"Let's get out of here." Craig looked across the kitchen at Esther, who had just returned from showering. Her long hair shone with freshly washed vitality, and she wore a white ankle-length prairie skirt that was dotted with tiny red flowers, and a red silk blouse.

"Out of here?" she asked.

"Out of here. Let's go to town. I'll buy you dinner at Maude's. Or if you want, we can try that new place just outside town."

She didn't go out to dinner. Ever. People had a habit of staring just enough to make her feel awkward. She started to refuse, then realized that this would be different. She wouldn't be alone.

Her father! The thought that she might encounter him in town made her stomach do a queasy flip-flop. She looked uncertainly at Craig and felt her heart catch with yearning. Oh, how she wished this man could want her as much as she wanted him!

"I'll be there, Esther," he said, as if he could read her mind. "He won't hurt you when I'm there."

That was certainly true. Intellectually she realized that her father was one of life's bullies, a man who would never attempt to take on anyone bigger and stronger. Her emotional perception was vastly different, however, and Richard Jackson was still the all-powerful, terrifying figure of her childhood.

She managed a smile. "I hear Maude's is wonderful."

"Maude's it is. But I'm warning you, if you're on a diet you'd better forget all about it. She fries just about everything."

"Sounds good."

"Great. I'll need to stop at my place to get a change of clothes, though. In fact, I guess I need to get a whole bunch of stuff since I'm going to be staying here for a while."

"Craig—"

"Shh. You didn't ask, and I'm not offering. I'm insisting. You shouldn't be here alone."

For some reason she couldn't take exception to his insis-

tence. In point of fact, he was only trying to help her out, and
making too much of a stink would appear ungrateful. She was
very grateful.

She did, however, insist that they take her Jimmy rather than
his pickup truck since it was easier for her to get into it with
her brace.

"That's fine," he agreed. "Do you want to drive?"

Esther held out the keys to him. He captured her hand as
he took them, and smiled down into her eyes. She caught her
breath, and felt as if the very earth beneath her feet shifted.
The whole rest of the world receded, becoming nothing but a
distant blur of color and sound. His hand felt so warm around
hers, the callused texture of his palm so exciting. She could
remember what those hands had felt like on her breasts, and
she ached to feel them again.

Guinevere chose that moment to thrust her nose, then her
entire head, between them.

Esther looked down, startled, then gave a chuckle. Guinevere wormed between them, then sat.

"Jealous, aren't we?" Craig said. But he let go of Esther's
hand and scratched the dog behind the ears.

Esther felt absurdly disappointed that he had been so ready
to let go of her and turn his attention to the dog. That fire in
his gaze must have been in her imagination. Well, of course!
she told herself impatiently. He didn't really want her! How
many times was she going to have to bang her head on that
wall before she accepted it?

Turning swiftly away, she managed a laugh. "She's *very*
jealous. She thinks everyone in the world ought to pet *her*."

"I can understand that. Who doesn't feel that way?"

Before she got very far down the hall, he touched her shoulder gently. "Look at me, Esther?"

Slowly, she faced him. Guin nudged her leg impatiently,
but she ignored the dog. "Yes?"

"Are you mad at me?"

Surprised, she took a moment to marshal an answer.
"No…"

"Then why did you turn away like that?"

Now how could she possibly answer that? Finally, setting her hands on her hips, she tilted her head to one side and frowned at him. "It was time to leave. We're going to town, aren't we?"

He looked as if he didn't believe her, but he dropped the subject. "What about Guin? Do you cage her?"

"Not since she was a puppy. She knows to behave herself, don't you, girl?" She patted the dog's head and began marching toward the door again, determined to get out of here before things got any stickier.

Of course, it was hard to march with any real dignity when she kept limping, but oh well. Her natural humor began to reassert itself, and by the time she reached the front door, she was actually smiling.

"Guin, you be a good girl and hold the fort while I'm gone, okay?"

Guin sat and thumped her tail agreeably, watching calmly as Craig and Esther walked out.

"I swear that dog understands every word you speak," Craig said as they drove toward his place.

"Of course she does. Doesn't Mop?"

"When it suits him. Oh, he's a wonderful sheepdog, but off duty he's a little stubborn and independent."

"Willfully deaf, you mean."

"That's about it."

While Craig showered and changed, Paula took charge of Esther. They sat in the living room with glasses of iced tea while the children played down the hall in one of their bedrooms.

"You like Craig, don't you?" Paula asked her.

"Yes. Of course. I like him very much." Even that small admission brought heat to her cheeks.

"My brother's an exceptionally good man," Paula said warmly. "That rape charge really wounded him. He hasn't been quite the same since."

"What do you mean?"

"Well…" Paula hesitated. "He lost so much. Even though they released him when they found the real rapist, he lost his trucking contract because he'd been in jail. And then he couldn't get another one. I don't know if it was because they think he really did hurt that little girl, or if it was because they decided he was unreliable because he was in jail. I don't know. Craig doesn't know.''

"That's awful!'' Esther felt a sharp pang of sympathy for him.

"So…'' Paula shrugged. ''He bought this ranch while he was still driving, and was saving up money so he could pay it off and buy sheep. Not because he wanted to ranch, because he didn't. But because he wanted to bring my family off the reservation and give us a life. He always meant for us to come here someday and work and live. When he couldn't find another trucking contract, he sold his truck and used all his savings and all the money from the truck to pay off the ranch, buy the sheep and move us down here.''

Esther nodded, feeling her throat tighten.

Paula sighed and pressed her lips together as if she were repressing tears. ''Anyway,'' she said after a moment, ''he believes it's better for the children to be raised here. I had my doubts at first. As awful as the res was in some ways, at least the kids would have been growing up among their own kind. They wouldn't be a minority, you know?''

Esther nodded. She could easily understand Paula's concerns.

"But, I guess he was right. Most people here are pretty nice. Nicer than the whites who live around the res. Mary started school this week, and everybody's been really good to her. There's the two Indian deputies, and one of the teachers at the school is an Indian, too, so…it'll be all right. And here they have better food and better shelter.''

Paula shook her head a little and looked away. ''But Craig had to give up so much. That worries me. He always said he couldn't stand to be nailed in one spot, and now he is. He gets this look to him sometimes, like he's gonna die if he can't get back on the road.

"Anyway, he even had to give up his gaming.''

"Gaming?''

Paula looked surprised. "He didn't tell you? He loves to war game. He has all these miniature armies that he's painted so they look almost real, and he used to have a big sand table that he could arrange to match the ground where big battles were fought, and he'd reenact them. It took a lot of time and a lot of money, I guess, because he gave it up, put the soldiers away and took the sand table apart. He said it was because the kids needed a bedroom, but he used to cast the soldiers himself out of lead, and he doesn't even do that any more. He says it's because he doesn't want the kids exposed to lead, but they wouldn't get exposed to it, because his casting stuff is out in a shed. So it's because we can't afford it."

Esther nodded, not really sure what Paula meant by his war gaming. "You mean he has these little soldiers...?"

"Like you see in a museum diorama," Paula explained. "Very little figures of men."

"And he reenacts battles."

"Right. To see if when he changes something the outcome changes. There are rules that have to be followed. Oh, it's all really complicated, but he plays by mail with some other men around the country, and he really enjoyed it."

It began to seem to Esther that Craig Nighthawk had sacrificed a great deal because of a crime he hadn't committed...and because of his love for family. He was a rare man.

Craig returned shortly, freshly showered and wearing carefully pressed jeans and a crisp white western shirt. In one hand he carried a duffel.

"We're outta here," he said. "If you or Enoch need me for anything while I'm staying with Esther, give me a shout, Paula. I'll come running."

"We'll be just fine," his sister assured him. "Just make sure that mean old man doesn't hurt Esther."

It somehow felt different this time when Craig helped her up into the Jimmy. It wasn't as if he were doing it because of her weak leg, but because she was his date.

Which she wasn't, really, she reminded herself sternly. They were just going out for dinner. He hadn't asked her out. "Paula says you used to do a lot of war gaming."

"Paula talks too much. I suppose she also gave you my entire history, along with a copy of my immunization record."

A laugh bubbled out of Esther. "Not quite."

"No? No pictures of me running around with my diaper falling off? No first grade report cards covered with frantic teacher notes? No memories of how clumsy I was?"

"Not a one."

"Hell, she's slipping. I'll have to talk to her."

Esther laughed again. "She's just worried about you having to give up so much."

He looked over at her and shook his head. "I didn't give up anything meaningful, when you come right down to it. And some things are a hell of a lot more important."

"You gave up your freedom."

Now that one was harder for him to answer, and she felt her heart begin to race uncomfortably as she waited. Not that she cared, really, because after all he would never be interested in her as more than a casual friend. But if he were unable to settle down happily...

"Sometimes," he said heavily, "I think I should have been born a gypsy. I've been suffering from wanderlust since— Well, ever since I can remember. It gets especially strong in the spring. I figure, all things being equal, that when we get the ranch on a sound footing and can afford to hire some help, I may look for a job as a long-haul driver again."

Esther had to confess that thought didn't really thrill her. Somehow the thought of not seeing Craig for days or weeks on end just...hurt. Not that she would probably see all that much of him after her father left the county. He'd certainly have no reason to be stopping over all the time.

"Anyway," he told her, "it's just a pipe dream, and I'm not really sure I'd even do it. Ranching isn't so bad most of the time. "I'll just be a whole lot happier when we've got a little cushion built up."

"I can imagine." Well, she didn't know exactly what to make of that. He missed trucking, but he hadn't exactly said he would die without it. "So what about war gaming?"

At that he laughed and shook his head. "I'll bet that sister of mine tried to make me sound like some kind of martyr, which I'm not. Never have been. Sometimes life just deals some tough cards. You do what's necessary to take care of your obligations and then worry about other things when you have time. I'm sure as hell not sitting around getting bitter about the past, or even moping. In fact, except for my sister's big mouth, I'd be having a great time right now.''

Esther could hardly pursue the subject after that. Smiling, she let it drop, but she figured Paula had been closer to the truth than Craig wanted her to know.

When they got to town, they were able to find a parking place only a half block up the street from Maude's diner. Craig came round to help her down.

Esther hesitated, because the curb was in the perfect position that if she didn't land just right she was going to fall. It was too close to the car for her to step down to the street, and too far away for her to easily step onto it. Craig solved the problem by holding out hands.

"May I?"

She bit her lip and nodded, allowing him to take her around the waist and lift her to the sidewalk.

"There you go."

Perhaps someone somewhere would be able to explain to Esther what happened just then, but as it was she could only put it down to extraordinary meanness. A man who was walking down the street looked toward them with a sneer.

"Hey, Injun," he said. "Moving on from kids to cripples?"

Chapter 11

For Esther, time abruptly slowed down. As if every detail were suddenly magnified, she saw Craig's nostrils flare and a white line suddenly appear around his lips. In the merest instant she knew what was about to happen. Craig was going to turn and confront the obnoxious ass, and the situation would only get messier. He might even get hurt. In the blink of an eye, she forgot her fear of men in an urgent desire to prevent violence that might hurt Craig.

She turned swiftly, heedless of her lame leg, and confronted the man herself. Pointing her finger at him, she said, "How dare you! This man was cleared of all part in that terrible crime! And what's more, I am *not* a cripple! You, however, are apparently suffering from a severe defect of manners and intelligence. Now get out of here before I get really angry!"

The man was so taken aback by her unexpected attack that for a couple of seconds he could hardly react. Then an ugly sneer began to spread across his face, but before more nastiness could come out of his mouth, a familiar voice interrupted him.

"You heard the lady. Move on, Lenny."

Nate Tate stood on the sidewalk behind them, legs splayed, hands on his hips, every inch a lawman who wasn't going to stand for any nonsense.

"I c'n say anything I want, Nate," the other man argued. "It's a free country."

"It's a free country except for fighting words, Lenny, and saying nasty things about a man's lady friend couldn't be anything except fighting words. So move on before Mr. Nighthawk takes a notion to deck you."

Lenny moved on, muttering about the country going to hell when the law would stand up for an Injun. Esther clenched her hands so hard that her nails bit into her palms, yet she still had to bite her tongue to keep from responding. "Oh, that hateful man!" she said finally.

Nate gave her a rueful smile. "Every place in the world has its share of his kind. Not a whole hell of a lot you can do to change their minds, unfortunately." He shook his head. "You two heading for Maude's?"

Craig nodded. "Join us?"

If Esther had cherished even a faint hope that this was a date, his invitation to the sheriff dashed it completely. Surely if this were a date he wouldn't have done that. She gave herself yet another kick for allowing her hopes to override her common sense. She knew better!

Nate shook his head. "I won't interrupt. I just wanted to have a few words with Esther. Maybe I'll have a cup of coffee with you while you wait for your dinners, then be on my way."

"Sure," Craig agreed. "Good idea."

Together they entered Maude's. In an instant every eye in the place fixed on them, and Esther was glad for Nate's company. It wasn't that any of them were overtly hostile, but she got the feeling they might be. That, she assured herself, was a product of her own paranoia. Most of the folks in this county were good people. Nice people. She hadn't had any trouble with them before. Of course, she'd been hiding out like some kind of hermit—

Oh, stop this now! she told herself. Enough! They're just curious.

Craig pointed to an empty booth, and Esther was glad to disappear into it. Craig slid in beside her and Nate sat across from them. Maude must have seen them come in, because she was upon them almost at once with plastic menus and flatware wrapped in cloth napkins. The napkins surprised Esther.

"Evenin', Sheriff," she greeted Nate. Then she turned her basilisk eye on Craig. "How you been, Mr. Nighthawk? I have some of that elderberry pie you favor, by the by."

After the incident outside, Esther was somehow surprised that this woman didn't treat Craig like a pariah. But, she reminded herself, the whole county didn't believe ill of him.

"And *you*," Maude said, turning her glare on Esther, "must be that artist lady I've been hearin' about for so long."

"Why yes! How did you know?"

"You got that lame leg." Maude shook her head. "Damn shame a pretty thing like you has to have a limp. Well, the good Lord knows what he's about, I s'pose. Now," she added, jabbing a finger at Esther, "I expect I'll be seeing more of you, now that you finally broke the ice and come in here. I tell you right up front, though, I don't cotton to this fat-free, low-calorie stuff we're getting shoved down our throats by them that claims to know what's good for us."

From the corner of her eye, Esther saw Nate struggle to hide a smile.

"My granddaddy lived to be ninety-seven years old eating eggs and bacon and steak and butter," Maude continued. "My momma and daddy both are in their late eighties, and they're still eating my cooking. Seems like to me it ain't the saturated fats that's the problem, but the way you live. Hard work'll keep you healthy."

Esther nodded, both in agreement and amusement. "I quite agree."

"Good." Maude fixed her with another glare. "Course, if a lady's watching her waistline, I can be persuaded to turn up a tasty salad with lemon juice dressing, but otherwise it's good, solid farm food."

"That's exactly what I'm in the mood for," Esther assured her. "I seldom feel like cooking for just myself, so I'm looking forward to a very hearty meal."

Maude nodded as if she hadn't expected anything else. "Good. Have the T-bone smothered in onions and mushrooms. The beef is extra good this week. Baked potato or fries?"

"Maude's fries are to die for, according to my daughter Krissie," Nate said. His dark eyes twinkled.

Maude snorted. "Can't imagine why anybody would want to die for fried potatoes."

"Fries it is," Esther told Maude. "Thank you."

"House salad, house dressing?"

Esther nodded. Craig ordered a dinner identical to hers, and Nate insisted he just wanted coffee, no pie. "Really, Maude, I've got to cut out the pie. I got my thirty-four-inch waist back and I aim to keep it this time."

"You need to get out from behind that desk more."

"You're probably right. But since I have to get home soon because Krissie is playing the organ at church tonight, I'm going to have to skip the twenty-five mile run that I'd need to burn off a piece of your pie."

Maude snorted again and stomped off. Nate looked at Esther with a grin. "Quite a character, our Maude."

"She certainly is."

"A few years ago, she took on Micah Parish. He hadn't been in town too awful long…less than a year, I think. Anyway, Jed Barlowe was up in the church belfry shooting at anything that walked, and Maude made some noxious comment about 'that Cherokee deputy' of mine." Nate shook his head, grinning reminiscently. "Damned if I know what Micah said or did, but she actually apologized to him a couple of minutes later. She's practically sweet on him now." He glanced at Craig. "Which may be why you haven't been treated to the sharper edge of her tongue…or have you?"

"She's always treated me like she did just now."

"Damn. Maybe our Maude is turning over a new leaf."

"You mean she's usually blunter?" Esther asked.

"Blunter and sharper. She's got a reputation for being able to skin a man at twenty paces with the sharp edge of her tongue."

Esther laughed. "That could be a truly valuable talent."

Craig glanced at her with a laugh warming his dark eyes. "Naturally *you'd* think so, being a woman."

She smiled demurely. "We use what weapons we have."

Nate cracked a laugh. "Okay, okay, let's get serious here for a couple of minutes."

Just then Maude brought the coffee and slammed it down in front of Nate along with a wedge of pie. "It's blackberry pie, and I won't be making it again until next year, so you'd better eat it."

Nate groaned. "Maude, am I going to have to send Marge over to talk to you?"

"Your wife don't frighten me none. She'll just have herself a piece of that pie and tell me how she can't understand why you'd pass up anything so good when you could always run them twenty-five miles tomorrow—chasing *her*." Head high, Maude stalked off, leaving them laughing behind her.

But Nate's smile faded quickly, and after a couple of mouthfuls of pie, he looked squarely at Esther, his expression serious. She felt her stomach sink.

"I found your father this afternoon," he told her. "About a half hour after I talked to you on the phone. I had a long talk with him, told him he was upsetting you."

"And?"

"Well...he insists he just wants to talk to you. He says he hasn't touched a drop of alcohol in fifteen years and that he's gotten clear on a few things. He just wants to apologize."

"Apologize?" Esther could barely take it in, and when she did a white rage filled her. "Apologize? That man beat me and my mother for years. He killed my mother! How can he think an apology... My God. My God!"

Nate looked down at his pie and shoved the plate aside. He didn't say anything for a while, and neither did Craig. Both men looked unhappy about the situation.

"Well," Nate finally said, "I don't believe he thinks the apology will make any difference to *you*."

"Then why bother? Why stalk me like this?"

"I reckon it's something *he* needs to do."

"Well, he's damn well going to have to live without it. My God, I never want to set eyes on that man again, let alone listen to him apologize for killing my mother and crippling me!"

Nate nodded. Craig reached under the table and took her hand, squeezing gently. Neither man said anything.

Esther turned her head, staring at the wallpaper that was only a few inches from her nose. Apologize! She couldn't even imagine the temerity of it! Why on earth would he think that she was willing to hear his apology?

"He's lying," she said suddenly, facing the sheriff. "He's lying about what he wants."

"Well," Nate replied slowly, "that's a possibility. I can't rule it out entirely, but it sure seemed to me that he was telling the truth."

"He might be," Craig agreed. "Selfish as it is, it might be something *he* needs to do."

"Strikes me that way, too," Nate agreed.

"*Selfish* is a good word for it," Esther said flatly. "Utterly, purely selfish. But that's so very much like him! He never gave a damn what anyone else might feel, not in all the years I lived with him. He was the absolute center of the universe, and treated everybody else like they were slugs on the ground." She shook her head. "I'm sorry, I'm getting all wound up and I'm sure you don't want to hear it, but that man has got to be the most self-centered scum that ever walked this planet. Whatever he's doing here, you can believe he doesn't care a lick how it affects me. Can't you make him go away?"

Nate shook his head. "Sorry. Wish I could. But the fact is, he hasn't done anything wrong in the eyes of the law. If he wants to camp out at the motel for the rest of his life he can do it. You might want to post your property, though. That way if he shows up at your place again, you can call me to remove him. I can even charge him with trespassing.''

"That's it? That's all? Trespassing?''

"That's it. Unless he does something else I can nail him on.''

Esther realized suddenly that she was squeezing Craig's hand so hard she must be hurting him, but when she tried to pull her hand away, he hung on. "What are my other alternatives, Sheriff?''

Nate took a couple sips of his coffee, then set the mug down emphatically. "Well, you could just ignore him and hope that he'll go away. Or, you could set up a meeting with him and make sure you're not alone when you see him. If apologizing is all he really wants, he ought to go away. If not, we'll find that out. In the meantime, though, there isn't a whole hell of a lot more I can do without setting my department up for some kind of lawsuit. The man has a right to go where he pleases until he breaks the law.''

A few minutes later Tate departed. Craig slipped around to the other side of the booth, then reached across the table with his hands palm up in invitation. Unable to resist, she placed her hands in his. "I'm sorry,'' he said. "This was supposed to be a fun evening out.''

She shook her head sadly. "It's not your fault. I'm sorry my problems are messing up your whole life.''

"Cut it out.''

Startled, she looked at him.

"You heard me. You're not ruining my life, or even messing it up. This is what friends and neighbors are for, and you're sure as hell not going to get any help out of law enforcement until something happens. There is no way I'm going to leave you to face this alone. Got it?''

She managed a nod. This was the man who had given up his truck driving and bought a ranch in order to ensure that his sister's family had a better life. She wasn't going to be able to argue with him about this, but she certainly didn't want to be another burden on him, either.

Well, enough of this, she told herself sternly. What was she going to do? Drown in self-pity because Richard Jackson couldn't be run out of Conard County? Absurd. Besides, Craig was right; even if they made him leave, he could just come back. If he really wanted to hurt her, sooner or later he would find the opportunity.

Maude brought their plates, large platters bearing big T-bones and enough fries for an army. She slapped the platters down emphatically, asked if they needed anything else, then stalked away.

"Well," Esther said, putting on a determined smile, "let's pretend my father never existed and enjoy dinner, shall we?"

The look he gave her was almost tender, and made her heart climb straight into her throat. "I just want you to be able to laugh," he said.

She almost made a fool out of herself then by bursting into tears. Nobody in her entire life had ever cared whether she laughed or cried.

"You're so beautiful when you laugh," he murmured. "All I want is for you to keep on smiling."

Her throat tightened until it ached. What could she possibly say in reply?

"Eat your steak before it gets cold," he said, giving her hand a last squeeze before letting go. "Then we'll take a drive."

The drive was beautiful. Evenings were long in the summer, but when night finally fell it was breathtaking. Without city lights or smog to restrict the view, the sky became a carpet of stars, more stars than she ever would have believed existed when she'd lived in Seattle and Portland.

Craig found a turn out along a dirt lane and they sat for a long time just watching the stars wheel overhead. They even saw a shooting star.

The breeze blew through the windows gently, relaxing Esther. She tipped her head back and looked out the side window at the stars, thinking that the sky looked so deep out here. Back home it had looked almost flat, with stars pinned to it like sequins on a dark velvet background. Out here it was so dark and there were so many stars that she could get dizzy looking up into them. Here she could feel the infinite vastness of the universe.

Relaxing though it was, there was one tension that wouldn't go away...her awareness of the man seated beside her. She could feel his warmth across the space between them. Her skin seemed to have become hypersensitive, acutely aware of each whisper of the breeze against her skin. And deep inside her she felt the throb of anticipation growing until she had to draw each breath lightly.

Finally even the stars vanished in her growing need to be kissed and held. In her need to be touched the way he had touched her before. Had she just imagined that entire episode in her kitchen? Had it really happened at all? And if it had happened once, couldn't it happen again?

Slowly, as if she were being controlled by a power outside her, she turned her head and looked at Craig. And suddenly she couldn't breathe, for he was staring straight at her, his eyes as dark and mysterious as the night sky above.

His dark gaze exerted a magnetic pull on her, drawing her toward him the way the moon drew the tide. She could feel herself leaning, though she was never sure if she really *did* lean toward him, or if she just felt as if she did.

But then he leaned toward her, closing the distance between them and answering the yearning in her soul with a kiss.

A hungry kiss. A devouring kiss, as if he couldn't get enough of her. A kiss that made her feel like a cool oasis in the middle of a desert. A kiss that made her feel desirable.

The force of his kiss and the tightness of his grip on her shoulders should have frightened her, but somehow they exhilarated her. She felt herself responding from an unsuspected well of fire deep within her, coming to full life as a woman beneath the questing pressure of his mouth.

Craig broke the kiss abruptly, pulling his head back, sucking air deep into his lungs. "Damn, I want you," he said hoarsely.

"Yes...yes..." Was that really her, gasping an affirmative with her head thrown back in utter submission? Was that really her...?

"Not like this," he said raggedly. "Not here."

His words reminded her that they weren't alone in the universe on some wildly careening planet. When he gently urged her back into her seat and buckled her seat belt for her, she struggled to hang on to the mood of moments before.

It evaporated anyway. The anticipation remained, but the passion cooled, leaving in its wake uncertainty and fear. What was she doing? And why?

Time sped by in a headlong rush as they drove toward her house. Almost too quickly to be believed, they were pulling up in front of her porch. Craig braked and switched off the headlights and ignition. The night was quiet. Too quiet. There was no one else around for miles.

Filled with unease, Esther stayed where she was as Craig climbed out and came around the car to help her down. She offered no protest when he unbuckled her seat belt and lifted her down. He made it seem as if she weighed nothing at all, reminding her afresh of his much greater strength. What was she doing?

He bent suddenly and gave her a quick kiss. "I can't do this," he said.

Disappointment was sharper than the uneasiness of moments before. Her stomach plunged until she felt as if she were falling from a tall building. "You can't?" Her voice was a mere whisper of sound.

He shook his head, his face nearly invisible in the night's darkness. "No, I can't. It's not...it's not that I don't want you, Esther. As God is my witness, I'm aching so hard for you I can hardly stand it. But I can't do this to you."

"Why?" And why couldn't she just let this go? she asked herself. Why did she keep asking questions to which she most likely didn't want to hear the answers?

"Why?" She thought she heard him make a soft, mirthless laugh. "How about this? I can't offer you a future. I can't even offer you tomorrow. I'm a wanderer and you sure as hell aren't meant to be a one-night stand. Now get inside before I do something I'll regret."

She did as he said simply because she couldn't see the alternative. He was upset, he was angry, and he was right—she didn't want to be a one-night stand. She wanted more, so much more.

Guin was moping. Apparently she didn't like Craig staying outside. She sniffed at the door and gave Esther long, reproachful looks. Finally, unable to stand it anymore, Esther threw open the door and let the dog dash outside. By the joyous barks she heard a half minute later, she knew Guin had found Craig.

"Traitor," she muttered in the Saint Bernard's general direction. Giving up hope that Craig would come inside so they could set all this to rights somehow, she finally limped her way upstairs.

It was a relief to take the brace off at the end of the day. Even after all these years she hadn't gotten used to it, even now when, instead of having to take whatever brace charity could provide, she was able to have one specially made. The straps still chafed a little, especially when the weather was hot, and the skin beneath was always happy to be set free.

She rubbed cream into the sore spots, soothing them. There was one place on the back of her thigh where the strap actually bit into her sometimes, and tonight it was almost too sore to touch. Of course, that was her fault. It had needed adjustment but she had ignored it, not wanting anything as unattractive as a brace to interrupt her Cinderella evening.

Cinderella? Had she sunk so low that being asked to go out for dinner at a diner could seem like being asked to the ball by the prince? God, was she never going to grow up?

Irritated and impatient with herself, she rose from her bed and dug a clean nightgown out of the closet. With no one to ever see her nightgowns, they were chosen to suit her: long, sleeveless, white cotton gowns with no more than a satin ribbon at the neck for decoration.

Slipping into one now was like settling into an old familiar chair. It reminded her that she was home and she was safe in her own bedroom. Everything else was locked outside.

It was a game she had taught herself as a child, to imagine

her bedroom a sanctuary where no one could intrude. It wasn't a perfect sanctuary, of course, but once she had been asleep her father had been very unlikely to focus his wrath on her. That old feeling of security came to her now as she crawled beneath the sheets and lay in the darkness with the summer breeze blowing gently over her.

She was dozing lightly when she heard Craig come in. Instantly she became alert, straining her ears to hear. After a few minutes all her fears that he might go home and leave her alone evaporated. She could hear him talking to Guinevere, heard him turn on the water in the bathroom downstairs, listened to the sounds as he showered.

His nearness was driving her nuts. The sleepiness that had been on the verge of overwhelming her vanished completely. The sheets were suddenly uncomfortably warm and she kicked them aside.

He was downstairs. In the shower. Naked. Oh, why couldn't she just *once* know what it was like to be loved by a man? Why had he gone all noble on her at exactly the wrong time?

Sleep had become an impossibility. Her body was aching and tingling with feelings she couldn't name, and restlessness kept her tossing on her bed. All she could think of was how much she wanted Craig to kiss her, hold her, touch her....

Her cheeks burned as she remembered him touching her breasts, and, as she wondered what it would be like to be kissed there, her entire body began to burn. She drew a shuddering breath and began to breathe rapidly as her mind unfolded a sorcerer's brew of enchanting fantasies.

What if he came up those stairs and walked in on her? What if he crossed the room and lay beside her without a word? Would the darkness conceal enough to make it seem like a dream as his hands lifted her gown and wandered over her flesh?

If she had a nightmare, and he lay beside her to kiss her awake and was wearing nothing at all...

A shudder passed through her that had nothing to do with the temperature. She couldn't go on like this. Understanding why Pandora had opened the forbidden box, she rose from her bed and walked carefully to the head of the stairs.

He was still in the bathroom. When he finished he would have to walk past the foot of the stairs to reach the living room. A band of yellow illumination fell across the hallway below where lamplight spilled from the living room. She would see him. Maybe call out to him. Maybe she would do nothing at all. She didn't know.

She just knew that she waited with bated breath and hammering heart, riveted to the spot as if held there by a wizard's spell, so full of yearning that she was helpless.

Suddenly Craig appeared, naked except for one of her ruby red towels around his waist. He was moving along the hall with his back to her. Guin was nowhere in sight.

Just as he turned the corner to pass the foot of the stairs, something alerted him to her presence. He looked up sharply, and froze when he saw her.

Except for the dim lamplight spilling from the living room, they stood in darkness, she at the head of the stairs in her long white nightgown, he at the foot wrapped in a towel. She looked like a pagan goddess emerging from the mists of night; he looked like a pagan warrior. Between them yawned a gaping darkness as treacherous as any chasm.

"Please," she whispered.

"No."

"Craig…"

"Damn it." He swore quietly, as if he were afraid to disturb the dark between them. "I told you…I have nothing to give you."

"You. All I want is you…"

His head jerked a little, as if the words struck him with the force of a blow. "No, you don't know what you're saying. I can't offer you any kind of future, Esther. I'm dirt poor, I'm a wanderer…hell, I'm an Indian. Do you know how some folks are going to treat you if you mix up with me? If you think you're a pariah now…"

"I don't care what people like that think. I never have." She wanted to approach him, but her legs were so shaky, and without her brace she would probably just tumble down the stairs and break something. "Craig...Craig, I'm not asking for the rest of your life." *Liar,* whispered a voice at the back of her mind. "I'm asking for one night. Please." Oh, God, had she really said that?

He turned so that he faced her fully. "Why, Esther?"

She stared at him mutely, unable to make herself explain. It was so humiliating.

"I'm not asking you to beg," he said quietly. "I'd never ask that of you. But I deserve to know why you're willing to settle for one night when you deserve a hell of a lot more."

She closed her eyes as she felt her hopes slipping out of her grasp like so much water. In a moment she would turn and go back to her bed...alone. No!

Forcing herself to look at him, she humbled herself as she never had before. "I... No one has ever wanted me. No one."

"I can't believe that, Esther. No way."

"It's true." She drew a deep breath, steadying herself and reaching for every bit of courage she had. "I'm crippled. Just like that man said tonight."

"Esther—"

"No, don't argue with me. It's true. I wear a brace, I limp, my bad leg is smaller than my good leg...anybody can see it. It scares men off. They want perfect women."

"Only *boys* want perfect women."

She shook her head and laughed, a sad little sound. "Trust me. I've been on the receiving end. Once..." Her voice trembled. "Once there was a man who... Well, he told me I ought to be desperate enough to settle for anything."

Craig swore. "I hope you gave him a good piece of your mind! I've never heard such hogwash."

She gave another sad laugh. "He was right. I know that. Except that...I've never been desperate enough to just settle, you know?"

"Thank God!"

"And I...well, you...you don't make me feel as if that's what you think of me. You make me feel..." She couldn't bring herself to say the word.

"Desirable," he said for her, stepping up onto the first step. "Damn it, woman, you *are* desirable. You've been driving me nuts."

Her heart began to lift a little, and her hopes to soar.

"But this isn't a good reason," he told her. "There'll be another man who finds you every bit as desirable as I do, someone who can offer you a future. A real future."

"I have a future," she cried out, holding her hands out almost desperately. "I have a real future, with a career and enough money and all the rest of it. What I don't have, what I need...is to be loved. Just once."

"Esther—"

She cut him off. "Craig, don't you see? Just once before I die I want a man's arms around me in love. And you're the only person I've ever trusted enough. The only one I want."

He hesitated visibly, looking like a man who could find no alternative that was acceptable. "I don't want to hurt you."

"You'll hurt me only if you turn away now. I know what I'm asking for, Craig."

"Do you? Do you really?" He took another step up. "I don't think you have any way of knowing just what kind of effect this can have on you emotionally. I don't want you to feel used later."

"I'm willing to take that risk, because you're never going to happen to me again. I'll never have this chance again with *you.*"

She meant that heart and soul. And it seemed as if he realized that, because he climbed another couple of steps. As he climbed he left the lamplight behind and became a figure of darkness. For some reason the way the shadows etched him gave her an atavistic thrill.

"Esther..." He barely whispered her name, and it reached her as if it were sighed by the night itself.

Her heart climbed into her throat and lodged there. The darkness that surrounded them was sheltering, protective, as if they were held within the womb of night.

Closer he came, and she felt the sands of time trickling away, closing off her option to change her mind. And with

that awareness a wildness began to rise in her. Somehow she
sensed that an incredible freedom waited for her on the other
side of tonight, if only she didn't back out now.

When he reached the top step and extended a hand to her,
the old wave of panic caught her again. A man at the top of
the stairs... So many of her nightmares began and ended with
a man on the stairs. She started to back up.

"It's okay," Craig murmured huskily. "It's okay. I won't
hurt you, Esther. I swear I won't hurt you."

She believed him, didn't she? Why else was she here with
him right now, torn between desire and sudden terror of shadows from the past.

"The stairs," she gasped. "It's the stairs..."

"The stairs and me." Reaching out ruthlessly, he caught
her up in his arms and began walking toward the bedroom.
"See," he said soothingly. "I'm taking you away from the
stairs."

She was gasping, as if she couldn't drag in enough air, and
shaking, but she didn't fight him. Clenching her hands so
tightly they ached, she forced herself not to react to old terrors.
This was Craig, not her father. This was Craig, the man who
had from the very beginning been so protective of her.

He set her down gently beside her bed, then stood in front
of her. With a careless flick of his wrist, he flung away the
towel and bared himself to her. It was so dark, but the star-
shine that came through her open windows was just enough
to let her see that he was a magnificent figure of a man, perfect
in every line. And for some reason the sight of him was easing
her fear and replacing it with something deeper, hotter.

"Esther?"

She licked her lips, nervous now in a different way. Shyly
she reached for her gown and began to pull it over her head.
Thank goodness it was so dark.

Suddenly his hands were there, helping her, and his voice
was whispering softly that she didn't have to do a thing, all
he wanted was for her to be very sure this was what she
wanted.

"Yes," she heard herself say. "Oh, yes, please...."

Then skin met skin and the world spun away.

Chapter 12

They lay face-to-face on Esther's bed. Craig drew her close, coaxing her head onto his shoulder, encouraging her to wrap her arms around him however she wanted. He even managed to nudge one of her legs between his, which left her feeling deliciously open and deliciously wanted.

He sprinkled kisses on her forehead and stroked her back soothingly, allowing her time to accustom herself to all the new sensations and experiences. "I've never made love to a virgin before," he told her quietly.

"That's okay. I've never done *any* of this before."

There was a tremor of laughter in her voice and his heart soared. It was going to be all right, he thought. She had rediscovered her laughter, and everything was going to be just fine. His anxiety about whether he would do everything right lessened, and his passion rose another notch.

"Touch me," he whispered raggedly. "Touch me anywhere…anyway…. It's okay…."

Shyly she reached out to run her hands along his smooth shoulders and down over his hard chest. The sensation electrified him, causing him to gulp a deep breath and reach for his wavering self-control. Damn! Had any woman ever made him so hot so fast? If ever one had, he sure as hell couldn't remember it.

But Esther was like a lighted match to his senses. Her shy explorations were as seductive as they were maddening, and he had to force himself to lie still beneath her caresses for fear of scaring her. He wanted to reach out and teach her the same lessons she was teaching him, wanted to stroke her smooth, warm skin the same way she was stroking him, but he restrained himself. First he wanted her to become comfortable with his male body. Then he would encourage her to become comfortable with hers.

Her hands wandered lower, tracing the contours of his abdomen, drawing achingly close to his manhood. It was torture of the most delightful kind for him, dragging a groan out of him.

The sound must have scared her, for her hand leapt away and only returned uncertainly when he managed to mutter, "That felt so damn *good...*"

Her fingers trailed down his back, branding him with fire it seemed, then across his hips and buttocks and down the back of his thighs. He loved it, loved her gentle touches and her growing boldness as she explored him, learning him.

She was getting caught up in it, too. Her breaths were coming quicker now, through her mouth, telling him that she was beginning to want him as much as he wanted her.

But he hesitated. Awareness of her virginity weighted him, making him cautious and almost reluctant. Everything would be new to her, so there was no way she could guide him to what pleased her most. There would be only trial and error, and a serious error could ruin the entire experience for her. He didn't want that. He dreaded that.

This woman had had so little goodness in her life, and almost nothing of love. He wanted with every cell of his being to make this experience one she would cherish for the rest of her days, but there was no road map to follow, no guidebook to lead him. Worse, the passion arcing across his own nerve endings was likely to make him rough and impatient when she mostly needed gentleness and patience from him.

He gritted his teeth as her hand tentatively found its way to the thatch of hair at the juncture of his thighs, holding back another groan that he feared would scare her. He wanted her to touch him, but was almost afraid that he would lose his grip on his precarious self-control. But then her hand darted away, as if she didn't have quite enough nerve.

That was good, he told himself, ignoring a surge of disappointment. There would be plenty of time later for him to know her most intimate touches. Right now when she was less afraid of his body, he needed to bring her on the journey with him, and lift her to the pinnacle of passion.

He nudged her gently over so that she was lying on her back. Taking care not to lean over her in a way that would seem threatening, he began to trace her contours with his fingertips. First the delicate line of her jaw—her bones felt so fragile!—then alongside her neck where he could feel her pulse steadily throbbing. Bending close, he pressed a kiss there, then resumed his exploration.

Down to her small shoulder, swallowed easily by his hand. Then to the graceful line of her collarbone, leading to the hollow at the base of her throat, where he pressed another kiss. As he did so, he heard her sharply indrawn breath, and knew that she was enjoying his touches.

Lower now his fingers wandered, passing tantalizingly between the hills of her breasts. They were small breasts, but soft and pretty and he had no trouble conjuring their image from memory. But they would have to wait, because he wanted to take this journey slowly. Carefully. Carrying her along one step at a time so that she never felt frightened.

He found her lower ribs, and traced them gently. Back and forth went his fingers, following the bones to her sides and back. He felt her stir, heard a soft gasp as he inadvertently tickled her, then felt the impatient rise of her hips.

Good. She was burning just as he was burning. The weight in his loins was heavy and hot, making him feel both edgy and slumberous. He imagined she must be experiencing a similar feeling of heaviness and anticipation. He hoped so.

Lower trailed his fingers, finding the hollow of her belly. There, between the points of her hipbones was the cradle that awaited him. Heat surged through his veins, and when he pressed his palm to her belly he felt her arch up as if to receive him.

Oh, she was responding to him. There was no doubt of that now. His touches were feeding the fire within her, and his fears began to ease a little.

Now his hand traveled lower, passing the delta between her thighs to concentrate on her legs. He heard her catch her breath again, and knew that this time the sound was one of apprehension. Recognizing it, he took his time as he traced her legs, learning the difference between them, discovering the disability of which she was so ashamed.

Yes, it was smaller, and he could feel how much weaker some of the muscles were. But there was nothing there that made her any less desirable. Nothing.

"Later," he whispered in her ear as his hand gently massaged the thigh of her injured leg, "later I'm going to turn all the lights on and look at you. When I'm done you'll know there's nothing you need to hide from me."

She caught her breath again, but before she could say anything, he plunged his tongue into the shell of her ear and sent a shudder running through her entire length.

Sweet heaven, had a woman ever been more responsive? The act of arousing her was arousing him like never before. At this very instant he could have buried himself in her and reached a height of climax that would have left him drained.

But the getting there was the fun part, and he wanted to make sure she had every bit as much fun getting there as it was possible to give her.

This time his mouth made the journey over her as he trailed kisses along her jaw, down her throat and onto her breast. This time he skipped nothing. Instead, drawing a low moan from her, he drew her breast into his mouth and sucked strongly, feeling her already engorged nipple enlarge even more against his tongue. His mouth was hot, her breast was cool and sweet, and he didn't think he would ever want to let go.

She moaned again, and her entire body tried to turn toward him, telling him so very much about what she was feeling. "Craig…" she whispered his name, then was lost in a fresh wave of passion that rocked her from head to toe. An undulation passed through her like a huge wave, exciting him even more.

But they had all night and he was a determined man. He moved to her other breast, sucking just as strongly, teaching her body things it had never dreamed about itself. Damn, she was so innocently sexy!

Fresh need burst in him like a nuclear explosion. He sucked again and another groan was ripped from her.

Now! He wanted her right now!

But no, not yet. Sliding his hand downward, he slipped it between her legs. She gasped.

"Sweet…" he muttered, his thoughts getting more scattered by the moment. She *was* sweet, all dewy folds and moist creases. He rubbed her gently, giving her time to grow accustomed to his presence in that most intimate of places, then he slipped his finger between her folds and found the knot of nerves that would lead her to the pinnacle.

She cried out this time, as if his touch were too much to bear, but she didn't pull away from him. Lifting his head from her breast, he watched intently for signs of distress as he rubbed her so very, very lightly. A whole range of expressions played across her face, and she kept her eyes tightly closed, as if she wanted nothing at all to distract her from what was happening inside her.

In the dark he smiled at her, and thought that she was incredible. Her hips began to rock insistently, and he pressed harder with his finger. She groaned and it seemed her entire body arched upward, demanding more and yet more.

He gave it to her, stroking her more firmly and sliding one of his fingers deep into her wet depths. She arched then, crying out, and her eyes opened wide in astonishment.

Perhaps the penetration hurt her a little; he couldn't tell. But she didn't try to push him away, nor did she complain. Instead her eyes closed and she pressed upward harder against his hand.

And then, so swiftly that it took him by surprise, she surmounted the peak with a long, low cry and convulsed against him.

Before her convulsions ended, he levered himself over her and pressed his erection to her entrance. Her eyes snapped open again, dark and glittering in the nearly lightless room. He restrained himself, suddenly remembering.

"I can't," he said. "I didn't bring protection."

"It's okay," she whispered. "Don't worry about it."

"But—"

"Shh…it's okay. Really. Nothing will happen…"

He couldn't restrain himself another moment. The woman was willing and he'd run out of excuses. His body demanded surcease, and his heart demanded his union with Esther. He wanted her, damn it. He was through considering consequences.

He slipped into her almost effortlessly, her discomfort evident in her suddenly indrawn breath, in the widening of her eyes.

When he hesitated, she murmured, "It's all right. I'm okay…"

And then he drove home, carrying himself higher and higher with each thrust of his hips. To his great joy he heard her soft cries of passion yet again.

And finally she called, "Harder…oh, please…"

He obliged readily and moments later carried them both over the precipice.

He rolled off of her and let the cool night air bathe their skin for several minutes, drying them off. Then he turned toward her and cradled her as close as he could get her. A woman's body was a miraculous gift, and Esther was more miraculous than most. She had given him a trust so profound that he felt confused. Even a little panicky.

Part of him wanted to run right now, but he figured that

would be about the worst thing he could do to her. Nor would it make things any easier for him. Against his better judgment, he had given them both what they thought they wanted. What he feared now was that they both were going to discover it had been a big mistake.

That *she* was going to discover she had made a big mistake.

He hoped the spirits were in a benevolent mood.

But what now? Should he climb from the bed and return to the sofa downstairs where he kept guard each night? Or should he stay where he was and feel the gossamer web of involvement grow ever tighter?

Esther stirred against him and her hand found his cheek, resting gently there. "Thank you."

She was *thanking* him? That had a curious effect on him, at once humbling him and terrifying him. "No, I should thank you," he said huskily, then cleared his throat. This conversation could get heavy in a real hurry, and that was the last thing he wanted right now.

Because right now he absolutely didn't want to have to sort through his jumbled feelings and thoughts, trying to make some sense of them so he could explain them to Esther. The last thing he wanted right now was any kind of postmortem.

So he sat up abruptly, and switched on the light. Esther made a soft gasp and tried to tug the sheet over herself.

"No," he heard himself say, tugging the percale from her hand. "I made you a promise."

Her blush was rosy, not only flooding her face but her shoulders and breasts as well. "Craig, no. Really, it's not necessary..." Her voice faded away as she lost air with which to speak.

But he wouldn't let her escape him. He had promised her something, and he always kept his promises. Never mind that he was going to back himself away from a relationship with her as quickly and gracefully as he could manage. The point was, from now on when she thought of a man looking at her body, she was going to see him and know that not everyone was revolted by her imperfection. She was going to remember that one man at least found her desirable.

Initially the experience was painful for her; he could read it in her eyes. She felt exposed and frightened of his reaction, not to mention embarrassed. But he wouldn't let her hide from him. Instead he scattered kisses all over her, trailing them from her neck to her toes.

Yes, her leg was smaller and not as well shaped as her uninjured one, but it was hardly repulsive. He strung extra kisses over it, and made a point of staring straight at it so she would know he wasn't avoiding it.

And finally her embarrassment faded, replaced by the blossoming of fresh passion. He kissed her everywhere again, this time lingering longer, making silent suggestions with his lips and tongue until she was in helpless thrall to the sensations he was giving her.

Then he slipped gently between her legs and drank deeply of her womanliness, giving her one of the most beautiful experiences a man could give a woman. And nothing, absolutely nothing in his life, had ever touched him as her rising cries of release touched him.

When he slid up over her and looked into her hazy hazel eyes, he murmured, "You're perfect in every way that matters."

Her eyes widened, then closed slumberously as he slipped within her once more. She cradled him perfectly, and even as he rode her to the stars he wondered how the hell he was going to live without her.

Dawn crept through the windows in a silver glow. Esther slipped out of the bed and paused to look down at Craig. She was surprised he had stayed with her all night. Somehow she hadn't expected that.

He was beautiful, lying there sprawled out with only a corner of the sheet to preserve his modesty. She probably could have stood there forever drinking him in except that Guinevere had emerged from somewhere in the depths of the house and was letting it be known that she needed to go out now.

Sighing, choosing to ignore the brace that leaned against the chair beside the bed, she made her cautious way down the stairs. Guin charged ahead of her, dancing impatiently in the hallway below.

Where had the dog been last night, Esther wondered. In retrospect she would have expected Guinevere to show up during their lovemaking out of curiosity if nothing else, but the dog had apparently chosen to spend the night elsewhere. Curious.

And oh, what a night! Remembering, she felt a fresh blush stain her cheeks. Craig had given her no quarter, demanding her full response. She tingled all over with memories of how he had touched her and kissed her, and how he had made her feel.

So beautiful! Nothing had prepared her for the breathtaking actuality of making love. Nothing *could* have prepared her.

She made coffee and sat at the kitchen table with a mug, all the café curtains pulled back so she could watch the start of day.

Nothing, she realized, was ever going to feel the same again. Nothing was ever going to look the same. She had been changed by last night in a way that few things in her life had changed her. A whole new world had opened up to her, and a man had given her the gift of knowing that she was a whole woman.

How was she going to live with the emptiness now?

With a sigh she looked down at her mug of coffee and understood why the fruit of the Tree of Knowledge had been forbidden. She hadn't expected the transition to be as earth-shattering as it was, and now that she actually knew what she would be missing, her isolation was only going to be more painful.

She sat on, watching the day lighten to the clarity of full morning, and felt deep within her a kernel of terrible rage at the man who had distorted her entire life. And now he expected her to listen to his *apology?*

A burst of black hatred filled her as she acknowledged for the first time that she wasn't only afraid of Richard Jackson. She was angry at him. Furious. And she hated him with a passion that nearly scared her.

How had those feelings been there but unrecognized for so long? How could she have felt things so strongly without knowing it? And why had last night opened the vault in which she had kept them buried?

Because her future was suddenly bleaker than ever before. She had promised Craig that she wanted only one night, and he had come to her only because of her assurances. He had feared hurting her because he couldn't offer her any kind of future. He had warned her. Repeatedly. And she had chosen not to listen. She had chosen to run the risk.

And now she knew exactly how much Richard Jackson had cost her. Last night had opened up long-ignored dreams and showed her that they could be real—but not for her.

To begin with, she couldn't trust a man. She had come to trust Craig only by long exposure. Another man would have run for the hills the first time she freaked out on him. And even last night when she had started to freeze up, he had been so understanding. She would have forgiven him if he'd called it off right then.

So Craig was unique. He had been patient with her beyond belief until he had surmounted her fears and her barriers enough that she could trust him. That was about as likely to happen again as the moon was to turn into green cheese. Hell, she'd gone her entire life and not one other man had attempted to get past her defenses.

Not that she really wanted them to, because she *was* afraid of them. They were bigger and stronger, and they were familiar with violence. Throughout her childhood she had watched boys beat up other boys, and in adulthood it didn't escape her how often men were behind crimes of violence, how often they beat their wives, children and dogs.

She didn't want to run this risk again. She was honest enough to admit it. Craig had gotten behind her walls only because of an unusual series of events that had brought them together often enough to encourage it.

But she could not consciously take the risk.

Another sigh escaped her and she sipped her coffee, frowning when she realized it was getting cold. She poured herself a fresh cup and resumed her melancholy contemplation of the world beyond her window.

She had to deal with this rage and hatred she felt for Richard Jackson, she decided. The violence of the feelings frightened her, but more, she felt they were probably keeping her from healing. How could she ever heal with that kind of virulence inside her?

But how could she get rid of something that had been a part of her for so long? Forgetting was apparently impossible. She'd tried before to just bury the past and treat it as something that had happened to someone else. That had only made her angrier.

But never before had she realized just how very angry she really was, or that she felt such hatred for her father.

Fear had been all she allowed herself to feel about him for so long that the strength of her hatred shocked her. She didn't want to feel that way about anybody, not even about Richard Jackson.

Unfortunately, there didn't seem to be any way to banish the feeling. It sat there in her mind like a lump of coldest lead, leaving her feeling sickened. It was awful to discover she was capable of such a thing.

A creak of floorboards in the hall alerted her. She looked up to see Craig enter the room looking tousled and only half awake. "You okay?" he asked.

"I'm fine." Sort of. He was gorgeous standing there in nothing but a pair of jeans. Even his bare feet were beautiful, strong and straight. The sight of him evoked memories of the night past and made her heart skip to a quicker rhythm. Just a few hours ago she had clasped him to her and felt him deep within her. Everything inside her clenched pleasurably at the memory.

He cocked his head, studying her intently. "You don't look fine."

Before she could protest, he closed the distance between them, bent over her and kissed her gently on the lips.

"Last night was wonderful," he murmured. "Regrets?"

She hesitated long enough that he lifted his head and looked intently at her. "You *do* regret it."

But she shook her head. Would she undo what had happened? No. And in her book that meant she had no regrets. "No. I don't."

He dropped into the chair next to her and looked at her seriously. "If there are any consequences because I didn't use protection—"

"I know what to do about it," she interrupted, letting him think she meant abortion. In point of fact, the mere possibility that she might be pregnant filled her with an almost unbearable yearning. To have a child! To have Craig's child... There was suddenly nothing in life that she wanted more.

He was still watching her intently. "If anything comes of it..." He hesitated. "I just want you to know I'll help in any way I can. You won't be alone."

She believed him. He'd already displayed his sterling character repeatedly. Craig Nighthawk was a man of great honor, and he would probably even offer to marry her if she turned out to be pregnant and expressed her intention of keeping the child. But she didn't want him that way. Would never want him that way. He would only feel like a prisoner, and he already felt too much that way.

And this was all ridiculous speculation at this point anyway. She found a smile and offered it to him. "I know, Craig."

Her smile seemed to relax him, and he rose, padding across the kitchen to get himself a cup of coffee. When he returned to the table, his expression was almost rueful. "This is awkward," he said.

"Why?"

"Just...not knowing exactly what to say."

Her smile became almost brittle. "Last night was last night. Today is today. We agreed that last night was...well, it was *last night*. It ends now."

Something flickered in the depths of his dark eyes. "Does it?"

"You said you're a wanderer, that you can't offer me a future. I understood that and I agreed to it." God, it was killing her to say this, but she didn't want to tie him to her with shackles of guilt and honor. That would be unbearable, like capturing a mustang and putting it in a small corral. He needed to be free. "All I wanted was the one night. I told you so."

Again that odd look flickered in his eyes. "You did," he agreed, his voice flat.

"So the subject is closed." She managed another smile. "You go your way, I go mine. No hard feelings, no regrets." Gee, did that sound grown-up or what? "Would you like some breakfast?"

He continued to stare at her until she began to feel distinctly uncomfortable. Finally he shook his head. "I'm not hungry this morning. Thanks, anyway."

"Okay. You have to go work at the ranch this morning?"

He looked surprised. "I'm staying with you to make sure your father doesn't cause any problems, remember?"

She was suddenly flustered, realizing that he was right. How was she going to survive having him around all the time?

She didn't particularly want breakfast either, but preparing one gave her something to do to evade his steady gaze. He was looking at her as if she were some kind of riddle to be solved. Tomato juice, toast, a slice of melon…she carried them to the table and forced herself to eat mechanically. Chewing and swallowing at least obviated the need to speak.

"Have you thought any more about Sheriff Tate's idea?" Craig asked her.

She looked at him, toast turning to ash on her tongue. She had to take a swallow of tomato juice to get it down. "I don't want to confront him. What good would it do?"

Craig looked disbelieving, as if he wondered if they had participated in the same conversation with the Sheriff. "It'll settle the issue of exactly what Jackson wants from you."

"No, it won't." She spread her hands. "If I talk to him with someone else present, he'll do exactly what he said he wants to do. He'll apologize. That doesn't mean he won't come back a couple of hours later to kill me. Whatever else he may be, Craig, my father isn't a stupid man."

"Oh, I don't know about that. Seems pretty stupid to me

when you beat up your wife and kid. Pretty stupid to cripple one and kill the other. If nothing else, that kind of behavior gets you in trouble with the law.''

"He didn't get into any trouble for throwing me down the stairs that time. He told a good enough lie that the doctor believed I'd fallen.''

"Only because you were little and didn't know how to fight back. You know how to take care of yourself now, though, don't you? You wouldn't let him get away with that stuff anymore.''

But somewhere inside her she was still the small child at the mercy of her much larger father, and all she could do was shake her head. "No way I'm going to face him. No way. I know what he can do to me.''

Craig looked as if he would argue further, but just then they both heard Guinevere's bark from the front door.

"I'll get her,'' Esther said, rising swiftly from the table and hurrying as fast as her unbraced leg would allow. It seemed as if everyone was expecting something from her that she wasn't capable of doing. How could anyone possibly expect her to face her father after all he'd done? Why couldn't they see how impossible it was?

She was aware that Craig was right behind her, but she ignored him, hoping he would leave her alone. Now that she'd accepted his protection it was beginning to seem as if she were going to have to accept his interference in every aspect of her life, even something as insignificant as letting the dog in.

She wanted to turn and confront him, but lingering caution prevented her. She still wasn't ready to get into a real confrontation with a man...although maybe that was something she needed to do. Maybe a whole lot of things in her life would get better if she would just learn to stand up to a man. Any man.

She flung the door wide. Guin darted past her joyfully, but right behind Guin was an elegant blond woman in a blue suit who puffed on a thin cigar.

"Hi,'' said Jo Fenster with a smile. "I thought I'd better

come stay with you since it's my fault that madman is bothering you, and you said you wouldn't hire a bodyguard."

Esther felt a blush rising hotly in her cheeks. She couldn't think of a thing to say.

Jo's smile widened as her gaze wandered from the nightgown-clad Esther to Craig, who wore nothing but a pair of jeans. "I should have known you'd have everything well in hand."

Chapter 13

Jo breezed through the door as if she owned the place. Esther had always envied that about her. Jo Fenster was brimming with the confidence that came from being both beautiful and successful, and it never occurred to her that she didn't belong wherever she happened to be.

She walked straight up to Craig and stuck out her hand. "I'm Jo Fenster, Esther's agent, and the person primarily responsible for this fiasco since it was one of my people who gave that criminal son of a bitch Esther's address. And you are?"

"Craig Nighthawk." He shook Jo's hand, smiling faintly.

"White knight and bulwark against the world, I presume," Jo said.

"No, just a sheep rancher," Craig told her. "Excuse me while I finish dressing."

Craig disappeared into the living room, closing the double doors behind him. Jo followed Esther down the hall to the kitchen, talking all the while.

"My dear, if I'd known they grew them like him out here,

I'd never have settled in the big city. But a sheep rancher? How...unique."

Esther was very fond of Jo, whose pretenses for the most part were humorous and not serious at all, but this time she felt a strong surge of protectiveness for Craig. She didn't want anybody viewing him as some kind of amusement. "He's a very nice man," she told Jo.

"I'm sure." Jo plopped down at the table and waved away the offer of coffee or breakfast. "He's also gorgeous, and I'm going to tease you mercilessly. But later. First I want to know if the man has given you any trouble. Your father, I mean."

"He came out here yesterday to try to see me. I refused to open the door."

"Good for you! I've been absolutely worried sick, which is why I came straight here once I concluded matters in Europe. By the way, you're going to have a show in Madrid, not Paris, after London wraps up, so you'd better paint just as fast as you can. I promised them a minimum of ten pieces, but I told them I couldn't set a date until I'd spoken to you."

"Ten pieces!"

Jo smiled. "You can do it, Esther. We both know damn well you can, so why don't you just admit it? But to get back to that south end of a mule you have for a father, just what exactly does he think he's going to accomplish by harassing you? Maybe they'll just throw him back in prison."

"They can't throw him in prison unless they convict him of something, and as I've been reminded more than once over the last couple of weeks, he has to *do* something illegal. Calling me, writing me, even showing up on my doorstep isn't illegal."

"Well, it ought to be!"

"That's what I thought, too, until I really started to think about it. If it was illegal for him to show up on my doorstep, it'd have to be illegal for you, too."

Jo frowned and pulled on her cigar. "Well, we can't have that, can we? So, how did you meet this gorgeous sheep rancher?"

"One of his sheep ate my flower garden."

Jo rolled her eyes. "Count on you to have a sheep devour your garden. Can't you do anything normally?"

Esther felt her own humor rising in response to Jo's droll teasing. "I wasn't doing anything abnormal at all! Really. I was just sitting on my porch sipping iced tea when this animal wandered up and began to dine on my marigolds."

Jo shuddered. "Can you imagine eating a marigold?"

"I was worried the sheep would get sick, but apparently it survived quite nicely."

"And this is when you met Monsieur Nighthawk?"

"Exactly."

"And how long was this man a sheep rancher next door to you before you met him? Or did he just suddenly spring out of the ground?"

"Oh, he's been ranching over there since long before I moved here."

"And it took you more than two years to meet him?" Jo shook her head. "What am I going to do about you, Esther? You're entirely too reclusive. It's one of the reasons I came hotfooting it out here to the end of the world. I figured you wouldn't have a soul to turn to."

Esther regarded her wryly. "If I make a whole bunch of friends, I'll have less time to paint."

"There is that. Oh, well, there's nothing really wrong with being a hermit." Jo's eyes were dancing, belying her words. "Well, if you can possibly stand it, I'd like to bring in my bag, explore your shower and change into something more suited to the locality. Then you can tell me that you don't need me, that Señor Nighthawk has the situation well in hand. I will listen and gratefully take myself back to civilization."

"Why don't you stay a couple of days and catch your breath?" Jo would make a wonderful buffer against the presence of Craig in the house.

"I'll think about it." Jo sighed. "Actually, I really *should* be heading back. Work has been piling up on my desk the entire time I was in Europe. I'll probably find myself buried in an avalanche of paper the instant I sit in my chair. But, oh well! It's waited this long, it can wait a little longer."

She rose. "I need to get my carry-on out of the car, then lead me to the bathroom!"

Esther walked along with her, feeling the wobbliness of her leg like a background warning of an earthquake to come. The muscles were becoming very fatigued from trying to compensate, and at any moment she would probably put her foot down and go for a headlong tumble. Exercising caution, she stayed on the porch while Jo traipsed across the uneven gravel walk and the driveway to her rental car.

"How did you find me, anyway?" she called to Jo.

The agent pulled her suitcase from the trunk. "It wasn't at all difficult. I just asked this very nice sheriff or deputy or whatever he was when I reached Conard City. His directions were very clear."

Which, thought Esther glumly, may have been exactly how her father had found her. Some helpful person—and this county was full of helpful persons—had probably given him directions. Why had she ever thought she would be impossible to find?

She showed Jo to the upstairs bathroom, then went to her own room to change.

The first thing she did after donning her underwear was to reach for the brace. Her leg was already aching from so much unaccustomed work without the aid of it, but she didn't want to put it on. Somehow that brace was a symbol of a bondage inflicted on her by her father. It was a visual symbol of the blight on her life.

She wanted to hurl it across the room and never touch it again.

The door to her bedroom opened suddenly, startling her. She gasped as Craig stepped in, closing the door behind him. Instinctively she tried to cover herself, but Craig's raking gaze made a mockery of the attempt. He noted every detail, right down to the delicate lace on her bra and the low cut of her panties.

"Delightful," he said with an enigmatic half smile.

"You shouldn't be in here," she told him breathlessly. "Jo—"

"Jo," he interrupted, "is in the shower. Anyway, she's already figured out what's going on here."

Esther stiffened her back, feeling that she was being boxed in somehow. "And just what *is* going on here?"

"I'm filling my eyes with the delightful sight of the lady I made love to last night." Before she could do more than feel a warm, curling thrill at his words, he was squatting before her, taking the brace from her limp hands. "Let me help with this."

She should have sent him on his way immediately, but somehow it was the last thing on earth she felt capable of. Instead she let him put that awful contraption on her, showing him how to fasten it so that it was just snug enough.

"Wonderful things medical science comes up with," he remarked as he tightened the last strap. "This has got to be better than crutches."

It was, and she found herself feeling almost ashamed for having resented it so much. He surprised her by bending forward to drop a kiss on her thigh between the rods of the brace. Then he helped her to her feet and drew her into a snug embrace.

"This," he said, "is how the morning-after *should* begin." Bending, he stole her mouth in a mind-stunning kiss that left her hanging almost limply in his arms. How was it possible to melt inside merely from the touch of lips? How was it possible that a kiss could drive away all the many things that had been annoying her and leave her so wonderfully relaxed, as if she were suddenly floating on a warm cloud?

She could gladly have stayed there forever, wrapped in his strength and his warmth. Eventually, though, his hold began to slacken and she knew it was time to step back.

"Since Jo is here," he said gently, "I'm going to run back to my place for an hour or so. Will you be all right?"

She managed a nod, even though his sudden desire to get away left her feeling bruised.

He seemed to sense her reaction because he hesitated, then added, "There's some business I need to look into. Really."

"Sure." She managed a bright smile, reminding herself that

216 *Nighthawk*

she had no claim on this man, and that he'd made it as clear as crystal that he didn't want her to have any claim on him.

"Tell you what. I'll wait until Jo is through with her shower."

He'd misunderstood her reluctance, and she was relieved that he didn't realize that she was simply disappointed, not frightened of being alone. "Really, it's not necessary. I'll be just fine."

After he left, she donned a long voile skirt with subdued roses on a beige background, and a beige cotton sweater. Jo would probably want to see what she had ready for the London show and there was little likelihood that she would get any painting done while she had company.

When she descended the stairs, her leg grateful for the added stability of the brace, she went to make a fresh pitcher of iced tea, wait for Jo and wonder how it was that her entire life seemed to have careened out of her control.

Ever since the letter from her father had arrived, she realized, little by little events had been slipping out of her control.

No, wait. The problem had really begun with Cromwell eating her geraniums and marigolds. Amusing or not, it had been the first sign that the universe had decided to play games with her mind. Cromwell and Craig Nighthawk, not to mention Mop.

Good Lord! Her garden had been devoured, her dog impregnated and her privacy invaded by a dark wanderer with eyes like windows on midnight. If she really thought about it, her father was the least of her problems. He, at least, was only exacerbating a fear she had never lived without. Craig and his animals, on the other hand, were turning her life on its ear.

She was thinking about Craig entirely too much, mooning over him when she ought to be thinking more seriously about her work. Then there was Guin, curled up in a corner of the kitchen, ignoring everything around her in favor of mooning over Mop. At least that was what she presumed Guin was doing.

"You are, aren't you, girl?" she asked the dog. "Thinking of that philandering komondor who's probably gone back to

Bucket now that he's had all he wants of you. But isn't that just typical of a man? They take what they want and then vanish, leaving the woman to deal with the consequences by themselves.''

Guin watched her with sad eyes but offered no comment.

"Oh, I know," Esther told the dog. "You're head over heels in love with that rake. Nothing I say is going to have any effect. A woman in love must be the most senseless creature on the face of the planet. But mark my words, Guin. Once a man has had you, he'll have no more use for you."

Guin yawned ostentatiously.

"Right. You don't believe me. But don't say I didn't warn you."

Just as Craig had warned her by listing all the reasons she shouldn't look for anything further from him. And just in case she hadn't taken the hint, he'd made it plain that he could hardly wait to get out of here this morning.

All of a sudden she was on the edge of tears. It hurt. It hurt so badly she wanted to cry out. How was it possible she could care so much about a man she hardly knew? Even her dislike and distrust of men in general hadn't protected her against Craig Nighthawk. He had slipped within her defenses almost effortlessly, and now it was costing her.

Glumly, she stared down at Guinevere and wondered why females cared so much about creatures who didn't reciprocate. And why females insisted on charging right ahead despite all the warnings.

"We take the cake, don't we, Guin?"

This time the Saint Bernard chuffed a sound of agreement.

Jo's footsteps sounded on the stairs, forcing Esther to put aside her melancholy thoughts. The important thing to remember, she reminded herself as Jo stepped into the kitchen, was that Craig had not once lied to her. She had walked into this with her eyes wide open, and now she had no one to blame but herself.

"So, what happened to the five-star hunk?" Jo asked.

"He had to run back to his place to take care of some business."

Jo waggled her eyebrows. "Well, he's certainly one of the most interesting specimens I've seen in a while. Yummy, actually. I don't suppose he has a brother?"

"Just a sister."

"Rats! But really, he's rotten, right? A not very nice person."

"Actually," Esther said on a repressed sigh, "he's *very* nice."

"I suspected he must be," Jo said in a serious tone.

Esther looked at her. "Why?"

"Because he got past your tower walls. I figure he must be a combination of Albert Schweitzer and Albert Einstein."

That statement jolted Esther. It created an image she didn't like. "What do you mean?"

"Oh, don't take it to heart, sweetie! It's just that you're so damn unapproachable I kind of figured no man would ever be good enough for you."

"I don't avoid men because I'm a snob. I avoid them because of…well, you know."

Jo cocked her head and pulled out a chair, sitting across from Esther. "Isn't it basically the same thing, Esther? Because one man was a dyed-in-the-wool, alcohol-soaked son of a gun, you've been assuming all men were no better."

"Not exactly."

Jo shrugged and smiled. "I don't want to fight with you about it. I like being your agent and would like to continue as your agent."

Esther was appalled. "Jo, I'd never dump you simply because we had a disagreement. You know that!"

But Jo's expression said that she didn't know that, and that disturbed Esther even more.

"Jo?"

The agent hesitated, then said, "Well, frankly, Esther, you cut everything out of your life that might even remotely cause you pain. You've moved out here to the middle of nowhere, as far as I can tell you don't talk to anyone except me—and now this gorgeous Mr. Nighthawk—and you don't even want to hear the reviews of your shows. You use me as a bulwark against everything in the larger world that might touch you. Naturally, I assume that if I cause you too much discomfort I can expect to be discharged.''

Esther could hardly believe what she was hearing. Was this how she looked to Jo, whom she had trusted implicitly for the last eight years?

"You've turned yourself into an emotional shut-in, Esther.'' Jo shrugged. "That's your prerogative, and I'm certainly not going to tell you that you have to do anything different. It just surprises me to see that an ordinary mortal has gotten past your defenses. Now, shall we go out and look at the paintings for the London show before you throw me out?''

They spent the next hour out in the barn studio sorting through Esther's accumulation of paintings. She had put those she considered the best for the exhibit in one portfolio, and those with which she wasn't nearly as pleased in another. Jo snatched some of the ones Esther didn't like and moved them over to the exhibit folder.

"You really underestimate your talent, sweetie. These are gorgeous! And that mountainscape you're working on...well, that's going to attract some attention, I can tell you right now.''

Esther looked over at the large painting she had been working so carefully on when the rest of life would leave her alone long enough to concentrate, and wondered what Jo saw in it. To her it was beginning to look...bleak. Barren. Forbidding.

Stepping over to the window, she looked west to the mountains, thinking they didn't look at all as she was portraying them. This morning the light painted them in a slate blue that wasn't at all forbidding, and the plains rolling away toward them were still abundant with the life of late summer. Admittedly it wasn't the lush grassy green of the northeast or of the tropical south, but it was the silvery green of sage and tall wild grasses. Jackrabbits, coyotes and deer could be found out there without looking too far at all.

She turned around and looked at the painting again, and wondered what had been infecting her that she had made those mountains looks like the walls of a prison?

But isn't that what she had done? Turned those mountains into a wall between herself and the rest of the world?

"I'm going to have to leave soon," Jo remarked. "Next time you decide to move to some exotic location, try to get closer to a major airport, would you? The drive here is ridiculously long after flying so far."

"Sorry."

Jo gave her a sudden smile. "Actually, I understand that it would defeat the entire purpose if you were too accessible."

"I'm apparently accessible enough. My father certainly didn't have any difficulty finding me."

Jo closed the portfolios and tied them snugly. "If someone is determined to find you, I seriously doubt that any place is inaccessible enough."

"So it appears."

"Let's go sit on that beautiful porch of yours and watch the day pass until I have to leave."

They sat on chairs on the front porch, facing the mountains. Esther wondered where Craig was and what was taking him so long, then told herself it was none of her damn business. She'd poured them each a glass of iced tea, and because Jo confessed to being hungry, she brought out a plate of crackers, cheese and raw vegetables.

It was a pleasantly warm day in the upper seventies and as dry as bone. The grasses rippled in the breeze and Guinevere stirred herself to chase a butterfly.

Jo spoke. "It'd be hard to find a place more bucolic than this."

Esther glanced wryly at her agent. "Suffering from urban deprivation so quickly?"

"Well, I have to confess to a fondness for the theater, museums and sushi, all of which appear to be utterly lacking here."

"Well, there *is* a movie theater, and I seem to recall that the library runs a small museum that focuses on local history."

Jo pretended to shudder. "I'm surprised you aren't stark raving mad after more than two years here. How can you stand it?"

"I like my own company."

Jo turned then to look at her. "Point taken. Oh, all right, I'm not so thrilled with my own company. In fact, I bore me. I enjoy the company of all kinds of interesting people with their diverse interests and quirks. Humanity is a great big Fourth of July parade."

"I suppose so."

Jo lit a cigar and cocked a sardonic brow at her. "So, what is humanity to you?" she asked. "A long line of serial killers?"

Esther gasped, stunned by the blunt frontal assault. Before she could reply, Jo reached out and clasped her hands. "I'm deliberately being a jerk here, Esther. I'm trying to make a point. You've withdrawn so far from the rest of us that you're living alone in a dusty, barren valley of your own making. I can't believe you let that man go this morning as if it didn't matter a damn if you saw him again."

"Jo—"

"Just listen to me, then I'll shut up and get on my horse, as it were, and ride into the sunset. Your entire demeanor when he left said that you didn't care. But you did. I could see it in your eyes. What makes you think he'll ever come back if you don't ever let him know that you want him to?"

Esther felt her stomach sinking in the most hideous way as Jo's justifiable question drove home. "We agreed beforehand—"

"Oh, baloney! Honey, those things are always open-ended. People have a lot of reasons to want to protect themselves when they feel they're starting to get involved, and they come up with all kinds of excuses and rationales for how they're just going to take one bite of the apple and then move on without a backward glance. My husband proposed to me the morning after what we both agreed was going to be a one-night stand without strings. If he hadn't had the guts to break our ground rules, I'd have missed a lot of fun."

"This is different."

"It always is. Oh, well." She puffed on her cigar and returned her attention to the mountains.

"I just met him recently."

"Mm."

"I hardly know him, Jo!"

"Yep. I hear you." Jo smiled and waved the subject aside. "I'm great at giving unsolicited advice. Just ignore me. Your life, your choice. You're the one who has to live with the consequences."

"Exactly." Suddenly, inexplicably, Esther laughed. "Did you fly all the way out here just to lecture me on my personality flaws?"

"Hell, no. I have better things to do with my time. And I'm probably all wet anyway. Who am I to judge how someone else chooses to live? My own lifestyle is pretty...eclectic. And the marriage after the one-night stand only lasted a couple of years, so take my advice for what it's worth...zip."

Esther's smile widened. "What? Backtracking, Jo? I never saw you as one to back down. Besides, you weren't offering advice, you were bashing my timidity."

A laugh escaped Jo. "God, what a bitch I am. Okay, okay, I'll go back to being an agent. Just make sure that whatever happens you keep painting those pictures, hear? I'm going to need a whole bunch of new ones for Madrid, and after that probably Vienna. You're becoming quite the international star, m'dear."

"I don't want to be a star."

"No, but you want to be the best. It shows in everything you paint. So enjoy your stardom. Being an artist, you're entitled to be unpleasantly reclusive and secretive. Just think, you get to have your cake and eat it, too!"

But finally Jo could linger no longer. She had to leave or miss the flight she'd booked after showering, although she offered to forgo the trip if Esther didn't want to be alone.

"After all, I came out here precisely to see that you had someone to look after you, and I was prepared to stay as long as it took to find someone to do it. But since you've already taken care of that...?"

Esther nodded. "Scat. I'll be just fine, and I'm sure Craig

will be back at any minute. Nothing's going to happen in five minutes.''

Twenty minutes later she watched Jo drive away. When the growl of her engine faded, Esther was once again alone in the vast silence of the prairie.

Craig hadn't expected to be gone much more than an hour, and he figured Jo was with Esther, which was a pretty good insurance policy against anything that Richard Jackson might be thinking of.

What he hadn't expected was to blow out a front tire and go into a ditch on his way back to her place. He stood there looking at his truck nosed down with its rear wheels in the air and figured he had a choice. He could walk to his own place and call for a tow truck, or walk to Esther's to call, because he sure wasn't going to get that truck out of there without a winch.

Damn! He brushed the sweat from his brow with his forearm and settled his hat back on his head. Double damn! If he'd been paying attention to his driving instead of mooning about Esther, he would never have lost control when that tire blew, and if he hadn't lost control he wouldn't now be looking at this mess.

He glanced up at the sun, judging that it was just pushing toward ten o'clock. He hadn't been gone that long and assured himself again that Jo was with her. He was primarily worried about Esther not being alone so she wouldn't get scared. Truth was, he didn't think Richard Jackson wanted to hurt her. Hell, if the man had wanted that, he'd had plenty of opportunity the first time he came out to her place.

Of course—and this was the possibility that began to eat him alive as he stood there staring at the wreck of his truck—he could be wrong. Richard Jackson just might be warped enough to want to play with his victim first, keep her in a state of prolonged fear, before he moved in for the kill. Stranger things had happened.

Hell! He kicked the blown tire, then climbed up the side of the ditch to the road. No one in sight anywhere. Not that there was much traffic along this road in the middle of a weekday morning. Most folks in the ranches around here were too busy working. It might be an hour, maybe two before the first vehicle came along. In that time he could probably walk most of the way to Esther's.

He swore at his cowboy boots, wishing he was wearing almost anything else on his feet, then set off at a fast walk toward Esther's.

He was getting mightily attached to that woman, and he was getting awfully tired of pretending he wasn't. Of course, she didn't feel the same way about him and he was resigned to that fact. Last night had been, well, wonderful, but it was still only an aberration for her. It hadn't been that she had wanted him, Craig Nighthawk, as much as it had been that she wanted to solve the mystery of her womanhood.

Well, he could understand that. And because he had wanted her so much, he hadn't minded being used. Although, to be fair about it, she hadn't made him feel used. Actually, she had made him feel special by letting him know that he was the only person in the world whom she wanted to share the experience with.

Thinking about that gave him quite a glow as he trudged along the road. No one outside his immediate family had ever given him such a gift of trust as Esther had given him last night. That would have touched him under any circumstances, but it was especially soothing to a soul that was still badly bruised from accusations two and a half years ago. From incidents like the one that had occurred when he took Esther out to dinner.

And that was why there was no real future for them, he reminded himself. That was why he had to keep his distance. For her sake. Not only was he a poor rancher with wanderlust in his soul, but he was an Indian who had been accused of a terrible crime. There were enough people who wouldn't forget that to make life hell for anyone who cared about him. He couldn't ask a woman to put up with a regular diet of that kind of abuse. And what about kids? How could he possibly put children through this?

Damn, how had he gotten so far down the road of speculation? Esther wasn't going to be part of his future, so it was pointless to ask himself how he could put her through such a thing. No need to even consider it.

But thinking about children had a melancholy effect on him, and as he tramped along the road with the sun and the breeze in his face, he found himself thinking about the kids he would never have. Kids he really would like to have.

He thought about trying to run, but looking down at his boots he cast the thought aside. He would break an ankle running in these damn things. Nor could he run barefoot safely, because here and there alongside the road were shards of glass. He was stuck walking as fast as he could toward Esther's place.

Damn cowboy boots, damn the blisters that were beginning to grow on his heels, and damn life in general. Sometimes it could be so in-your-face unfair.

Everything he wanted was just out of his reach. Well, he shrugged inwardly, what was new? He was used to wanting things he couldn't have. Nobody in this world got everything and he was damn lucky to have as much as he did.

But, man, did he ache for wanting Esther Jackson.

Esther thought about going out to her studio to paint after Jo left, but she didn't feel like painting. Not today. What she wanted to do was find a quiet place where she could curl up by herself and think over the events of the past night.

She'd noticed in the past that when something major happened to her she needed to run it over and over in her mind, as if to assimilate all the important details and make sure she forgot nothing of significance. Last night had been an earth-shattering event for her and she wanted to savor every detail, wring from every remembered moment everything that she could. And until this very moment, she really hadn't been alone so she could do it.

So instead of going to the barn, she curled up on the pillows of the wrought iron chaise longue at one corner of the porch and closed her eyes. The breeze tossed her hair lazily, and she could faintly hear the buzzing of bees in her flower garden. Guin settled down beside her and watched the breeze play with the grass.

Last night had been simply perfect. She wouldn't have changed one moment of her time with Craig...well, except that she wished she could be sure he had wanted it as much as she did. Having asked him left her feeling a little uncertain about that part of it.

But he had acted as if he wanted it every bit as much as she did, once she had asked him. But that might just have been because he was so kind.

No, she didn't want to think about it that way! She didn't want to tarnish a memory that was always going to be one of the most beautiful of her life.

Smiling inwardly, she hugged a throw pillow and snuggled down in the chaise. Not even in her wildest imaginings could she have conceived that a man could make her feel so wonderful, so wild, so...exquisite.

And she was determined, absolutely and positively, not to let anything at all rob her memories of their joy.

Wondering what was taking Craig so long, she gradually drifted off into a doze, lulled by the quiet beauty of the warm Wyoming afternoon. She never noticed the thunderhead building above her.

Chapter 14

"Esther. Esther, wake up."

She stirred on the chaise, vaguely realizing that someone was calling her. Thunder boomed hollowly, and the breeze that blew over her skin was cool.

"Esther…"

She didn't recognize the voice. As soon as that realization penetrated the fog of sleep, adrenaline hit her with a sharp jab. Instantly she was awake, sitting up swiftly, looking around.

And facing her worst nightmare.

Richard Jackson stood not more than six feet away, looking down at her. Guin, for some reason, seemed not to be disturbed by his presence.

"Nice dog," Richard said, and smiled.

"Get out of here!"

But he shook his head and sat in a wicker chair facing her. "I need to talk to you, Essie. Just for a few minutes. Then I'll go away."

"I don't want to hear anything you have to say! Just get out of here." Inside she was shriveling. As if something about Richard Jackson reached into her very soul and blighted it, she could feel the tender buds of life withering and dying. God, he terrified her.

Pushing herself off the chaise, she began to back away from him. Run! She had to run!

Turning, she hurried as fast as her brace would allow her, away from him. Away from the threat that had stalked every day of her life.

Guin followed her, whining her disturbance. Jackson followed her, too, calling her name. "Essie—"

"Leave," she sobbed, hurrying as fast as she could, steadying herself against the porch railing when she nearly stumbled. "Get out of here! I'm going to call the police!"

"Essie."

Guin suddenly turned on him, standing stiff-legged with her hackles raised and growling deep in her throat. Jackson drew up sharply.

"Look," he said, "I just want to talk to you."

Esther backed up, holding on to the railing for dear life, aware that she had twisted her leg somehow while she ran, and now it throbbed with fiery pain. Oh God, she had to get to the phone in the kitchen. "I don't want to hear anything you have to say."

He held out his hands imploringly. "Look, I won't come any closer, I swear. Just hear me out."

She shook her head almost wildly, torn between fear and a rising anger. He was too close. Guin's growling seemed to be holding him at bay, but she couldn't be sure that would deter him for long.

"Essie, please."

"Go away!" she sobbed. "Just go away and leave me alone!" Another backward step and her leg buckled beneath her. Desperately she clung to the rail as she started to fall, and just managed to catch herself. "Get out of here!" Oh God, if she lost her footing she would be totally at his mercy.

But suddenly Richard Jackson turned away. "Sorry. I thought maybe after all this time you'd want to know that I finally learned something."

Guin followed him, growling low in her throat.

The fact that Richard was turning away, not threatening her at all, finally penetrated Esther's terror. And suddenly, as clearly as if he were standing right there, she heard Craig say, "You have to face the demon...."

Shaking, shivering, she gripped the rail with both hands. The urge to flee was overpowering, but where could she run? She'd just proved that there was no way she could outrun anything but a two-year-old. Richard would be able to catch her in less than a half-dozen steps—and would have if he had wanted to.

She felt cornered. Trapped. There wasn't even anything handy that she could use for a weapon if he tried to hurt her. The only advantage she had that she could see was that if he threw her off the porch she would only get a few bruises.

But he wasn't coming any closer. In fact, he was walking away, looking back at her over his shoulder.

He had aged, she realized with a jolt. The demon of her youth looked old, with white hair and a sunken face. His shoulders were stooped, as if he were hunched in expectation of a blow. Even the hands, big hands that had once terrified her by their very size, suddenly looked shrunken.

Everything about him looked shrunken, she realized. He was no longer the huge, threatening menace of her childhood, but a shrunken, ordinary old man.

Taking heart from the fact that he wasn't much bigger than she, she dared to halt him. "Why should I listen to you?"

"No reason, I guess." He hesitated. "Except that maybe you'll be able to sleep better knowing I don't intend to hurt you."

She felt another uncomfortable jolt. How had he known? Then she remembered that Sheriff Tate had spoken to him just yesterday. Maybe the sheriff had let him know how terrified she was. She felt a sudden burst of hot anger at that, fury that Tate had told Richard about her fear, fury that Richard was able to scare her so much.

"I'm just supposed to take your word for that?" she heard herself demand hotly. "Why the hell should I do that, Richard? Every time you came crawling back after you beat up

Mom or me you said it would never happen again. Every time you came back you said you were sorry, that you'd never meant to hurt us. But I'm still crippled and Mom is still dead!''

He kept his face averted, but she could see the way his hands clenched and his jaw worked as she shouted at him. A long time passed before he spoke, a time in which the only sound was the wind in the grass and Guin's warning growl. Finally he said, ''Yes, you are.''

It was as if he punched her. All the air rushed out of her lungs, making her feel dizzy and weak. Her voice deserted her, leaving her helpless to lash out. She couldn't believe he'd admitted that. Couldn't believe he'd admitted it so easily. So calmly. What was this? A sham?

But he turned then, and she doubted he could have manufactured the terrible look in his eyes.

''I killed her, Essie,'' he said simply. ''I killed her and I have to live with that. I crippled you and I have to live with that. I have to live with the memory of every blow or nasty word I hurled at you. Do you know what I dream of at night? Your face when you were little, looking so god-awful scared and hurt. The way you skittered away from me as fast as you could if I came into a room. I have to remember what I did to you and your mother.''

''So do I,'' she said defiantly. Was she supposed to feel pity or sympathy for this man?

He nodded. ''I'm not asking for your forgiveness. I don't have a right to that. But I want you to know I learned. I had fifteen years in a prison cell to give me time to think without alcohol getting in the way and I figured a few things out.''

''So?''

He looked down, as if hoping he could find answers on the plank floor in front of his loafered feet. When he lifted his head he looked even more shrunken. ''This isn't for you, I guess.'' His voice cracked on the words. ''I can't take back what I did to you. I know that. There's not one damn thing I can do to make it any better. I guess I gave you nightmares you'll have for the rest of your life. I sure as hell gave you that leg.'' He indicated her leg with a jerk of his chin.

Esther compressed her lips and folded her arms tightly around herself, wishing the earth would just open and swallow the man. But the earth didn't open, and she kept hearing Craig's urging to face the demon. Somehow that gave her courage to keep standing there looking at this nightmare monster from her youth.

"I'm here for me," he said abruptly. "It's something I need to do. To tell you to your face that I'm sorry as hell about the kind of creep I was and about how bad I hurt you and your mother. I know you aren't going to believe it, but I always loved you."

"You sure had a strange way of showing it!"

He nodded. "I guess so. I wish...I wish I could fix it, Essie. Really. But I can't. So I just gotta stand here and tell you how god-awful sorry I am. I had a weakness for alcohol and I was too weak to fight it. I was a weak man."

"And you're not now?"

"No. Not like I was." He looked at her from those haunted eyes. "I don't drink anymore. I don't go anywhere near the stuff. And I'll never hit anyone again, ever."

He averted his face for a moment, then looked at her again. Before speaking, he drew a long, shaky breath. "I loved your mom. I loved her too damn much. I got...too possessive. She loved to flirt with guys and dance with guys and...I used to get so mad I couldn't even see straight because of the way she was looking at some guy. I know it's no excuse but...I don't know why, but I kinda figured that if I hit her she'd stop fooling around. She never did, and I shoulda just had the sense to leave, y'know? But I was stupid, and she was mine, and I was going to fight for her. Only problem was it was her I was fighting."

He drew a ragged breath and Esther felt an uncomfortable tug. She didn't like the image he was painting of her mother. She had known that her mother drank, too, and got violent sometimes when she did, but she hadn't thought of her as being cheap. "Are you blaming *her* for what you did?"

"No." He shook his head. "No, I'm not. Nothing she ever did deserved being beaten up. It sure as hell didn't deserve getting killed. I'm just trying to..." He hesitated. "I guess I'm trying to explain. It ain't no excuse, Essie. There isn't any excuse for what I did. I was just a bastard. I was too quick to hit. Too quick to get mad. They had me take some counseling about that when I was in prison. Anger control counseling. I think it helped because I don't get near as angry as I used to."

God, he was pathetic, she found herself thinking. As he stood there and exposed more of his weakness he was resembling the monster of her nightmares less and becoming more just a poor excuse for a human being.

He shifted from one foot to the other and shoved a hand into his slacks pocket. "Anyway, your mom made me mad a lot, but there was really no reason for me to get mad at you except...I was jealous."

"Jealous?" She couldn't fathom it. Jealous of a small child?

"Jealous." One corner of his mouth twitched. "You took so much of her time and she was so crazy about you. I resented it, Essie. Pretty dumb, huh? I mean, you were my kid. I still don't understand why I was so jealous. I can remember..." His voice broke. "I can remember when you used to...crawl into my lap and call me daddy. I remember that and..." His voice broke again and his breathing grew ragged. "I can't explain it, what happened. I can't explain why I started to see you as a nuisance. You weren't a bad kid. Hell, you didn't even cry very much. And that time that I...that I..."

He broke off and turned away, visibly fighting for control. Several minutes passed before he spoke again. "I don't know why I threw you down the stairs. Your mom and I had been fighting, I remember that. I was pretty angry, and I put away a couple of six-packs, and then you started screaming and it was like something exploded in my head. I remember picking you up, but I honest to God don't remember throwing you down the stairs."

She spoke, her voice dripping ice. "I remember every detail."

He swore and walked a few steps away, as if he wanted to

escape. "I'm sorry," he said finally, turning to look directly at her. "I'm sorrier than I can ever tell you."

She simply looked at him, wondering if his apology was somehow supposed to make it better for her. It didn't feel like anything at all. How could saying you're sorry ever make up for anything? "I'm not sure you have any right to apologize," she said finally. "You knew you were causing harm."

He nodded. "I surely did. I just didn't admit it to myself. I had some red-hot teeth biting my tail and driving me on like I was some kind of madman. I don't know what the hell it was that kept pushing me, but I should've had better control. I shouldn'ta let myself get out of hand the way I did. And I'm sorry for it, Essie. I truly am sorry. I know it doesn't make a damn thing any better for you, but I had to tell you. I know I did wrong and I'm sorry."

She looked at him with a detached, cold sort of curiosity. "Did it make you feel better to tell me that?"

He shook his head. "No. Nothing's ever going to make me feel better. That isn't why I did this."

"Then why did you?"

"Because I had to own up to what I did. And I had to face up to you." He shrugged. "So, okay, I did it. Maybe someday you can even see your way to...letting me back into your life."

She was horrified. "Never!"

He nodded sadly. "I kind of figured you'd feel that way. You have every right to."

"Well, how wonderfully generous of you to admit that!" Her voice curled with scorn. Her fear of him was beginning to evaporate like a puddle on a hot summer day. "I'd have been happy if I'd never seen you again period."

He nodded, not even flinching, acting as if he were accepting just punishment.

"I've had nightmares every night of my life because of you! I never knew the simple safety a child is supposed to know from its parents. I had no childhood to speak of, and I suffer pain every single day of my life because of you. How can you possibly think an apology would make any of that easier to take?''

"I don't. I never did. I'm not a fool, Essie."

"Stop calling me that! My name is Esther."

"I called you Essie when you were a baby."

She knew that. What she hated was the skin-crawling feeling she got when she heard him say it now. "Well, you've apologized so now you can go."

But he hesitated and she found herself wanting to scream with frustration and a billion other emotions that seemed to have been building for so long. This man had made a wreck out of her life and now he stood there as if he had a right to be on her front porch. As if he had any right to anything at all.

"I'm sorry," he said again, and turned to walk away.

It was watching him walk away that at last broke the shackles of her prison of fear. She had faced him, she had stood up to him, and now he was walking away. She had triumphed in the most elemental way possible—she had faced the demon, and he was a demon no more.

Instead, she suddenly saw him as a pathetic excuse for a man who had ruined his entire life for lack of simple self-control. He could neither control his rage, nor control his drinking, and so he had killed his wife and permanently alienated his daughter.

And suddenly she knew she wasn't going to let it end this way.

Craig was about a half mile from Esther's driveway when he saw the battered metallic blue car turn into it. Even at that distance he recognized the vehicle and felt his heart slam into overdrive.

My God, Richard Jackson was going to see Esther! A multitude of horrible images crossed his mind, and he found himself clinging desperately to the hope that Jo's presence would be enough protection. Or that Richard Jackson really was harmless, that all he had wanted to do was apologize.

None of that helped ease his anxiety. Esther had needed

him and he wasn't there and there wasn't an excuse good enough on the entire planet.

He was already burning some huge blisters into his heels, but now he ignored them, spurring himself to a run. Two miles. He could do two and a half miles even in these damn cowboy boots in maybe fifteen minutes. Damn! He was going to scrape together the money and get himself a decent pair of jogging shoes so he didn't have to wear these damn cowboy boots except when he was planning to ride.

Esther. Fear for her raced up from the pit of his stomach and burned his throat. God, how could he have been asinine enough to think he could safely leave her alone for a couple of hours...a couple of hours which had turned into over three what with one thing and another.

He swore under his breath and spurred himself to an even faster pace. She had to be all right. She absolutely, positively *had* to be all right.

Because he couldn't live without her.

All that hogwash he'd been dishing out about being a wanderer, about being Indian, about having nothing to offer her...well, maybe it was true, but he could damn well change all of it except his being Indian, and that apparently didn't strike her as any kind of a big deal. Hell, she hadn't even asked the usual curious questions. Nope, Esther Jackson saw him as a man, plain and simple, and something about that was like a balm to his soul.

Because never before in a relationship had his heritage seemed so insignificant. Among his own kind it had dictated whom he could date, and in the white man's world it had either acted as an attractant or a repellant. With Esther it seemed to have no effect at all.

And he liked that. He liked not being continually faced with a whole set of preconceptions that he either fulfilled or failed to fulfill, like some kind of script he'd never been allowed to study before the play began. He liked the feeling that anything he happened to be at a given moment was good enough because it was *him.*

Nobody in his whole damn life had made him feel that way except his sister, God bless her.

And his fear that Esther wouldn't be able to put up with the disapproval…well, she'd shown her stuff pretty clearly when they went out to dinner and she told that jackass off. In fact, everything about her life said she wasn't the kind to wimp out when the going got tough.

On the other hand…he wasn't sure she felt anything for him, even though she'd trusted him last night.

The memory was like a jolt of adrenaline, spurring him to an even quicker pace. The blisters on his heels were hurting like hell and he felt some new ones growing on the side of his foot. So much for the protection socks were supposed to offer.

He said prayer after prayer for Esther's safety, all the while trying to convince himself that she was going to be just fine because all Richard Jackson wanted to do was apologize to her. He didn't want to hurt her. He wasn't crazy enough to hurt her. Hell, the man had just gotten out of prison. Why on earth would he want to put himself right back in?

But arguing for sense was grasping at straws and he knew it. The man had been capable of grievous harm to Esther and her mother in the past, and there was no good reason now to believe he was any different.

Craig cursed himself for all the times he had tried to tell Esther that she probably had nothing to fear from the man. He'd meant it at the time, but now he could only think what an optimistic fool he'd been. Of course she had something to fear from this man. She'd helped put him behind bars for murder, and it was entirely within the realm of possibility that he wanted revenge.

But no, he reminded himself. He'd come to her door, then left when she didn't answer. If he'd wanted to hurt her, he could have broken in. No, he didn't want to hurt her. He couldn't want to hurt her.

His thoughts were revolving like an out-of-control Ferris wheel, round and round over the same ground. He tried to stop them, but they wouldn't let go of the single-minded insistence that Richard Jackson couldn't possibly hurt Esther.

His feet seemed to become numb, the pain from the blisters receding until he felt it only as if from a great distance. Intellectually he knew he was getting closer to her house with each step, but emotionally he felt as if he were getting nowhere at all, even when he recognized a landmark and it confirmed that he had covered a quarter mile, a half mile, then a mile.

And then he saw Richard Jackson's car coming back up the drive. He considered trying to stop the man, then realized it would do no good. If Jackson had hurt Esther, he would probably just run Craig down. If he hadn't...then it made no difference.

Their eyes connected, just briefly as Jackson drove by and Craig stepped to the side to give him room. Jackson nodded, and in some odd way Craig found that reassuring.

Then he hit the road again, running for dear life, needing to get to Esther the way he needed to breathe.

As he rounded the last corner, he knew that everything was all right, because Esther stood there on her porch, looking out over the prairie. She was okay. Scared, maybe, but unharmed.

He stopped running, giving himself a desperately needed chance to catch his breath. Now with each step he could feel the blisters like fiery brands on his feet. Muscles he'd almost forgotten about were shrieking a protest.

Esther, who had been looking toward the mountains turned and spotted him. The smile that spread across her face was like a ray of sunshine after a rainy week. It reached across the distance separating them and touched him deep inside, making a connection that he knew would never be severed.

All this time, he thought as he walked toward her, he hadn't even realized what was happening to him. Now, please God, she would someday come to feel the same.

"Where's your truck?" she called as he crossed the hard earth and walked up the path between the flower gardens.

"I had a blowout and ran into the ditch."

"Are you all right?" Concern creased her face as she hurried toward the steps, limping visibly but ignoring it in her haste to reach him. "Craig? Were you hurt?"

"I'm fine," he assured her, wincing as his blisters sent up a shriek of pain. "Except for some blisters. Damn cowboy boots weren't meant for walking."

She reached him and caught his hand. Did she have any idea, he wondered, of how that felt to him? The touch of her skin, so seductive and warm, the feeling that she cared even more seductive and warm, the concern in her beautiful hazel eyes drawing him to her until he was filled with yearning.

"How far did you have to walk?" she asked, gently tugging him up the steps and into the house.

"Oh, maybe five miles."

"Your feet must be a wreck."

"They do feel like it."

In the kitchen she pushed him gently into a chair and then helped him get his boots off. Her help with his boots was so cute he didn't have the heart to do it himself. She turned her backside to him, giving him a fine view even if she was wearing a skirt, and wobbled a little until she found her balance.

When she pulled his boots off, it was obvious he'd gone past the blister stage. His socks were soaked with blood.

"Oh, Craig! This is terrible! How could you keep walking?"

"Because I was worried about you."

Esther caught her breath, looking at him, tumbling headlong, it seemed, into the dark pools of his eyes. She looked from his gaze to his bloody feet, then back again, as if unable to believe anyone had done so much for her.

Suddenly feeling embarrassed, he bent to pull off the bloody socks. "I'm gonna mess up your floor."

"Don't worry about it," she said softly. "Just sit there and let me get a basin of warm water for you to soak in."

She had a galvanized steel tub, just the right size to soak both his feet in. Using a pitcher, she filled it with enough warm water to cover his feet to the ankles and brought a blissful smile to his face.

"Ah, that feels good," he told her.

She smiled. "You just keep soaking. I'm going to look for some gauze and ointment to put on those blisters."

They were pretty bad, he thought, taking a look at his feet. It would be a while before he would want to wear shoes again. Still, it had been worth it. He would never have forgiven himself if he hadn't busted his butt to get here.

She returned a few minutes later with a towel, gauze, scissors and antibiotic ointment. She set everything on the table next to him.

"What did your father want?" he asked her.

She sat facing him and smiled. "You were right."

"Right? About what?"

"That it's better to face the demon." Her smile grew and she gave a little laugh. "I faced him, Craig. I faced him and he's nothing but a pathetic old man who messed up his entire life. He can't hurt me anymore."

He wanted to shout for joy, but he contained it. "No, he can't. Not if you're not afraid of him. That was always his leverage, wasn't it? That you were afraid of him. Your mother probably was, too."

"Not scared enough, apparently. He told me she used to like to flirt and dance with other men, and it drove him crazy with jealousy."

"That's no excuse to beat her up."

"That's what I said. He agreed." She tilted her head a little and smiled more deeply. "I'm free of him, Craig. That's the really important thing. I feel completely free of him for the first time in my life. I'm not frightened anymore. I don't have to live in dread that he'll suddenly turn up on my doorstep to kill me. It's in the past and I'm free!" She threw up her arms as she said the last, and he found himself laughing with her.

"Free," he agreed. "It must feel wonderful!"

"Nothing's ever felt better...well, except one thing," she added mischievously.

Understanding brought him to his feet, heedless of his blisters or the tub he was standing in. Bending, he swooped in for a kiss and found himself welcomed with a warmth that had previously been reserved to his dreams.

Lifting his head he smiled down into her hazel eyes. "It *was* pretty good, wasn't it?"

Even as she nodded, he realized how little that meant. She had asked for one night, had been insistent that she wanted nothing more from him, and this morning had made it plain through her actions that she had meant what she said.

Suddenly deflated, he sat back down and considered just how hopeless his situation was. There was no reason on earth she should reciprocate his feeling. Absolutely none.

"Craig? Is something wrong?"

He shook himself and looked at her. "No, no, nothing. So you're free of your fear. That's wonderful."

She looked at him oddly, as if guessing he was redirecting the conversation. Then she reached for the towel. "I think we can dry you off now."

"I don't want to ruin your towel."

"Don't worry about it. It's just a towel. Here." She handed it to him and opened the package of gauze while he toweled his feet dry. The bleeding had just about stopped. He took the antibiotic ointment from her and spread it over the raw patches that covered his feet. Then she insisted on holding his feet in her lap while she wrapped gauze over the blisters.

It was emotionally touching, but it was also one of the most stunningly sensual things anybody had ever done for him. When she was done and he stood on his feet, there was only one thing he wanted in life, and that was Esther Jackson in his arms.

He reached for her and she hesitated. "Esther..."

She looked up at him, her gaze uncertain. "We agreed to one night."

"Damn our agreement," he said forcefully. "Esther, I want you. I need you."

A soft little sound escaped her, something like a sigh, and she leaned into his arms. "I want you, too," she admitted.

Wanted but not needed. The distinction pierced him with a sense of impending sorrow, but he forced himself to ignore it. He would gratefully accept however much or little this woman chose to give him right now, and hope that someday she would come to feel about him as he felt about her.

They went upstairs hand in hand, Craig mindful of her dislike for being picked up and her fear of stairs. It was, he thought, a triumph that she could climb stairs beside him. Old fears must surely haunt her.

But if they did, there was no shadow of them in her eyes as she smiled at him. God, how he loved her smile! In her room, with sunlight streaming over them, they undressed each other slowly, savoring each newly revealed secret. Once or twice Esther was almost overcome by shyness, but when he pulled her close and kissed her, she relaxed and gave way to their rising passion.

There was something incredibly special about loving this woman in the daylight with nothing concealed. He stood over her without embarrassment and let her look her fill. Then, determined to prove a point, he bent over her and began to kiss her from head to toe with his eyes wide open.

"You're beautiful," he whispered again and again, and he truly meant it. What he wanted was for her to believe it, too. If his lips could convince her, they would do so.

By the time his lips had trailed to the soles of her feet, she was quivering from head to foot and breathing through gently parted lips. Only then did he lower himself over her, covering her with his heat and his strength. At once her arms lifted to encircle him and hold him close.

"Am I too heavy?" he asked.

"No...oh, no! You can stay here forever if you like." And she truly meant it. Being pressed head to foot against him in this intimate way was one of the most exquisite and soul-satisfying experiences she had ever had. Only her art brought her close to this sense of completeness.

He took her mouth in a deep, evocative kiss, telling her how much he wanted to be inside her. She responded immediately, opening her mouth, opening her legs, taking him inside as if she wanted to consume him.

His penetration thrilled her, sending widening waves of pleasure and desire through her. She arched upward to take him deeper, and it was as if she were trying to draw him into her very soul.

But then he teased her, pulling away, hushing her protests with a sprinkle of kisses as he slid down over her until he was kissing her in the most intimate place imaginable.

She felt as if she were caught on a pinnacle of sensation so intense that it was almost painful. She cried out, torn between begging him to stop and begging him never to stop. She had never dreamed that anything could feel so good that it bordered on agony.

Her climax was an explosion that made her see stars and lasted so long that she thought it was never going to end. And just when she thought it was almost over, Craig entered her again in an easy sliding movement, filling her and enhancing her pleasure a thousandfold. This was what she needed, she thought dimly. This man with her, this man inside her. Always.

Later they lay tangled in the sheets, damp from their exertions and so tired they could hardly move. Craig cradled her head in the hollow of his shoulder and made some contented little sounds that caused a bubble of laughter to rise in Esther.

"You sound like Guinevere when she's rolling in clover."

"I probably feel *better* than Guinevere when she's rolling in clover." He turned a little and snuggled her closer. "So our agreement from last night is off."

"So it appears."

"Do you mind?"

This time the laugh escaped her. "Do I look like I mind?"

He lifted his head and studied her quite seriously. "Guess not."

"So it's over."

"Good."

A silence ensued. Guinevere, who had been left outside the closed bedroom door, moaned, reminding them that she was there.

"Is she always this pushy?" Craig asked teasingly.

"She gets even pushier."

"Hm. Why do you put up with it?"

"Because I love her."

Something seemed to gleam in his dark eyes, making her catch her breath, but then he changed the subject.

"Do you still feel good about facing your father?"

She smiled widely. "Absolutely. In fact, I'm almost euphoric. I had no idea how trapped I felt until finally I was free. It's…as if I've been walking up the side of a mountain with a crushing burden on my back, and all of a sudden I'm on level ground and the burden is gone. I feel lighter than air!"

He hugged her tightly. "I'm so glad," he murmured, feeling his throat tighten. "I'm so glad."

Esther boldly kissed his chin and then, when presented with the opportunity, kissed his mouth. "I wanted to tell you…when he was leaving, I couldn't just let him go."

He pushed himself up on an elbow and looked down at her, surprised. "You invited him to stay?"

"No! Oh, no! Never. I'm sorry, but there's no way I could ever trust him enough to let him back into my life. Now that may not be very charitable, but…well, I can forgive but I can't forget."

"Did you forgive?"

She nodded. "That's what I told him when he was leaving. I told him I forgive him."

"And do you?"

"Oh, yes. I felt so sorry for him. Craig, he has nothing left. He ruined his own life and drove everyone away. He's pathetic. But…I knew I forgave him, so I told him. And as soon as I said it…"

She hesitated, then looked up at him with shining eyes. "I let go of another burden. I let go of a crushing load of hate and anger that I hadn't even realized I was carrying all this time. As soon as I made that decision and felt it strongly enough to actually say it to him, it was gone." Tears sprang to her eyes and began to run down her cheeks. "It felt so good to let go of it, Craig. So good to finally just let it all go…"

He held her close and rocked her gently for a long, long

time. The afternoon began to wane, and Guinevere became a little pushier, scratching on the door and barking.

"I need to let her out," Esther said finally. Her tears were dry now, and she lay contentedly against Craig, wondering how it was possible to feel so good, so right, as if nothing could ever be better.

"I'll do it," Craig said. "Be right back."

After pulling on his jeans, he opened the door. Guin barked joyously and dashed down the stairs. He looked over his shoulder at Esther. "Impatient doesn't begin to cover it. I think she's about to pop."

He descended the stairs to find Guin sitting right by the front door, her tail thumping impatiently.

"Okay, okay," Craig told her. "Some of us take longer to get moving than others. You have to remember I only have two legs."

Guin whined and wiggled. Craig reached for the doorknob and threw the door wide open. Guin pushed the screen door open herself and dashed out.

Craig looked out over the yard and felt his jaw drop. "Well, I'll be." Mop had gotten over here somehow and engaged in a game of tag with Guinevere that made it plain how overjoyed the dogs were to see each other.

But what really stunned him was Cromwell. The ewe stood placidly in the middle of Esther's garden, munching happily on flowers, just as she had weeks ago when he first met Esther. How the hell...?

"Craig? Is something wrong?" Esther stood at the top of the stairs in a hastily donned bathrobe.

"Can you come down here, honey? You aren't going to believe this."

Honey. A pleasant quiver ran through her, and a stab of yearning so strong it hurt. If only he would always call her that. She didn't have her brace on, so she took extra care descending the stairs, gripping the banister tightly. Craig watched her, his smile deepening with each step she took.

"You're really something, lady, you know that? Enough guts for ten people."

His praise left her feeling flushed with pleasure. When she reached his side it seemed the most natural thing to slip her arm around his waist. His arm promptly settled around her shoulders.

"You see that?" he asked, pointing outside.

"Mop, you mean? He must have come for..." She trailed off. "Cromwell? What is Cromwell doing here?"

"Damned if I know. She's sure done a number on your garden. Guess I'm going to have to turn her into stew."

"Don't you dare," Esther said severely. "She's only being a sheep."

"Well, I need to do something about her. This is getting ridiculous."

Esther shrugged and laughed. "Just let her be. When the flowers are gone, the temptation will be gone."

He looked down at her, his dark eyes capturing her gaze and holding it. "Do you suppose it's an omen?" he asked, his voice going suddenly husky.

She suddenly couldn't breathe. "Omen?"

"Cromwell brought us together, remember?"

She managed a nod.

"Maybe this is telling us that we ought to stay together."

Now she really couldn't breathe. Her heart was hammering so hard she could hear it. "Don't joke."

"Believe me, I'm not joking. I did a lot of thinking while I was walking over here. It's kinda been growing on me for some time that...well, I can't live without you."

Esther's eyes began to shine, whether from tears or happiness he couldn't tell. "What about...what about wandering and all the rest of it?"

He shrugged and looked rueful. "That was just a lot of talk, sort of an image I had of myself. You come right down to it, I was wandering because I hadn't found my home. I think I found it, Esther. Right here with you."

She drew a quick breath and looked up at him as if her every hope in the world hinged on his next words. That look made him feel a little easier about plunging ahead.

"I know I can't support you yet, but—"

"But I'm perfectly capable of supporting myself," she stated firmly. "I have been doing so for quite a few years now."

He grinned. "I noticed. Anyway, I kind of figured you'd feel that way, so that bit about not having any money doesn't really mean a whole lot, I guess. I support myself, so it's not like I'm asking to live off you." He fell silent, as if he didn't know where to go from there.

Esther, growing impatient finally, prodded him. "Just what *are* you asking?"

He drew a deep breath and squared his shoulders. "Well, I reckon it's too early to ask if you love me, so I'd just like to ask if you'll give me a chance to court you. I'm hoping that maybe, eventually, you might... Well, I love you, Esther, and I'd kinda like it if you'd love me back. Do you think you could see your way to giving me a chance?"

The smile that spread across her face was like the dawning of a new day.

"Oh, I think I could see my way to that, cowboy. Indeed I do."

Then she threw her arms around his neck and hugged him tight. And Craig finally let out a whoop of sheer joy.

Epilogue

Four furry little puppies tumbled around Esther's feet as she finished adjusting her wedding veil. Craig had insisted on the wedding dress and veil, saying he wanted her to have it all.

Esther looked down at the puppies and laughed. She had it all, all right. Four puppies that might look like their father, if their present furriness was any indication, a komondor, a Saint Bernard, a sheep that devoured flowers —and, a baby of her very own on the way.

She hugged the secret to her, keeping it as a surprise for tonight after everyone had left. Tonight, which would be their first night together as man and wife. She knew Craig would be as thrilled as she was, because he'd more than once said he would like to have a couple of children.

"Ready?" Paula asked from the doorway.

"Ready." Picking up her bouquet, Esther stepped carefully around the pups, paused to pat Guin on the head, and headed downstairs.

If she limped, for once she didn't notice it. Even the stairs today seemed to provide no obstacle. She felt as if she were walking on air.

The yard was full of people when she stepped out onto the porch, and her breath caught in her suddenly tight throat as she realized that she had never been as isolated as she had felt. Here she was, surrounded by all the people she had come to know since moving to Conard County: Nate Tate and his family, Janet and Abel Pierce, Mandy and Ransom Laird, Micah and Faith Parish, Maude Bleaker, Verna Wilcox and Velma Jansen and their families, Gage and Emma Dalton....

Her eyes were suddenly misty with tears as she realized how many friends she had. And now she had a family as well, because Paula and Enoch Small Elk had all but adopted her. Little Mary Small Elk, all dressed up to be the flower girl, tugged on her dress. "Now, Aunt Essie?"

"Now, Mary."

There was no one to give her away, but that's how she wanted it. To the sound of the prairie wind, she walked down the porch to where Craig and Reverend Fromberg awaited her. When Craig took her hand and smiled into her eyes, she felt everything else in the world vanish.

Dimly she heard Reverend Fromberg's voice admonishing them then reciting the vows. She heard Craig say, "I will," and then she heard her own voice say it loud and clear, "I will."

The next thing she knew she was tightly held in Craig's arms as he kissed her, setting her senses on fire, reminding her of all the delights that lay ahead of them.

Then she turned to greet her smiling friends and neighbors and realized that Craig wasn't the only one who had found a home.

For the first time in her life, so had she.

* * * * *

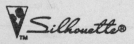

Take 4 bestselling love stories FREE

Plus get a FREE surprise gift!

Special Limited-time Offer

Mail to Silhouette Reader Service™

3010 Walden Avenue
P.O. Box 1867
Buffalo, N.Y. 14240-1867

YES! Please send me 4 free Silhouette Intimate Moments® novels and my free surprise gift. Then send me 6 brand-new novels every month, which I will receive months before they appear in bookstores. Bill me at the low price of $3.34 each plus 25¢ delivery and applicable sales tax, if any.* That's the complete price and a savings of over 10% off the cover prices—quite a bargain! I understand that accepting the books and gift places me under no obligation ever to buy any books. I can always return a shipment and cancel at any time. Even if I never buy another book from Silhouette, the 4 free books and the surprise gift are mine to keep forever.

245 BPA A3UW

Name	(PLEASE PRINT)
Address	Apt. No.
City	State	Zip

This offer is limited to one order per household and not valid to present Silhouette Intimate Moments® subscribers. *Terms and prices are subject to change without notice. Sales tax applicable in N.Y.

UMOM-696

©1990 Harlequin Enterprises Limited

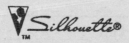

As seen on TV!
Free Gift Offer

With a Free Gift proof-of-purchase from any Silhouette® book, you can receive a beautiful cubic zirconia pendant.

This gorgeous marquise-shaped stone is a genuine cubic zirconia—accented by an 18" gold tone necklace.

(Approximate retail value $19.95)

Send for yours today...
compliments of **V** *Silhouette*®
™

To receive your free gift, a cubic zirconia pendant, send us one original proof-of-purchase, photocopies not accepted, from the back of any Silhouette Romance™, Silhouette Desire®, Silhouette Special Edition®, Silhouette Intimate Moments® or Silhouette Yours Truly™ title available in February, March and April at your favorite retail outlet, together with the Free Gift Certificate, plus a check or money order for $1.65 U.S./$2.15 CAN. (do not send cash) to cover postage and handling, payable to Silhouette Free Gift Offer. We will send you the specified gift. Allow 6 to 8 weeks for delivery. Offer good until April 30, 1997 or while quantities last. Offer valid in the U.S. and Canada only.

Free Gift Certificate

Name: _____

Address: _____

City: _____ State/Province: _____ Zip/Postal Code: _____

Mail this certificate, one proof-of-purchase and a check or money order for postage and handling to: SILHOUETTE FREE GIFT OFFER 1997. In the U.S.: 3010 Walden Avenue, P.O. Box 9077, Buffalo NY 14269-9077. In Canada: P.O. Box 613, Fort Erie, Ontario L2Z 5X3.

FREE GIFT OFFER
084-KFD

ONE PROOF-OF-PURCHASE

To collect your fabulous FREE GIFT, a cubic zirconia pendant, you must include this original proof-of-purchase for each gift with the properly completed Free Gift Certificate.

084-KFD

And the Winner Is...
You!

...when you pick up these great titles
from our new promotion at your
favorite retail outlet this June!

Diana Palmer
The Case of the Mesmerizing Boss

Betty Neels
The Convenient Wife

Annette Broadrick
Irresistible

Emma Darcy
A Wedding to Remember

Rachel Lee
Lost Warriors

Marie Ferrarella
Father Goose

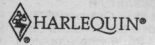 

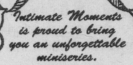

Intimate Moments is proud to bring you an unforgettable miniseries.

BEVERLY BIRD

The Wedding Ring

Wrapped in the warmth of family tradition, three couples say "I do!"

LOVING MARIAH
(Intimate Moments #790, June 1997)
Adam Wallace searches for his kidnapped
son...which leads him to the Amish heartland
and lovely schoolteacher Mariah Fisher.

MARRYING JAKE
(Intimate Moments #802, August 1997)
Commitment-shy Jake Wallace unravels the
ongoing mystery of stolen babies and helps
Katya Essler learn to believe in love again.

SAVING SUSANNAH
(Intimate Moments #814, October 1997)
Kimberly Wallace needs a bone marrow donor
to save her daughter's life. Will the temporary
nanny position to Joe Lapp's children be the
answer to her prayers?

▼INTIMATE MOMENTS®
™ *Silhouette®*

Look us up on-line at: http://www.romance.net

WEDR

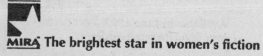